punkPunk!

An Anthology of
Punk-Inspired Fiction

Edited by
Andrew Hook

Selection copyright © 2015 by Dog Horn Publishing
Stories copyright © 2015 the contributors
Introduction copyright © 2015 by Andrew Hook
Cover art and design © 2015 by Adam Lowe

All rights reserved. No part of this publication may be reproduced, stored in a retrieval system, rebound or transmitted in any form or by any means, electronic, mechanical, photocopying, recording or otherwise, without the prior written permission of the author and publisher. is book is sold subject to the condition that it shall not by way of trade or otherwise be lent, resold, hired out or otherwise circulated without the publisher's prior consent in any form of binding or cover other than that in which it is published.

'You Can Jump' originally appeared in *Death Dance*, edited by Trevanian (Cumberland House, 2002), and was subsequently reprinted in *Crimewave* #7 (TTA Press) and also in *You Can Jump and other stories* (Alia Mondo Press).

ISBN: 978-1-907133-89-3

First published in the United Kingdom in 2015 by
Dog Horn Publishing
45 Monk Ings
Birstall
Batley
WF17 9HU

doghornpublishing.com• andrew-hook.com

British Library Cataloguing-in-Publication Data
A cataloguing record for this book is available on request from the British Library

punkPunk!

INTRODUCTION

Andrew Hook

In January 1978 I was ten and a half years old. I had been a *punk* for some time without really knowing what punk was. I was at the nebulous age where reality was only just starting to form around me and my world view was naïve and malformed. Initially it wasn't even clear to me that punk was about music, but I knew it was political because a few of us at school had plans to sneak up behind Margaret Thatcher and pull down her underwear. But that must have been 1979, so memory is challenging me now. What I do know is that one day my mate, Mark Dullea, said: 'If you're calling yourself a punk then you need to buy a punk record.' That weekend I did.

I went with my mum to the Jarrold's department store in Norwich where she asked the salesgirl if she had five minutes, whilst I saw the cover of The Stranglers' '5 Minutes' single beneath the glass counter. The lettering was LED red on a black background. I now go giddy even thinking about it. It would be the first 'proper' record I would buy.

'5 Minutes' is a song written by Stranglers' bass player JJ Burnel about a rape that occurred at a shared flat he had once lived in and his frustrations over finding the five men who committed the attack. Those lyrics went right over my ten and a half year old head, but I sensed the record was dangerous, dark, and sinister. It was unlike anything I'd ever heard and so my Stranglers' obsession began. Speaking to JJ about it after a gig some years later he suggested I became a punk through peer pressure, but I disagree with him. It didn't feel that I *became* a punk because I already *was* punk.

Admittedly even in 1978 I was coming a little late to punk, and also coming at it too young, but these were my formative years and as a result *I am a punk*. I know that as well as I know my parentage. And I'm positive that the music, the DIY-attitude, the whole *punkness* of it fired my creativity, both in fiction and editorially. And that *can do* energy has also meant that I've flung myself into all manner of projects, foolishly or otherwise, because I've been given the self-belief that everything is worth a shot.

So how did this anthology come about? Over ten years ago, I read the short story 'You Can Jump' by Mat Coward in *Crimewave* magazine. That piece pinned down for me what it meant to be punk. It's a reflective but not nostalgic slice of fiction, shimmering with hindsight and an underlying thread of crime. I felt then – as I do now – that it's a perfect punk story, and I knew at some point I would write my own punk story. It took me a further ten years to do so, and 'The Last Mohican', published here, is just that. These two pieces fuelled the urge for an anthology, but something else did too.

At the 2010 World Horror Convention, I was on the fringes of a conversation with Lavie Tidhar and some other writers when steampunk was mentioned. As was cyberpunk and Hebrewpunk. Lavie wondered what might come next. I've always been aggrieved at the appropriation of 'punk' by those genres, so I said, 'Why not punkpunk?' We joked about it. But the seed was there.

So here, now, is *punkPunk!* What has the reader got in store?

Some of the stories are snapshots of punk: L A Sykes and Mark Slade's 'The Boys' and Joe Briggs' 'Real Reggae' are ground roots tales about punters working out what punk is all about; two stories use The Stranglers as (in one case literal) jumping off points: Stephen Palmer's 'Blanknoir' takes its inspiration directly from their 'Black and White' album, and Douglas Thompson's 'Out of the Box' puts a fictional spin on a real life event which occurred at one of their gigs; humour runs through Richard Dellar's 'The Rock Star' as his protagonist follows a flawed blueprint for success; and in Adam Craig's 'What Use Optimism?' a forty-something's attempt to revive his punk youth is aided and abetted by ghosts of the past. The fragility of musicians is explored in both Terry Grimwood's 'What It Is' and P A Levy's 'Breath of Fresh Air'; whilst fantasy fuels the characters in Jude Orlando Enjolras' 'The God-Fearing Crack Dealers' Songbook', where punk is a cosmic revolution; and in Richard Mosses' 'Starfire' acolytes of a mock religion see punk in another light. The association of being around musicians is the driving force behind three stories:

Gary Couzens' Australia-set 'Spinning Fast', Gio Clairval's 'Punk up Your Road Blues' and Sarah Crabtree's 'Quantum Punk'. The anthology's remit was open beyond the summer of '76, and Alexei Kalinchuk's 'Cowboys and Mohawkers' deals with alternative music in 1980s Texas, whilst both Douglas J. Ogurek's writing and his characters rebel against convention, as his scenester protagonist tries to overcome his desire for admiration in 'Jester Punk Fuffery'. Finally, 'You Can Jump' by Mat Coward, is reprinted here in all its glory and my own 'The Last Mohican' rounds off the anthology in agreement with the publisher.

This eclectic mix of stories shows punk is not simply a static component of history, but a process of evolution and revolution which extends from the heady days of 1976 right into the now, and presumably beyond. Are you ready to jump into contemporary punk-inspired fiction? It's not a nostalgia trip.

Contents

THE BOYS

L A Sykes and Mark Slade

I was stood at the bar in The Roaring Lion. I took a long swig of whatever Bernie the landlord was passing off as mild. It made my saliva curdle and had my stomach acid trying to escape before they became acquainted. I necked the rest of the pint and my eyes watered with the heartburn. Ordered another four and lashed pound notes onto the drip tray.

'Take it easy on that shite, Horton. You'll be out cold lad. Pace yourself,' warned Bernie.

I had to respect Bernie's honesty. It was shite. It was watered down shite. Recently I wished it was more water than my body and brain could cope with. I didn't want to drown my troubles any more, I wanted to drown full fucking stop.

Christ's porcelain eyes burned into mine from over Bernie's shoulder. A five foot crucifix was propped up underneath the optics. The facial expression looked to me like the effigy was staring right into my self pity, saying *you think you've got it bad? Don't bother praying lad, He didn't do nowt for me neither.*

'You joining the God Squad Bernie? Just, I don't think this is the best place for holding AA meetings.'

The stupid old fucker stared at me confused for a moment. Beer rusted cogs creaking into motion. I nodded at the cross.

'Oh. That. No, I'm holding it until Father Jiggins pays his tab. Can't turn nothing into whiskey for ever, can I?' He gives me a wink. Two inch ridges indent in his face, like knife scars under his eye sockets.

I laughed and shook my head, which span a bit. Lit another fag.

Even the clergy were pickling themselves on the brewery's slate. In hock. Indebted.

'You ever feel guilty that Christ died for your sins, Bernie?'

'Don't remember asking him to, be quite honest,' he said.

'Me neither.'

'Thinking big thoughts, Paul? He's at university, this one,' Bernie says to a miner who should have retired a decade ago. He's clutching a pint jug with jet black fingernails. He looks into the distance between me and Bernie, coughs and shits his pants involuntarily. His eyebrows raise and he farts. Says nothing. Nothing at all. Just motions for a refill with his half empty glass.

I look at Bernie and back at the miner, who's now wriggling on his stool.

'How's your dad, Paul?' asks Bernie.

'Still a pretentious cunt,' I reply, without even thinking or considering. I am sober again.

Because my father has threatened to kick me out onto the streets this afternoon.

Because I am not in university any more.

Because this has brought intense shame on my mother and father in their circle of friends.

Because I quit.

Because I was bored of regurgitating the same information the other thousands in the lecture hall were.

Bored and tired of the same old shit. The same old shit everyone else copied down and sent back in for bits of paper with red pen marks and fancy lettering and a black gown like a demented magician and all that bollocks. Just so they could write it on a C.V and send it to some tosser in a drab, faceless office, begging to swap their only years on this forsaken planet for bits of fucking change. To escape the dwindling mills and mines and sweatshops. So they can go to the bank and sign their freedom away after they've proved they can afford to be a bit of gravel in the ultimate pyramid scheme of economic enslavement and profit creation for those on the top, hoping that a bit of dust might one day trickle down and they can take a week off from their pointless activities. And that's just the ones with a modicum of intelligence.

What about the rest? They were never even told that there was a possibility of life beyond the menial labour and production lines. Shit wages and shit conditions and a pittance that they had to be grateful for because there were millions unemployed and dying in the wings, ready to come and scrap for their jobs. The unions were living on past glories and would not sustain a credible force for the working class. I didn't want to be labelled. I didn't want to shimmy from my working class roots up to lower middle class respectability. I didn't want to play the categorisation Game. I didn't want a cushy local government job.

I'd seen through the Big Game. The Big fucking Game of a nation of tax paying dogsbodies to big business and banking and economic theory and a fucking monarch who takes everybody's pennies and pounds and sloshes them all together. Not mine. I vowed there and then to never contribute my taxes to this affront to democracy.

I was nobody's butler. Nobody's good citizen. I wanted better. I wanted to go and tell the lot of them that I was having no part of this societal construct. I just didn't know how. Yet.

I was feeling trapped in this shithole of a pub. In this shithole of a small town in a large county of a small country in what was once the largest empire in the world. I only had one outlet. One retreat from this all powerful urge to run fucking rampant. One last bastion of bothering to be a human being in England in nineteen seventy six.

My mates.

*

Sat down at the table and chinked the glasses, one by one. On my right, Dennis 'Den' Chaddock. Same age as me. Arse end of eighteen. Sat holding open my battered copy of *A Clockwork Orange*, pretending he can understand its contents. Pretending he's contemplating free will and determinism and the implications of enforcing a morality that should hopefully have been inbuilt to our species' DNA.

Instead he's scanning for the sex parts, frustrated that Brenda, his missus, won't let him get into her knickers yet. Not before they get married. He's a rough bastard is Den. Fought anyone at school. Didn't need a cause either. He was like a rocket propelled grenade, just needing someone to line him up and let him go. Loyal as fuck too.

'Need drain the main vein, girlies. No gobbin' in my pint you pack of twats,' he shouts, heading to the bogs.

Thinking was not one of his habits though. Ever since his mother had died he'd gotten edgier and touchier. The only thing holding him together was Brenda. And myself, doing my best to keep his seams together, which was difficult given my own sparking fuse.

Him and Brenda, that was his reason to live. The other boys couldn't understand it however. Den was a sharp looking fella, making his ragged jeans and top look like a fashion trend. The birds would have never kept their hands off him if he'd let them touch him. He wouldn't have though. He was Brenda's, end of fucking story.

Mickey Hughes said, 'What's with him hanging onto Brenda without a shag? He a secret queer or what?'

I put it down to him trying to create the ideal relationship that he never saw in his own parents. His dad, Den Senior, was a shocking alcoholic. He'd had a major accident down the pit in the early seventies and lost a hand. Never got over it. Took out his perceived unmanliness about not being the bread winner on the boy and his ailing mother. I pitied the bastard but Den harboured nothing but hate, which was understandable really. His mother was moved to a hospice before Den got big enough to spark Senior out. She wasted away for years and Den spent an hour every day with her until she went, never missing a single evening.

Mickey 'Tubby' Hughes wouldn't hear it and was adamant it *was* about Brenda's fantastic tits. I offered the idea he was supplanting his own helplessness from his mother's terminal illness onto Brenda as a symbolic way of being able to act out looking after her. Maybe I was just an old fashioned romantic and it was all about Brenda's fantastic tits. I'd never have asked Den, he'd just have clammed up and told us to fuck off.

Matty Clancy had simply suggested that Brenda was a nice girl with a heart of gold and a strength about her person. Me and Mickey exchanged raised eyebrows and Tubby said, 'He's such a sensitive soul is our Matthew.'

'Fuck off you cunts,' he laughed. Kicked Tubby under the table, forcing his knees to wobble our jars and spilling precious loopy juice.

'Oi, knock it off the pair of yous. I'm running out of funds, this is the last of my grant money,' I shouted.

Tubby Hughes was nicknamed Tubby because he was about three stone piss wet through. Brought up on a diet of chips and pie and mash and potato grated on his fucking cornflakes, he should have been built like a red brick outhouse. One of five kids, all different dads, scrapping for bread and butter might have explained his emaciated, bony form. He'd never admit it though. Too proud to ever say he was hungry. Too proud to ever hear anyone say his mum was a whore as well, without wishing they'd kept their soon-to-be toothless gums clamped shut. We'd all heard the rumours, of course—that his mum was on the game, but I believed Tubby when he said that she just picked losers. Soon as the going got tough, the useless skiving cunts upped and shot off into the night, leaving her another mouth to feed. His sixth step dad seemed a good bloke. Affiliated with the Salvation Army. Strict bastard. Wanted a quid a week off Tubby as rent for him sleeping in the fucking bath. Cheeky cunt.

Matty was away with the fucking fairies. A dreamer. An introspective is what I think they're called. You could stare into his eyes and see he was miles away in his own mind. Wicked sense of humour though. Always thinking, like he was walking in a constant daydream. I'd ask occasionally what he was muttering to himself about, always giggling to himself. He'd always deny it. He was a good kid and me and Den never let anyone near the boy when they tried it on because he looked a soft touch. He lived with his old nan because his dad had hung himself before he was five and his mum had had a breakdown and was still in the old funny farm thirteen years later. Matty told us she'd been electroshocked that many times she was a walking mannequin.

*

Den came back from the toilets and plonked himself down, resting his boots on the table.

'You lose a kidney or what?' said Tubby.

'He was wanking over the old *in out in out*,' laughed Matty.

'Fuck off you wankers. Can't a man use the restroom in peace,' he snarled.

I pointed to the book. 'Hang about, what the fuck have you done?'

'Sorry. There was no bog roll. Had to improvise. Only the first five chapters anyway,' he replied, making over the top dough eyes.

'You cheeky bugger,' I said, unable to stop myself from laughing at the bastard.

The sight of Auntie Tracey knocked me back in my chair. She sauntered in with her mate chatting, looked over, winked and caressed her lips with her tongue, staring right into my eyes. She wasn't my real auntie, just a throwaway auntie by way of being best mates with my mum. Me quitting university causing shame and embarrassment? How about Auntie Tracey giving me tit wanks and hand jobs from the age of twelve. How's that for a fucking napalm shame bombshell mummy and daddy and your precious wannabe middle class conservative twats?

How about Auntie Tracey making her impotent husband watch as he's tied to a chair and dressed in Tracey's lingerie, while she begs me to take her up the arse? Next door but one, while you're watching the fucking *Good Life* and worrying about when the bins are being emptied.

*

Tubby drags me out of my reverie for Tracey with a sobering question. 'What do we do when your grant money is gone?'

Den sits upright and leans in. Says, 'Money frees you from doing things you dislike. Since I dislike doing nearly everything, money is handy.'

He takes off his Aviators. We look at him blankly.

'Hate to name drop, but that was Karl Marx,' he said.

'Wrong Marx brother.'

'What?'

'That was Groucho Marx, you knobhead.'

He narrowed his eyes and replied, 'Well I knew it was one of the buggers.'

We struggled to stop bursting into laughter in case he went apeshit.

'There's only one thing we can do. We'll have to get jobs,' I say with a straight face. We all crack into hysterics.

We are not lazy or work shy. The truth is there are no jobs. This country is on its knees. Those geniuses in power have fucked up big time with the collective enforced money pool. Great Britain is no longer Great. It is merely Britain. Where electricity goes off all the time, plunging the smog ridden inner cities into unfamiliar darkness, forcing co-habiting strangers into uncomfortable chit chat so they can stare at each other and wonder who the fuck they've been sleeping next to for the past forty years. Where rubbish is teeming in the streets, and the pavements are pounded with the worn shoe leather of the disaffected and the disenchanted. Where the police do what they want and the once noble ideals of a society of helping out those falling behind you is regarded as potential communism, branded backward and sinister. In a small town relying on unproductive mine shafts and dwindling cotton mills and no more nail factories which is what it was famous for in the fucking first place over two hundred years ago. Pubs called the Kings Head were actually places where kings stayed on their way traversing the thriving old towns, now just home to the man in the street hell bent on drinking themselves into oblivion because they can't handle the harsh existential realities of life as an unprivileged human being who thought we were all born equal. An age who'd forgotten the free thinkers of Ancient Greece and even the Enlightenment. The New Dark Ages of Man. We laughed for ten minutes straight.

I looked around the Roaring Lion and had an epiphany. We were never going to be productive members of the illusory societal structure we never wanted to be a part of in the first place. We were never going to end up shitting in our pants involuntarily at the bar of a run down public house. We were never going to be alcoholic priests who had taken to ticking with a giant crucifix. Even religious organisations wouldn't have stooped so low as to be hiring us even if we'd be deluded enough to consider it a half decent aspiration after analysis of basic critical thinking.

No. I took another, more focused look around. Fuck university. Fuck school. Fuck the joke shop. Fuck the DHSS. Fuck every cunt who demanded we fit in with their failing and constrictive orders to bow down to authorities we could see full fucking well just wanted the sweat off our backs and a chunk of our pay packets.

I stared. I watched. I heard juke box boom the gormless drivel of *Brotherhood Of Man* chirping *Save All Your Kisses For Me*. Den was even nodding along and mouthing the words. Hard Den Soppy Den. But no. He hadn't even realised he was doing it. The miner was wiggling his shitty arse and miming the words. Aunty Tracey was mouthing the words to me as she opened her legs and flashed her sweaty gusset, stray black pubes spidering out of the sides of her lacies. Even the priest who'd just stumbled in was singing, corrupting the lyrics from 'kisses' to 'whiskies'. Big Bernie did the dance, the 'swinging at the knee kick' as he ejected the priest and theatrically booted him through the door.

And this song was complete horseshit. This was all it was. A song. A pop song. Mindless entertainment. Mindless, yet it had infected their minds. It was in their heads. It was shite. There was the epiphany once more in all its majestic glory.

Why hadn't I thought of this before?

How else to spread a message? Our message. To finally be heard.

Music.

Infect their minds. With a Message. Our Message.

We were going to tell the whole lot of them to get fucked.

To get fucked.

Right in their ear drums.

And they were going to sing our words and dance to our tune and pay us for the privilege.

And every one of them thrown in the gutter will be with us. Be one with us.

We were going to start a revolution.

Smash this horrible status quo.

Be free.

We were going to rock the country out of apathy and revitalize its denigrated youth.

We were going to fucking punk rock before punk rock ever fucking existed.

Cowboys and Mohawkers

Alexei Kalinchuk

I put on my rings that morning because I expected trouble at school. All eight of them were made of chrome, which I liked because my name was Peter Kromer, but in high school everyone called me Pete Chrome which gave me a secret buzz because I loved all kinds of alternative music, but especially punk rock, and the Dead Boys' drummer called himself Cheetah Chrome. Little things like that impressed me then.

Wearing my rings made me feel like my hands were armored so I was ready for anything the dumb-assed cowboys of our sleepy little Texas town wanted to hand out.

The night before we'd done something to them.

I'd been home all that first week of school, and my mom was working graveyards at the hospital, so I was alone when a tapping started at my bedroom window one night. Curious and wanting to test whether the fever had got me hearing things, I drew the curtain aside and there was spiky-headed Stan and Mud wearing a Dirty Rotten Imbeciles t-shirt.

'Meet me out back.' I waved them towards the rear of the house, thinking I must've missed out on something from the gleeful looks on their faces. I missed out on a lot the last two weeks because my father forced me to visit him in Montana and I caught a chill doing the fly-fishing he wanted me to like.

'Why can't we come in?' Mud asked me when I met them under the light on the back stoop, both of them bobbing there with moths passing around their heads.

'Y'all smell like cigarettes, my mom'll know you been here and I'll get the whupping, that's why. Hey. What's that smell? Where you coming from?'

'We sprayed it.' Mud smiled. 'Just like we said.'

'You didn't wait for me?'

'You were sick,' Stan said, grinning, now holding up his palms smudged all over with black and red spraypaint. 'We need a favor. We gotta wash. We seen Officer Ricks car up the street, so we had to sneak here.'

'Okay, just wait. I'll be back.'

I dressed fast as I could, understanding how Officer Ricks was someone they shouldn't oughtta see, especially with paint all over their hands. Like everyone else in our town, Officer Ricks had it in for us. Us. The Mohawkers.

No, I wouldn't let my friends down.

I came back out, helped look in the garage for some paint thinner among all the junk my father left when he left us. We found it, got Stan and Mud's hands clean so that if Officer Ricks stopped them on their walk home, they wouldn't be the first suspects come tomorrow when everyone saw their handiwork.

We'd get blamed, of course, but there'd be no witnesses, no evidence, just a lingering anger to punish our crowd.

So that next morning I put on my chrome rings thinking of how even just recovering from my fever, I'd lend a hand if a fight found us. I hoped I'd smash some cowboy faces.

*

On the walk to school I saw it. In big black and red letters on an abandoned rice mill two blocks from our high school it said: KICKERS SUCK. The shitkicking cowboys were going to go berserk today.

We'd been fighting a one-year war with the kickers at school. Kickers. Guys in cowboys hats. After two of them whaled on a friend of mine, we fought back. Slashed truck tires. Broke windshields. They beat on us. Then Trank cut one with a linoleum knife and Spaz got a gun drawn on him. I broke a guy's thumb wrestling with him in the Dairy Queen parking lot.

DON'T GO IN TODAY IF YOU DON'T FEEL RIGHT, my sleeping mom's note said on the table that morning.

I had to, my friends needed me.

Cops, parents of kickers, and teachers decided we were at fault, so we were mostly alone in our struggles. In our community all that mattered was how our high school football team went to state years ago and now most of those players had bred our enemies, the kickers, and all of them lapped up all that glory days talk, let's recapture the state title hoo-hah. People living in the past, just like the team name: The Rebels.

I hurried down the street, looking around for pickup trucks full of hard faces, but trying not to look jumpy.

We represented a future people didn't like or understand. Kickers called us mohawkers. It wasn't even a real word, but after a while even we called ourselves mohawkers. Like it was an honor or something.

Didn't I tell you that small things impressed me back then?

*

I stood with Sarah, Trank, Stan and some other punk rock kids in the main hallway of our school. Times like these, safety in numbers felt right.

Principal Farner watched us from nearby.

'So visiting your dad in Montana sucked?' Sarah asked.

'Maybe. I don't know. *He* sucked.' I talked but looked at people streaming in through the front doors, ready for confrontation. 'And I hate the taste of trout.'

We all laughed. Nerves, I guess.

Mud walked through the doors, grin on his face you couldn't jump across if you had a ramp and a motorbike.

'They're all out there in the parking lot by Kevin Carnes' pickup. They're talking.'

This sounded like some kind of a war conference, so Mud's joy bothered me enough to ask why in the hell he was so happy.

'They're pissed about the spraypaint,' Mud said, 'but they've got bigger problems. My dad's on the school board and he told me something this morning over cornflakes.'

'Talk already,' I said.

'I thought something was weird, how they hadn't tried to jump us since school started, but now I know. Now I know.'

'Goddamnit, talk,' Sarah shoved Mud, he laughed.

'My dad tells me there's education budget cutbacks coming.'

'Oh no,' Sarah waved her hands in a fake tragic way, 'how am I going to study geometry now? C'mon, Mud.'

'School merge, they're talking school merge,' Mud said.

Then came details. Budget problems raised talk of merging two school districts; the black one with the white one. Theirs with ours. *That* would drive the kickers crazy.

Just as we were discussing it, in came broken-legged Gary Parr on crutches with two of his Wrangler-wearing buddies carrying his books. I'd already heard that he'd rolled his truck while driving drunk so he wouldn't be playing football for a while. Would he even get a QB slot next year? The Cougars, the team from the school we were merging with, they went to state last year, so they had the talent on their bench and maybe Gary Parr, Brian Gerber and the others wouldn't just be *given* their slots after the merge.

'Y'all queers want something?'

Even on crutches, Gary Parr was a dick. Why did he bother with the shiny pie plate belt buckle and the boots if he couldn't do his High Noon strut? If I were him, I'd be thinking pajamas were the right choice.

'Hey Gary,' I said, waving.

'You shut your mouth, pasty.' He pointed at me.

Did I really look like someone coming off a fever? I hoped I'd still be able to fight. Looking at the kicker closest to me, Donnie Roscoe, I wondered where I'd hit him with my fists of chrome so I could shatter his head like glass.

Principal Farner approached. All of us, kickers too, took notice. Gary Parr said, 'Lucky' to us. I guess meaning lucky for us the principal was there.

After they left, Sarah said, 'Yesterday I was in the girl's bathroom in a stall when two kicker girls came in. They were talking at the sinks and one of them said Gary Parr got drunk that night because Wendy Aubrey said that Prince was cute.'

'Prince? I bet he liked that.' I started singing Prince's *When Doves Cry* in a jokey voice because I didn't want my friends to suspect I liked his music.

I knuckled under a lot back then.

'Gary's losing his world.' Sarah shook her head. 'If he wasn't such a violent racist human stain, maybe I'd even feel sorry. You know he slapped her? Wendy Aubrey?'

I didn't know how to respond, because Sarah was always miles ahead of us on these things. I should've said Gary was wrong. Or told her that I liked Prince's music.

I sensed her waiting for a response to Gary's hitting Wendy, but I was too slow and she rolled her eyes and walked off. Her dyed black hair with the red stripe in it moved down the hall. I know *now* what I would've said, but then all I could think about was how I'd kissed her once at a party.

'Time of the month,' Trank joked.

'Shut up.' I chewed my lip.

'If the war's over,' Mud said, 'maybe it's time we focus on the band. There's this new kid in school. You should talk to him, Pete. He's a drummer in Band. We need a drummer.'

And that was the first I'd heard of Calvin Carr.

*

Stan was right. With Gary's injury and the upcoming racial tensions at our school, kickers couldn't focus on fighting The Mohawker War. Now that we didn't have to worry about getting jumped while walking home, maybe now we could give Deadman's Earlobes another shot. That was our band.

But finding drummers wasn't easy.

I'd have to finesse talking to Calvin. All those other times we'd failed to recruit guys from Band, most couldn't get past what we wanted to play versus what they were taught, the rest couldn't see a future in becoming a target for kickers. Or else they saw us as troublemakers. Total bullshit.

But since Calvin transferred into our district, that might make him more open to joining us, or so went my hope.

*

My second day back in school, I caught Calvin in the hall and he nearly threw his schoolbooks at me and ran. Our reputation, of course.

'It's okay,' I said, 'I just want to talk.' I made calming motions with my hands. 'So you play drums, right?'

He shrugged.

Looking at Calvin up close, I decided that despite his wiry forearms, he looked rabbit-like. That twitchy nose. A tuba player named Schloss stood by him trying to look hard. Funny.

I made my pitch, handing him a cassette of stuff I'd recorded from my record collection. 'Just give it a listen and if you like it, you should think about playing with us. Or at least come by, you know, to jam.'

'I'm busy today, um, tomorrow?'

'Tomorrow then.' I laughed it felt so good.

*

I don't know if Calvin was gifted or some kind of robot who only needed to hear something once to imitate it, but when we ended up at his house the next day after school, he played drums like I'd never heard anyone play drums.

'Keep doing that,' Mud yelled at him while picking out a crunchy riff, smiling, buckling his knees in time with the beat.

'You really never heard Scream or DRI before?' I asked during a break. They were two of the bands on the cassette I gave Calvin and the way he could sustain a driving beat or make an abrupt change of time, he must've heard *some* punk.

He shook his head behind his drum kit, hit the pedal on his bass drum a few times. 'Never, but I like 'em.'

Yeah, that first practice ripped.

We ran through the entire set and Calvin did drum fills that added teeth to some songs and cymbal-splashed menace to others. I wanted to drop my bass and jump in the air.

Stan, our singer, didn't say anything, but he leaned on the mike stand until Calvin's mother came into the garage and told us dinner was ready. Everyone perked up at that.

My mom had run us out when I tried hosting practice.

'I don't break my back at work just so I can hear the neighbors the next day complain about the noise,' she'd told me.

Calvin's mom did things differently. She asked us in to sit at her table and served us something unpronounceable that she learned to make when she studied in France years ago.

'Whatever this is, it's good,' Mud said through a mouthful.

Mrs. Carr blushed and when she left the room, I told Calvin while lifting my fork, 'Best fucking food ever.'

Calvin's face locked up until he saw his mother wasn't around and then he relaxed. He had a good smile. Probably he should smile more, not look so serious, but having my dad walk out like his did, I understood why he might not want to.

'My mom used to run a catering business when we lived in Boulder,' Calvin said.

'Where's Boulder?' asked Mud.

'Colorado. It's where my dad lives. We're just renting my cousin's house until he sends for us. He got a job there.'

He looked hopeful when he said it, but I knew he didn't believe his father was sending for them. A lot of nights in my bed, I used to imagine my father was coming back too.

'Thanks,' he told us. 'Thanks for coming over. I don't know a lot of people at school and this is great.'

'Boulder's a dumb name for a city,' Stan said.

We all looked at him.

'Sorry, I just...sorry.' Stan scratched his chin, then asked, 'Hey, why does she limp like that?'

Calvin's mom *did* drag her left foot behind her. But I wasn't dick enough to point it out, so I smacked the back of Stan's head and let him get mad.

It turned out Calvin's mom had some kind of neurological disorder. Her inner wiring was all fried so sometimes she had complete mobility, other times not. She treated us kindly despite our hair, our noisy music. I liked her.

But mostly I liked that we now had a drummer.

*

The next three practices also kicked ass.

But personality or creative differences came up, and by then I knew I'd have to be the one to fix them.

'Your hair looks gay,' Stan said to Calvin at the third practice. 'Not trying to be rude or anything, but it does.'

Calvin sprayed his hair into spikes, finally breaking with his conventional look and starting to wear old t-shirts and ripped jeans instead of his preppy polos. If focusing on his personal style sounds shallow, well, maybe we were and didn't know it then.

'What's wrong with my hair?' Calvin looked hurt.

'What I said, it looks gay.'

'Don't be a dick, Stan.' To Calvin, I said, 'Looks good.'

But Stan loved attention like worms love dirt. And he wrote half the songs, so I had to put up with him. In the face of kicker harassment we'd all learned to put up with each other.

'Calvin,' Mud said, but looking at Stan who must've put him up to saying it, 'if you're going to do all them drum fills, you're going to overpower the guitar parts in this song.'

'I am?' Behind his drums, Calvin frowned.

'That's true and I wrote this song,' Stan chimed in, leaning on his mike stand, 'so I should know.'

I put my head against the cabinet of my bass amp, biting the inside of my cheek, playing a scale over and over. This totally childish shit. I saw where it was going.

But I didn't gather this group just to have it fall apart.

I'd rescued Mud by introducing him to the music of Minor Threat, Fear and the Bad Brains. I got him going to punk shows. I got him excited about music. But he brought Stan along, and they knew each other longer, so I had to tread carefully.

'Let's fucking make music,' I said. Then we got back to it, but all the while we played songs about hating Reagan and smashing windows, I kept it in the back of my mind that I had to fix things between everyone in the band.

*

I got the opportunity to fix things thrown to me days later. A show coming up. There hadn't been a punk show in weeks and now we'd use this time to square things between us.

The night of the show Calvin had to cook for his mom before he left. She was having a bad motor skills day. Then he snuck out. I'd promised we'd get him back before his mom knew he was gone. She would never have let him go.

The show was on a school night.

After picking Calvin up at the corner of his block, I drove us all to my place. With my mom at her nursing job, there'd be nothing to keep us from a bottle of cheap red wine I'd bought with a fake ID in the next town over. Each overly sweet mouthful of Boone's Farm brought us closer to friendship and punk rock immortality, I thought.

We polished that bottle off, then the four of us went to GOLDEN LOTUS TAKEOUT. The Chinese restaurant didn't last a year, but the new owners left the sign up when they converted it into our town's punk rock venue. Not a lot of bands visited because they usually skipped us to go to Austin or Houston or Dallas, but when they did visit, they came here.

This being a school night, most mohawkers didn't show. And this wasn't the Dead Kennedys or Flipper playing, but instead an outfit out of Utah called The Revolting Medusas.

But I had their album because I ordered it through the mail and loved it and wished there'd been more of a crowd. Calvin could've met people we knew from out of town. But maybe it being less crowded, that'd give us a chance as a band to deepen the friendship between all of us.

When we walked into GOLDEN LOTUS TAKEOUT, a girl with blue hair named Marcy came up and asked me to make an Ill Repute/Angry Samoans tape for her. I said I would. She'd given me a ride to a Really Red show in Austin once.

'Hey, where is everyone?' she asked.

I shrugged and she left me to talk to someone else.

The Revolting Medusas had no opening act. A damned shame because they deserved it.

'They got a chick singer,' Stan said, smirking. 'Man, I wish I'd known.'

I was glad Sarah wasn't around to hear him.

Anyway, I thought the Medusas sounded good and tough.

They blasted out their music and I wanted to show how much I loved it, so I started slamdancing. Thrashing. Moshing. You know. Before metalheads stole the idea of a mosh pit, while dumbassed cops still thought they were witnessing riots and shutting down punk shows in some cities, *that's* what we were doing. Before '92 when all music became 'alternative' that year if you believed the station identifications in between commercials for fast food and used car lots.

Anyhow, so there I was, bouncing off other punkrockers, body against body, and it was cool because no one used elbows or swung spiked wristbands. Fifteen people dancing total.

I danced three songs.

And then a few folks started stagediving. Crazy. There just wasn't enough crowd to catch anyone diving off stage. I'd never done it myself, though one time a stagediver landed on me. We bonked heads and I had to go to the ER to get stitches in my scalp. They had to shave a postage stamp-sized wedge in my hair to do it, which was fine because then I used that as an excuse to checker my hair with a bunch of those bare-scalp wedges.

My mom was not pleased.

So anyway, the crowd was stagediving.

And Calvin slamdanced. Sweating, resting, he stood a few feet from me laughing while Stan whispered into his ear. Good. Maybe they were finally getting along. But when I turned away, the next time I turned back I didn't see Calvin, and Stan, grinning, was talking to Mud.

I got a bad feeling.

I looked up at the stage and there was Calvin on it. And me too far to reach him. Goddamned Stan must've talked him into it, I decided.

Calvin stagedived.

Arms flapping, the poor kid realized the cushion of the crowd had pulled out from under him. He landed on his palms, breaking his fall, but hit his chin on the concrete a moment later. Shit. Along with some other kids, I carried Calvin to a side stage not used that night.

The Revolting Medusas stopped playing.

The singer, black lipsticked lips pursed, came over to Calvin who lay there flat on his back, holding his face. He looked scared. Then he took his hands from his chin.

Blood jetted. The singer yipped. People recoiled.

And I had to take Calvin to the emergency room.

Stan and Mud decided to stay. Stan looked sorry, so for a moment there I wasn't sure about his involvement. But then he grinned so I punched him in the face. He fell down.

*

At the ER, Calvin holding an icepack and gauze to his chin while we waited, I told him not to worry. Stan was out.

'If he wants to sing, it's going to have to be solo in the shower.' Comforting him, all the while I was thinking it was a good thing my mom didn't work at this hospital. She'd have strapped me with a belt.

Calvin didn't speak, stared at the polished floor.

Then his mother showed up with a neighbor since she couldn't drive because of her disorder. 'Go home, Peter. Your mother has to be as worried as I am about Calvin.'

'My mom? Nah. She's at work. She doesn't even know I'm out.' Because I'd been reassuring Calvin all this time, I didn't think to watch my words in front of his mother. Shit.

Calvin's mom frowned, sniffed me and said, 'You've been drinking. You snuck my son out of his home to take him drinking at a concert on a school night.'

I thought she was going to slap me, so I just waved at Calvin who didn't respond and I left them there.

*

Calvin transferred schools to Boulder with his father.

His mom stayed in town for a few years after, but she rebuffed my attempts to be her friend and said she told Calvin about my requests that he call me.

But he never called.

And that next fall at school, with the kickers ripe for another Mohawker war, that's when it happened. They merged schools. Our school went multicultural. Kickers didn't hunt mohawkers that fall, and forget taking the state title because the football team didn't even break out of district that year. Then the black kids' parents started attacking the idea of a team being named The Rebels in the first place, while the white parents said that it was tradition and anyway, what did that have to do with their win-loss record?

What a mess.

Meanwhile Stan and I made a truce. He apologized for being a dick, but also said, 'I never told Calvin to stagedive. I was stupid jealous, but all I said was about grabbing your moment, these crazy guys jumping with no crowd to catch them.'

Grabbing your moment.

A week into the fall classes, Mud's father illustrated this by taking a job as oilrig supervisor in the Gulf, and moving his family to Galveston. That killed any hope of a band.

But I had memories of practice, that last one we played. The crackle-pop of amplifier feedback, the fading hiss of cymbals, a guitar chord hanging there a moment before getting eaten up by the quiet.

It's a sound that hasn't left me in all of the years since.

BLANKNOIR

Stephen Palmer

Hate Leaders

Dave's tank rumbled along Hammersmith Road as bricks and mortar fell from the buildings to either side, crashing to the tarmac to smash into billows of dust. He'd sprayed the band name Blanknoir on one side in red, the other side concealed behind branches and iron railings that he'd picked up on the way. Strikers stared open-mouthed at him; scabs sneaking past. Then he was gone, leaving tread marks in the mortar dust that covered much of west London.

He was going to get the band *noticed* whatever it took. He was going to get the debut album made. And nobody else was going to help, so Blanknoir had to do it themselves.

The first one who saw the tank was Blag. She looked like a taller, skinnier, paler Joey Ramone. Dave parked the tank outside the band's squat and poked his head out of the turret, brushing dust off his hair and 'tache.

'You fuckwit!' she yelled, 'what you gone and done now?'

'For the Marquee tonight,' he replied.

'You drove that joyriding through - '

'Yes! Why not? Five hundred people have seen the name already. It's called publicity.'

'Fuckwit.'

Matt and Sue appeared, both bleary eyed – it had only just gone noon. Matt was wearing his Hawkwind jacket, Sue some kind of khaki green T and a Mao cap. They stared.

'What?' Dave said.

Sue nodded, a grin on her face. 'Good Dave, it's great publicity, but also symbolic – the vehicles of the others used against them, that's a nice turnaround. No, I like it. I can write lyrics for a tank. Maim! Maybe a new song for tonight - '

The rest of Sue's sentence was drowned out by planes returning from strafing Croydon. Dave jumped down to the road and slapped the side of the tank. 'No way are we writing new songs half a day before a gig. The set stands.'

Tension again, springing up between them. Blag preened her dyed black hair. 'Says you.'

'Says us,' Dave corrected. 'We are this tank.'

Matt shrugged. 'A concert is a concert. I need some breakfast, I shall be back later.'

'We're turning up in this tank,' Dave said. 'It's a stunt. I could blow a man's arm off.'

'You're a stunt,' Blag replied, before heading off into the squat.

*

<u>Girls + Boys =</u>

The Marquee was rammed to the rafters. They turned up in the tank, crushing bricks and cans and discarded dry trees beneath the treads. Every striker, dosser and malcontent along Oxford Street saw them and it was like a self-made homecoming. Even Blag smiled – once. Matt was high on shrooms and Sue writing ideas down in her little red notebook.

Mart, however, was not pleased. 'What d'you think the police - '

'The police?' Dave interrupted. 'You see any police today? You saw more than fifty of 'em on the TUC march this morning?'

'Your set tonight had better be the best ever, or I'm dropping you - '

'Dropping us?' Blag said. 'You still think we're *with* you?'

Mart scowled. 'So, what are you doing?'

Dave stood in front of Blag, an arm's length from Mart. 'The entire album, twelve tracks in order, and nothing more. The album is the album, that's what Blanknoir is.'

'No encores,' Blag agreed.

Mart sniggered. 'They Long To Be Close To - '

'Fuck *off!*'

The gig was a sell-out, a triumph. Blag mesmerised the audience, dressed black from head to foot, scarier than Siouxsie. Matt wore his multi-coloured coat and coaxed electronic heaven from his synths. Sue pounded like Maureen, while Dave's bass thrummed, bestially. Classic Blanknoir.

The crowd went berserk when they realised the band had gone after twelve numbers and there wasn't going to be any more, but already the quartet were in the tank and heading off down Dean Street. Mart ran after them. In sleazy Soho they paused, getting out of the tank to stare at the fritzing neon, the poster-garbed dosser hideouts, the roadblocks. Even Dave was uncertain about smashing through Soho roadblocks – this was a place of revolution.

From the West Sea came a gang of skinheads, a dozen at least, attracted by the tank. Goss had spread across the area – the tank, the gig, the electric atmosphere... Blanknoir had enemies, everyone knew that, but these bastards were armed with spanners, mallets and chainsaws.

'I am not sure I like this,' Matt said, necking a coke then throwing the can aside.

Even Blag quailed. Sue stood between them, arm in arm, and said, 'These people are our class enemies. We can rightly hate them, even though hate is a negative emotion and beneath the Blanknoir philosophy. If they have chainsaws, we ignore the chainsaws, and that will be our response. They just want to be noticed. We ignore. It is the correct response - '

'But the tank!' Dave said. 'We need it!'

'We used it,' Sue insisted. 'We move on.'

Mart ran up, gasping for breath. He glanced at the approaching mob, then pointed his finger at Dave and said, 'You've gone too far this time.'

'*I've* gone too - '

'Yes! Any more of this madness and I'm not making the album. Publicity is publicity, but this is nothing more than vandalism.'

The skinheads began shrieking.

A man appeared from a side alley, bald, tall, wearing a sheepskin coat and DMs. 'Follow me,' he said. 'I know a place of safety.'

'Who the fuck are you?' Blag replied.

'My name is Lucifer.'

*

Lenins Leaning

Lucifer came from a Soho nightclub called Tokyo; turned out he'd been a fan of the band since their Surrey days in Matt's parents' mansion. Outside Tokyo, beneath buzzing neon, and with a thousand newspaper pages rolling in the cold street wind, they listened to him.

'I know a man,' he said, 'a Swede, who used to be a factory worker. He created Time Records. Interested?'

Dave frowned. 'You mean, he owns a record label?'

'His concept of ownership is nugatory,' Lucifer replied. 'Time Records is a concept. To be part of Time Records you have to symbolically buy a watch. He's made fifty million of them. With a strap. Interested?'

Dave glanced at the rest of the band. 'Uh... maybe. Why's he interested in us?'

'He's never heard of you. But I have, and I know him well. Interested?'

'Uh... maybe.'

Dave looked at Sue and shrugged. Sue said, 'The concept of ownership in a dead capitalist society is nugatory, yes, but let's not forget that we can use the weapons of the enemy against them. They *do* have a concept of ownership. So... this man's concept of ownership is different to that of the West, that doesn't mean it's a good one. Does it *work?* Does it strike at the self-satisfied, smirking, malignant heart of our shitty government?'

Lucifer shrugged. 'He's a Swede. They aren't British over there.'

Blag spat. 'He'll sell out. They always do.'

Lucifer shook his head. 'If he sold out, that would be the end of Time Records.'

'This Swedish man sounds like a decent bet,' Matt said. 'I think we should test him out, meet him, see what kind of man he is.'

Blag shrugged. 'Having the record out is better than no record.'

'Exactly,' said Lucifer.

*

<u>London Ladi</u>

Next morning the streets of west London were pandemonium. Overnight, truckers from the Hyde Park dugouts had moved west, shredding everything before them, the streets little more than rivers of rubble. Dust hung smog-heavy in the air and the sky droned with planes. There was little sign of the police. Government choppers like black insects rose from their hideaways by the Thames, flying north, while the people of the city sought food, water, clothes, batteries. The TUC soup kitchens were overwhelmed by starving Londoners.

'It's a revolution,' Sue said, approvingly. 'By default.'

'So long as we can hijack it for the band you can call it what you like,' Dave replied.

'Everything's an image, a prank for you, isn't it?'

Dave nodded, a grin on his face. 'Yup.'

Lucifer brought his Swedish acquaintance to the squat around noon. 'This is Björn Olsson,' he said, 'the man associated with Time Records. Björn, this is the band.'

Björn spoke through a heavy accent. 'I make one thousand copies,' he said, 'which we sell at gigs, to make a buzz on the underground. The circuit, you know? The vinyl is black, the label is white, with black writing. You have the master tapes?'

Dave nodded. 'They're buried, safe and sound. Our treasure, you see – our *power*.'

'Nearby?'

'Never you mind, blondie. Where, only the band knows. This band is everything. We're tighter than car wheel nuts, nothing can split us. Not even the government.'

Björn laughed. 'You think, so, this government is a joke? No. They make a big panic, then come down heavy. I see it before. How many album tracks, what are they?'

'Twelve,' Dave replied. 'The album opens with Hate Leaders – big crowd fave – then Girls Plus Boys Equals, Lenins Leaning - '

'No apostrophe,' Sue remarked.

' - London Ladi, Spite, Stroboscope, then on side two Arthur Ransome Is Dead, Intensify, You Dance Everywhere, Heatseeking, Proles, then we end with 1984½, with Matt and Blag trading riffs from the other eleven tracks. We often get that one up to ten minutes live, working the crowd 'til they're berserk. Ace.'

Björn made to reply, but a strange sound from outside stopped him. Dave ran out of the squat front door, into the street, where he saw cider-addled dossers being herded by what appeared to be shiny silver men.

Matt joined him. His face turned white. 'Versatran, series F!' he whispered.

'What?'

'Metal made into men! We are toast. Run!'

Dave looked more closely. The robots were no larger than a man, but their strength was obvious, mere human beings standing no chance. Government robots: no need for the cops, then.

Now Sue appeared. She shook her head. 'Good workers,' she said, 'they won't get bored. Matt's right. Run. The government is cleansing the city, but we can't get angry about it yet.'

Björn shouted over the noise, 'Come with me to Sweden, we get the album pressed up, then return in triumph to bring music revolution. You with me?'

As one all four of them said, 'Yes.'

Lucifer had vanished.

*

Spite

But first they had to dig up the master tapes.

Dave had buried them next to his mother's grave in Fulham Cemetery. They had to wait until sundown before they dared leave the squat, and with Versatrans everywhere – 'Get out of the way!' – it was always going to be difficult. They crossed the Talgarth Road under cover of gunfire from some distant huddle of shelters, but the A219 was impassable, choked with refugees from the pits and smoking stacks of Charing Cross Hospital. In the end they had no choice but to slip and slop along the Thames bank, until they found the green of Rowberry Mead, where they headed east.

The tapes were in metal boxes, PIL-style. Dave checked they were all present then dropped them into his rucksack. 'Blanknoir are going for the eastern front,' he declared. 'It's the place to go.'

They headed back to the Thames, where they had concealed a boatlet; with this they crossed the river to the ferry laid on by Björn. The first short stretch along the U-bend was okay, but by the time they got to Chelsea Embankment they were under fire from both rioting crowds and the Versatrans trying to shepherd the crowds into chicken-wire cages. Björn set up steel netting to deflect or catch missiles. Luckily almost nobody had guns, and with it being dark all the bullets hit water and nothing more delicate.

The big river U-bend around the Isle Of Dogs was similarly dangerous, but this time, because the locals had been under siege from government forces for well over a fortnight, and because the TUC forces hadn't been able to approach, the level of weaponry was tribal: spears, sharpened disks, catapults. All the ammo missed, the river too wide, the light too poor.

Eventually they passed the docklands... Woolwich... Dagenham... the Rainham Marshes Reserve. Gravesend was a nightmare, a hint of dawn now in the sky: clouds of spears, Greek fire, even some ack-ack taken out of the heavens and aimed at them. Their luck held. Dave found himself swearing oaths to all and sundry that he would not let the master tapes fall into enemy hands.

It clouded up as the sun rose. As they slipped into ocean proper between Sheerness and Shoeburyness all four of them stood at the ferry bow and watched the sun appear. Nimbus streaked the orange-tinted sky. Cumulus began to bubble up from nowhere. They were on their way to Sweden: safe at last.

*

Stroboscope

The ferry was named Laura Logic, and on this woman-ship they headed east, their plan to make overseas towards Denmark, then dock at Gothenburg. The seas were cruel, waves dashing themselves against the ferry hull, spume fleck everywhere, Blag seasick, Matt little better, Sue and Dave okay, though at times they had to scream. Denmark looked grey under grey skies.

Approaching Gothenburg, they realised that they had left the hold unlocked. As water poured into the ferry they followed emergency procedures to the life-rafts, in the freezing water all five of them heading for the nearest harbour at Gothenburg. Desperate times, scrambling ashore where they went aground on the rocks. Flocks of territorial seagulls screeched and squawked above their heads. Björn appeased the immigration officers they met, but Gothenburg was awash with aliens escaped from Britain, refugees from Hull, Lowestoft, Scarborough. A British exodus was underway, sweary, boozed up and fighting.

Björn lived at a commune, where he had his record plant. The spiral scratch chamber stank of vinyl. In less than a week he had a thousand copies of the album pressed up, sleeved gatefold style (a *hell* of a lot of argument over that little prog hangover) with stark B&W images of four heads on stakes: Dave looking down, Sue staring at the camera, Blag also staring down, Matt seemingly out of it as if on shrooms or dope.

They rebuilt the ferry then retraced their steps, arriving at the mouth of the Thames a week later. Radio reports said Britain was disintegrating by the day. Landing in a dense fog, they lost Björn.

With London aflame, the radio becoming garbled and fog shrouding the coast, they knew it was time to head up north, if only briefly, to marshal their forces.

Then south, to the capital, and the release of *Blanknoir.*

End of side 1.

*

Arthur Ransome Is Dead

Chaos in the capital.

The government fled overnight to Scotland, parts of Westminster razed to the ground. A dark mist created by clashing factions covered the centre of the city, turning day into night. The band headed south along the old A10, halting at the end of Kingsland Road when the rubble got too much, too high for their van to cope with. It seemed as though their dream of playing gigs and selling the album was to be dashed. Then they ran out of petrol. No garages remained open.

Mobsters shouted through loudhailers. 'Stay in your homes. Nightfall, you need to be indoors. The Scots have joined the government!'

Some order did arise from the dust. The TUC merged with the GLC to provide a skeleton of organisation covering the city and half of Greater London. Yet the skeleton was weak, and mobs prowled the streets, focussing their attention on the many TUC food banks. The Versatrans were already rusting.

For Sue, chaos was no bad thing. 'The government began all this,' she pointed out, 'and that's why the city was paralysed with protest marches. It's only right that they flee to Edinburgh. All we have to do is stand alongside the TUC and their associated bodies.'

They unpacked the van and waited for Blag to return with a Mini, which they hoped they could drive all the way to Westminster. An hour passed. They got scared. Then Blag appeared, telling tales of anti-TUC protest mobs, GLC vigilantes and worse.

Matt said, 'We very much have to ally ourselves with the TUC. They will put on gigs as soon as anybody, I would think - '

'You fuckwit,' Blag interrupted. 'This is *Blanknoir*. We go it alone!'

'We can't ally ourselves to anybody,' Dave agreed. 'The whole point of this band is not to rely on authority. Not to rely on anybody except ourselves.'

'But we relied on Björn,' Matt said, 'without his excellent help we would have no record.'

Dave felt anger welling up inside. Band tension... again. They needed to be *tight* at this time. He replied, 'That's different, you cretin. He made the record. A one-off deal. We didn't compromise on that, we demanded it exactly how we wanted it, and we *got* it.'

'Yeah,' Blag said, stuffing a ciggie into her mouth. Her lighter clicked. 'And we do whatever we want with 'em. Sell 'em, give 'em away, get 'em reviewed.'

Matt shrugged.

Dave eyed Sue. She would not be so easily mollified.

*

Intensify

Dave managed to get the band a gig at the Houses Of Parliament, or at least in its smoking ruins. Though Big Ben tower stood tall, the rest of the building was torched. Already starving mobs had taken all the furniture, the adornments, the filing cabinets, the booze. College Green was almost hidden beneath market fairs bartering this stuff.

And then Dave got a shock.

An hour before the gig, when the band had soundchecked, networked, and selected a couple of hundred copies of the record with which to barter (selling now being a meaningless activity), a skinhead approached him.

Dave looked the man up and down. 'Yeah?'

'You're in Blanknoir?'

'Sure. Bass. Front-man, some say.'

The skinhead nodded. 'Probably best not to play tonight.'

'What?'

'If there was an accident, you know?'

'An accident?' Dave said. 'You threatening me?'

'I'm in a band too. Front-man, some say. We are The Territorials. We're going to bring some order around here - '

Dave laughed. 'The TUC are doing that already, mate. You'd better stay off our turf.'

'Really? Hah... my existence isn't threatened by you, *mate*.'

'Who the hell do you think you are, telling this band where to play? This is *Blanknoir*. If you've never heard of us you're in the wrong country.'

'Unfortunately I had heard of you. Seems you hadn't heard of us. Seems you were part of the exodus to Denmark and Sweden. Nasty little cop out, that.'

'You don't scare me,' Dave said. 'This band is quite safe. We've got our own philosophy - '

The skinhead took a step towards Dave, so that Dave could smell his lagered breath. Suddenly there was a flick-knife between their faces. 'This is the philosophy of The Territorials. And we're a five-piece, one more than you. Worst case scenario, one of my band remains. You understand?'

Dave decided it was time to back away. 'We don't use weapons. No need.'

The skinhead stepped back. 'Stay away from the TUC, from anything anti-government. Don't believe the propaganda, okay? Then nobody will get hurt round here.'

'You don't understand, this band does its own thing. We do it ourselves. We ain't into hurting anybody.'

The skinhead smiled. 'I knew you'd understand. Just don't forget what I said, *Dave*.'

'But we can't cancel tonight's gig. Too late.'

'You got no choice.'

'So... you're going to play here?'

The skinhead offered Dave a look of contempt. 'What d'you think our fans would say if we played a gig in the house of politicians?'

Dave shrugged. 'Right.'

*

You Dance Everywhere

Was it a coup? Nobody could tell. Nobody had any information, just gossip, rumour, a word or two floating through the mist and smoke that covered London Town. Dave, frightened, got the band into a blitzed building behind Waterloo Station, where they hid their thousand records under rotting floorboards. Snot-defaced posters advertised a gig by The Territorials at the Ministry Of Defence. The symbolism was undeniable.

'We gotta get a gig *some*where,' Blag insisted. 'If not at parliament – I s'pose that might have been a bit pushy – then somewhere else.'

Dave glanced at her. This was not Blag's usual confrontational style. She was scared.

'Where?' he asked.

'TUC headquarters,' Sue said.

Dave rounded on her. 'We are *not* gigging with them, or the GLC, or anybody else. We do this *ourselves*. Our fans are all still in London. We've got a thousand records. We can barter, we can survive in this place, we can still make waves, make the people believe in us, follow us. The record is our front, our *word*. We do it ourselves. If we let anybody help us, we kill ourselves.'

'Crap,' Sue replied. 'Nobody can stand alone forever - '

Dave shouted, 'This band *can!* This is *Blanknoir!*'

'But every venue that puts us on is helping us. What's the difference?'

'Venues are part of the world of music, not politics or authority,' Dave insisted. 'They want bands. The TUC marched explicitly against the government.'

Matt said, 'We cannot gig properly in this environment, people are too worried about putting food on the plate for the next day.'

'They'll come to see *us*,' Dave replied. 'They need something to believe in, something to take them away from all this chaos. We supply that feeling for them, that emotion, that release. If we do it on

TUC territory we betray our philosophy, we dilute our music. So we do this on our own terms. The people need something hot, strong, totally *tight*, like this band is tight. They aren't going to follow any compromise band.'

Blag nodded. 'No fucking sell out. Sell out stinks.'

'Crap,' Sue said, shaking her head. 'I'm not having this crap.'

'It is too dangerous to go it alone,' Matt agreed.

'Then we're splitting?' Dave said. 'On the edge of greatness, we split? With a thousand copies of the album pressed up and ready to make music history, we split?'

No answers to any of these questions.

*

Heatseeking

Seeing little alternative, the band decided to suss out what The Territorials were up to. On the street grapevine they heard about a second gig at the MOD, so they went to check it out. At once Dave was struck by the paradox of this band, who despised trad power – or seemed to – playing shit punk-lite in a house of authority.

Blag's bull detectors had gone off too. 'This stinks,' she said.

Dave nodded, glancing at the night-dark street behind him. The torch-lit parade of black leather jacket clad fans appalled him. 'These sheep know nothing better than to die here for their band's cause,' he said.

'What are we gonna do, Dave?'

'Don't you worry. Our band won't split. We can handle a difference of opinion so long as it's about band philosophy. If Sue and Matt want to ally with the TUC, they can. We'll play there and be rubbish. Then you and I will follow the true path, with Sue and Matt beside us.'

'What is the true path?'

'It's all about what you show. The symbolism. These cretins think playing at army headquarters gives them power. It doesn't. It just allows them to temporarily wear the mantle of power worn by somebody else, in this case the MOD. Don't you see? It's about the symbolism of what we do and what the *fans* see us do. It's the beating punk heart.'

'So... we stick to our guns?'

Dave nodded. 'We line up a tour of London. We play symbolic venues. We barter with the album. The Territorials haven't got an album because they haven't realised the importance of a front that exists away from the band itself – they've got no artefact representing them. *Blanknoir* is our body of work, our weapon and our statement.'

Blag grinned. 'Let's tour.'

Dave nodded at the MOD building. 'Don't you worry, the pigs will become men. I can see their rotten thoughts. Let's hope they make enough rope to hang themselves.'

*

Proles

They played a gig at the TUC headquarters. They were rubbish.

The Territorials played a third and a fourth gig at the MOD building. But, although this appeared to indicate success, Dave noticed as he skulked in the shadows that the band's following did not increase. Blanknoir, meanwhile, were adding twenty punters per night to their crowd by playing pubs and bombed out clubs in the Hammersmith area.

Lucifer turned up one night, and Dave took him to the band's dressing room.

'I've got a job for you,' Dave said.

Lucifer handed over a copy of the album. 'Sign this?'

Dave nodded, signed, then passed the album around for the others to sign. Important not to upset the core fans. When Lucifer had his album back Dave continued, 'I need you to infiltrate The Territorials fan base.'

'You gonna blast them?'

'No! That's loser talk. If we attack we're no better than them, and we'd be using their weapons too. What we do is stay true to our vision. We *ignore* them. We gig locally and build up our following, basing it on our gigs and the album, like always.'

'What do you want me to do?'

Dave said, 'Get the guys in The Territorials to play St Paul's Cathedral.'

'St Paul's? Why?'

'Isn't it obvious?'

Lucifer's gaze went blank for a few moments. Then he smiled and said, 'Yeah.'

'None of us can do this job,' Dave continued, indicating the other three. 'The Territorials understand that we're the opposition, that we're the blood of the streets, potentially with a crowd to match. All of London is up for grabs now. That's why they're playing at the MOD. But we want their fans to see the truth. I reckon that band will play St Paul's if you get a chance to mention it to them. And then...'

'Then?'

'The ultimate prize. What I want them to do, what I hope they'll do.'

Lucifer nodded. 'Gotcha.'

Sue smiled. 'It is always a mistake to pervert the symbols of the enemy,' she said.

*

1984½

The penultimate night of the Blanknoir tour took place at the Hundred Club. It was a dump, a mess, a pit of lager and vomit and gob, but it was home to Blanknoir. Dave knew they were following the right path. Blag knew, Matt knew, and even Sue knew, though she still hankered after the welcoming arms of the TUC. But the statistics did not lie. Eight hundred copies of the album gone. Fifty given as freebies to the core fans. Twenty broken during a punch-up. One given to John Peel.

Had they got enough time? Dave did not know. The sky had gone black with war fog coming down from Scotland and the north. Rumour begat rumour begat rumour. What if there was no way back for Blanknoir?

But they had the album. They always had the album.

And then Dave heard the news he had been hoping for. Blag ran into the squat and shouted, 'They're doing it!'

Dave perked up. 'Eh? Who? What?'

'The fucking Territorials are playing the Houses Of Parliament!'

Dave laughed. 'We *got* them. They can't survive now. They've played all three of the venues that'll poison their fan base.'

'And us?'

'We play our last night of the tour - '

'Where, Dave? Fucking *where?*'

'Here! The squat. Our home, our origin. Where else?'

That day the band seemed to move at random, like a coin in the air. The buzz amongst the fans was incredible. Dave reckoned a thousand would turn up, maybe more. The rickety stage outside the back of the squat was made of MDF and gaffa tape, but it would do. The PA was half dead and slimy with saliva, but it would do. What mattered was the message, the heart.

The gig was a triumph. The music was white hot and perfect. They even had a phalanx of fans defect from The Territorials, fans tonight sporting green Sue-T-shirts.

So it came to 1984½, the last song of the set. Throughout the tour they had played the entire album, twelve tracks in order, and nothing more. The album was the album; that's what Blanknoir was. Usually they ramped up the adrenalin levels for the last track, spinning it out into a ten, a fifteen minute epic. Dave knew that tonight this magical cut could go on forever.

He stood at the front of the stage, Blag beside him. He glanced back at Matt, half concealed by a stack of synths. Sue glistened with sweat behind her drum kit.

Last song. Last night.

'This is the last one tonight,' he said.

A massive roar from the crowd.

'And it's the last one ever. We've made our statement.'

Blag stared at him. 'No!'

'Yes,' he said. 'We can't top this. We were looking for a better way, but we were living it all the time.'

Some fans were booing, but others were cheering.

'We needed to restore everyone's sight,' he continued. 'The album does that. We can't do anything after the album, it stands alone.'

More cheering.

'So, this is it. 1984½. I hope none of you bastards are taping this gig! It's the ones that don't get bootlegged that people never forget. So get out there, all of you, and follow your paths! And *never* get the feeling you've been cheated.'

End of side 2.

Breath of Fresh Air

P A Levy

Storm had smashed her way through bricks and mortar to get her paws on the new Damned album; Machine Gun Etiquette. She had played a certain scenario through in her mind, fast forward > rewind < pause :: , eloquently holding a machine gun, in such a manner so as not to damage her sharpened nails she had painted Love-Lies-Bleeding Red. Rat! Tat! Tat! Tat! Thundercat. Smash it up.

Screaming obscenities in her native Anglo-Saxon, like an Evangelist on cheap amphetamine, she marauded the High Street dressed in zips and leathers, kicking and punching her way through an invisible cage of air that surrounded her. Smothered her. Fighting for the right to have oxygen. Fighting for oxygen. A snakebite rosy glow couldn't mask her determination, and Storm stormed off, a Stormtrooper marching into Poland.

*

Machine gun in hand.

*

She thought to herself how much she loved this place. The London streets. The London stories. The London dirt. The London Underground and the underground. The overgrown London pavement cracks. The London sound; the changing London sound; louder, faster. She knew three chords and a drummer boy and they were ready to go to war.

This 'hands off' relationship with drummer boy had developed over many years, they grew up on the same estate, were in the same class at school, drunk Red Stripe and smoked spliff on the same swings in the same playgrounds. They both saw the Bill Grundy 'Filth and Fury' interview with the Sex Pistols. They both decided, then and there, cosmically at the exact same time, they would become punk rockers. It was their destiny. Her fate. And for him, a commitment that was so heartfelt, it was as good as a love song serenade.

*

This is how legends are made.

*

To find a bass player they advertised in the 'Exchange and Mart'. The ad had been misplaced between two Ford Escorts and yet they still managed to get a reply. Escort, as he became known, was offered the position because: 1) he could play a little, had his own guitar and amp. 2) Storm was getting bored. 3) He had a van, and a job, which meant disposable income, and by disposable income it was understood to mean spare cash for Storm to spend on drugs.

*

'Noise Heroes # 9' became their name.

*

As they couldn't afford rehearsal rooms they practiced acoustically, unplugged, in drummer boy's bedsit. The smell was rancid. The two month old air heavy with the detritus of overthinking and soiled, sweaty underwear. Above him was a brothel; a heaven with a suited and booted brick shit house geezer at the Gates of St Peter, and angels that spoke with northern accents. Influences that worked their way into the songs now becoming framed by the sounds of those very angels sighing and calling to their god as in prayer, a mantra, a chant to bliss. These were Storm's songs. The three minute goddess of crash and burn baby, burn. Storm's songs about her crumbling landscapes awash with grey, about the dereliction of her mind, and about a body she's forced to share a life. In the mind fallen brick rubble, encased inside a skeleton of cracked walls and bomb blasted windows, riot and the blue flashing lights of Babylon's three minute warning she chewed gum, overused her eye liner, wore a razor wire tiara.

They had their first gig lined up. Debut. Supporting some band they had never heard of. They needed posters, they needed flyers. Storm had decided she would do the artwork. She did two large lines of speed, opened a fresh bottle of gin, and sat cross-legged on the floor with a pile of magazines and newspapers in front of her. She started cutting out pictures, words, anything that caught her eye, and it became obsessive; carefully trimming snip snip snip everything with neat and true straight lines. Her mind was getting cut and pasted on to the white pages that haunted her like ghosts. With neat and true straight lines of speed the debut flyers needed a fresh bottle of gin. They cut pictures from the magazines and newspapers of words, obsessively trimmed snip snip snip everything, and sat cross-legged on the floor of their first gig supporting some band they had never heard of's artwork. That caught her eye. The two large lines of speed in the magazines and newspapers in front of her. It was her debut for obsessive cutting, but the anti ghost riddled white page attack worked. The artwork was a triumph.

Escort and drummer boy began to question Storm's sanity after she announced that she had fallen into an all consuming and passionate love affair with her fuzz pedal; 'I can get a decent fuzz high ride, man. I can melt into electricity,' she would say. She would smile, and a switch was turned on behind her eyes that flickered, that flickered, that flickered until it finally caught hold so that they could see a passageway that appeared to lead deep inside her. Neither of them took up the offer to venture to such a place.

*

Boys and girls come out to play.

*

As soon as they arrived at the gig the initial excitement had given way to despair. This was clearly not the place for Noise Heroes. Escort was sent to Coventry for booking a gig supporting a disco diva in a twelve pound Chelsea Girl outfit. They stacked up the doom and plugged it into the gloom but remained committed to the cause and so carried on regardless, even though there was a real danger they would be bottled off stage. No surrender, especially to the D-I-S-C-O squad with their backing singers on remote control. Stepford singers. Storm said they were Christmas sweets all wrapped up in their glittery colours. All that glitters is not...

Drummer boy and Escort were, not so much worried more, anxious, as they hadn't heard Storm on a powered up guitar, only acoustic during practise sessions, but they had to admit to being impressed when she started building up her Marshall stack. By comparison, Escort's Orange bass bins looked inadequate however serviceable. Drummer boy's kit was no frills basic. A simple, yet authentic marching machine. He hit them hard. He hit them hard 'cos he hated them so. He hated being drummer boy.

*

The stage is set.

*

As soon as Storm inserted the jack plug into her guitar, like a ritual act of sexual penetration, the room buzzed, a low humming prickly buzz. She stepped into her own imagination and screamed out feedback to get everyone's attention. Then they launched, and I mean launched, into the first number firing out a volume of energy which the small enthusiastic crowd pushed back with a rush to the front of the stage. This was going to be one of those gigs that urban legends are made from; this was the invention of nitro-glycerine sonic revolution, held together with safety pins, tethered to reality by bondage straps and buckles and belts; straining; torturous distortion.

The energy for the final number came to them via cloud nine. Although drummer boy and Escort both picked up on the vibe that something was going wrong. They understood Storm's anger towards her equipment as a way out of this predicament without ruining a great gig. They understood wrong. To be fair they had connected with something existing that wasn't going right. True. But Storm's mind had broken and she witnessed before her the shattered remains of a dream. Storm felt rejected. She was hurt. She stomped on lover fuzz box's switch, no response. No love. She tap danced on it, she kicked it, she jumped up and down on it, she stamped on it. Spat on it. Screamed at it. No response.

*

No future.

*

Hurling her guitar towards the stack she pulled the cabinets to the floor: Smash it up! Bounced the curvaceous bottom of the guitar on the stage: Smash it up! But each time she caught it, and she cranked out a chord that built into a progression. In a whirlwind of feedback she kicked the back of one of the cabinets and took out a machine gun, using the gun's barrel to create a bottleneck sound she played the blues; the band, with confused expressions on their faces, jammed. (My baby's left me and I am sad.) She then turned the gun on the audience and opened fire.

*

'I blew them away: Did it my way.' Storm. January 6th 1980

SPINNING FAST

Gary Couzens

A hot December day, the last of term. Clytie and Josie, in the toilets, pull down their grey school tights, ball them up and stuff them into their bags. Standing by the mirrors above the washbasins, they put on the lipstick they've hidden from the nuns. Josie undoes the top button of her white blouse, flapping the collar for air. Clytie's glasses have steamed up; she wipes them on her royal-blue skirt.

Josie leans forward, rubbing her lips together. 'Glad that's over, Clyte.'

They stride side by side out of the gate and down the road, their blazers draped over their shoulders. Clytie fans herself with her free hand, the heat oppressive on her bare legs, her armpits damp with sweat. Christmas decorations are in the shops they pass.

Although Clytie is half Greek – *half wog* – she hasn't inherited her mother's Mediterranean complexion and curly hair. Clytie's hair is the same shade of dark brown but straight to her shoulders, her scalp itchy in the heat. She doesn't *look like a wog* but her given name is Greek and she's the only Clytie she knows. It only took the first day at this school and Sister Teresa's mispronunciation in her Polish accent – *Clitty Robinson?* - to sniggers from the girls behind her, to make her hate her name.

They stand by the tram stop, the only ones there, shaded by a plane tree. They smoke while they're waiting, Josie gazing impatiently up and down the road, pacing back and forth along the pavement. Clytie feels exhausted watching her.

'Hi girls.' A man comes up to them. About six feet tall, making him about four inches taller than Josie and nine more than Clytie, and square-jawed, he's only about nineteen, so three years older than them. His hair is uncombed, untidy, damp and glossy with perspiration.

'Hello,' says Josie, pushing out her chest a little.

'Wanna hear some good music?' He holds out a leaflet; Josie takes it. 'Champion Hotel in Fitzroy. Little Band Night on Saturday.'

'Isn't that a bit daggy?' says Josie, her eyelids slightly lowered.

'Nothing daggy. Nothing shit. Guaranteed good.'

'What do you think, Clyte?' says Josie. 'You're the music fan? You and Theo.' Theo is Clytie's brother, a year older. Music is one interest they've shared for years, from younger days sat in front of the television watching *Countdown*.

'Yeah, why not?' Clytie isn't sure her parents will allow it. Maybe if Theo and Josie, or both of them, were with her. Should she tell them?

'Great! See you there.' The man holds out his hand. 'It'll be good. You seen The Ears? Primitive Calculators? Too Fat to Fit in the Door? Thrush and the Cunts?'

Josie smirks. 'You shouldn't use words like that in front of us convent school girls. I'm Josie.'

'Hi, Josie. I'm Sam.'

'This is Clytie.'

She's always speaking for me, thinks Clytie.

'See you girls there. Ask for me at the door. I'm in Dead Kids, guitar, vocals. Ask for Sam.'

*

Clytie and Josie take the tram to Flinders Street Station, changing for the tram to Fitzroy. Theo isn't with them: his music tastes don't extend to punk and he's out with his friends tonight. Clytie hasn't told her parents where she's going. She was prepared to insist – *It's 1979, Mum, and I am sixteen, nearly seventeen* – but in the end just told her she was staying the night at Josie's. Clytie is in jeans and a David Bowie T-shirt, slightly too big for her, borrowed from Theo. The Champion is on the corner of Brunswick Street and Gertrude, two storeys, white and brown with a cupola overlooking the street. The man on the door looks them up and down, his eyes lingering on Josie's chest, before he lets them in.

'Is Sam here?' says Josie. 'He said to ask for him.'

'Never heard of him,' says the doorman.

'He's in Dead Kids.'

'Don't push your luck, girlie.'

There's a crowd already, and Josie and Clytie have to squeeze in at the back. It's tight, with the smell of sweat and leather and denim. Clytie can barely see the stage as she's surrounded by people taller than her. Once or twice she's jostled, her glasses almost knocked off. Someone's hand rests too long on her bottom; she twists her hips to move away.

A blast of distorted, feedbacked guitar, a clatter of drums and a bass hammering in the pit of Clytie's stomach. It's loud, very loud. Beside her, Josie begins to jump on the spot. Clytie does the same, Josie draping her arm about her shoulders.

Each band plays for fifteen minutes or so, using the same microphone, guitar and bass amps, the same drumkit, sometimes the same keyboards. Some of the bands don't look much older than Clytie and Josie. Most of them are male, though one band has a girl singing in a bikini and fishnets, and there's a very serious-looking all-female quartet. Clytie can't play an instrument, though she's tried Theo's old acoustic guitar when he isn't looking. She's a soprano in the school choir, singing well enough, not so well as to be a soloist.

Could I do that? I could do that.

Soon, it's as if she's not in her body any more. No thought, just the sight of the band, the noise filling her ears, the taste of her own blood as she's bitten her lip. The throb of the bass, root notes eight to the bar; the crack of the snare drums, sheets of guitar chords.

'Hey, it's Sam!' Josie shouts in her ear.

And it is. He's on stage in a ripped T-shirt and jeans, black eyeliner ringing his eyes, barefoot, legs astride, leaning forward into the microphone, slashing at his guitar strings with his pick hand. A fleck of spittle catches the light. Behind him and to his right, a girl in a T-shirt, denim miniskirt and torn fishnets, short hennaed hair and dark red lipstick, thrusts her bass towards the crowd, her fingers strumming fast. All Clytie can see of the drummer is a pair of muscular arms and flailing sticks.

By the time Dead Kids stops playing, fifteen minutes and seven songs later, Clytie can hardly hear anything.

Dead Kids are the last band on. Josie and Clytie push their way to the front, against the press of the crowd towards the bar or out into the night. Sam is bent over, unplugging his guitar. His T-shirt, sticking to him, has a dark perspiration stain in the middle of his back. He glances up. 'Hi.'

'That was fucking great!' says Josie.

'Hey, thanks.' For a moment, he seems shy, at odds with his display on stage only minutes before, but he recovers. 'We're going on to Dan's for a party. Wanna come?'

Josie and Clytie exchange glances. Clytie knows her mother won't approve. *But she's not here now. What the hell.*

They follow Sam to the van outside, Deb the bassist behind them. They all sit in the back while Sam drives. Clytie has to rescue Deb's bass from cracking Josie on the head as Sam turns a corner too sharply. Josie laughs, shifting sideways crosslegged.

Soon Clytie is completely lost and doesn't know which part of the city she's in. It's a dark hot night, streetlights blotting out the stars. Carlton? Collingwood? Richmond? She has no idea.

The van stops at the end of a sloping street, outside an end-of-terrace house overhung by an unkempt elm tree. The house has two storeys, lights on in both. Music from inside, a bass pulse.

Josie's laugh, behind her and beside her. Clytie turns, but Josie has gone. 'Josie...?'

Deb laughs. 'You won't see her again any time soon.' She's standing on the pavement, one leg bent back, one trainer flat against the low wall dividing the scraggy front garden from the road. She holds out a cigarette packet. 'Want a ciggie?'

Clytie takes one. Deb lights it, and her own.

'Looks like even daggy little bands like us get groupies.'

'I'm not a groupie.'

'Didn't say you were. But I could see what was on your mate's mind all the way here. Sam always gets the girls. Can't see it myself. Wish he'd ask before borrowing my eyeliner, too. What's your name?' She exhales a big puff of smoke.

'Clytie.' She's about to add *Robinson*, but decides against it at the last moment. She curses her shyness. Her bladder is becoming uncomfortably full.

'I've never met a Clytie before. What kind of name is that?'

'It's Greek.' She has the explanation down pat. 'My mum's Greek. So I'm half wog.'

Deb cocks her head to one side, an appraising look. 'I can see it, now you say it. My grandmother's Sicilian. My *nonna*. So I'm quarter wog.' She holds out her hand; Clytie takes it. 'Pleased to meet you, Clytie, fellow part wog.'

'Hi Deb.' A man, about twenty years old, has come up behind Clytie. He's six feet tall, with close-cropped dark hair. His jeans have holes above the knees. He has a stubbie of Vic Bitter in each hand. 'Hi,' he says to Clytie.

'This is Clytie,' says Deb. 'She was at the gig earlier with her mate...what's your mate's name?'

'Josie.'

'You know, the blonde one, pink top, with Sam. We were saying he gets all the groupies. Girls don't get them.'

'You looked like you were doing okay.'

That startles Clytie. Is Deb a lesbian? *Does he think I'm one?* She's never knowingly met a homosexual, though she hears her parents and relatives speculating about an uncle on Dad's side, unmarried in his forties. And the nuns talking about sin. Come to think of it, there are rumours about one or two of the nuns. And the whispering: *D'you think Clitty's a lemon? She must be – I saw her looking at Alice in the showers.*

She's not. She knows she's not.

'Nah,' says Deb. 'Don't think she's that way inclined. We were just chatting about our wog heritage. And you better introduce yourself. Rude not to.'

He holds out his hand. 'Hi, Clytie. I'm Zack. I'm...not a wog.' He takes a cigarette from Deb.

As if given licence, Clytie starts talking, words rushing out after having been dammed up. She repeats what she told Deb about the origins of her name. 'I was at the gig earlier. Me and Josie.'

'Did you like it?' says Deb.

Clytie nods. 'My ears are still ringing!'

'Hey, all down to my bass playing. A girl on bass is a cut above. Well, there's Janine in the Young Charlatans, Cathy in The Ears. There are some of us getting the message out.'

'How long have you been playing bass?'

'Two months?' says Zack.

'About that. They couldn't get anyone else. It's just notes. Piss-easy. I could teach you if you want.'

Yes, I'd like that, Clytie thinks.

'A full-size bass might be a bit big on you, though. You are a bit petite. Little hands, too.'

'So you're not musicians...full-time?'

Deb laughs, a full-throated sound, leaning her head back. 'Yeah, and I like fucking starving! No, I'm a film student.'

'So am I,' says Zack. 'I'm just about to start my graduation film.'

'Yeah, he directs and photographs and I do the editing.'

'Abso-fucking-lutely. And I even got you to act in one of them.'

'Any excuse to get me in a bikini.'

'You didn't need one.'

'Yeah, and Helen Morse can sleep at night.'

'With you next to her?'

'Wouldn't kick her out of bed. I've seen *Caddie* five times now.'

'Someone must watch all those period pieces they make in Oz these days. It's not *real*. Hey, I've just seen something.' He steps behind Clytie, his hands reaching over her shoulders and taking off her glasses.

'I can't see.' Clytie has a moment of panic as Deb's face instantly devolves into a tanned-pink blob.

'Don't worry, you'll get them back.' The side of his hand brushes the nape of her neck as he gathers up her hair, tugs it gently back.

'What are you doing?' says Clytie.

'Don't you see it, Deb?'

'Nope.'

'Jean Seberg.' Pause. 'Y'know, *A bout de souffle*? Put her in a *New York Herald Tribune* T-shirt or a stripey top and you'll see it.'

'Yeah, sort of. The hairstyle's all wrong, though. Too long.'

'The face, though. The *face*. I could film that. In black and white Academy Ratio thirty-five millimetre.'

'You wish. Colour sixteen-mil, more like. Like the stuff they show at the Co-Op.'

'Who's Jean Seberg?' says Clytie. Zack lets her hair fall, presses her glasses into her hand. They've steamed up; she hurriedly wipes them on the thigh of her jeans before putting them back on.

'Who's Jean Seberg? Oh, the youth of today.'

'I'm sixteen,' she mutters.

'*A bout de souffle?* It's only one of the greatest films ever made. Godard, France, 1960. She did Hollywood too – *Saint Joan, Bonjour Tristesse.* Seen those? She died this year – only forty. Such a fucking tragedy.' He grinds his cigarette out underfoot. 'Christ, it's stink hot tonight. Want another beer?'

They go inside. Clytie asks Deb where the toilet is and follows where she points. She opens the door. Sitting on the throne is a man, a needle in a shaking hand poised over the crook of his bare left arm. He glances up and yells at her, face red with veins standing out on his forehead. *'Fuck off!'*

Clytie backs away, shutting the door hurriedly.

She's standing in the hallway. Driving rock music from a record player in the next room. She can't see Josie anywhere. She looks round the door into the front room: cans and empty bottles litter the old ratty cigarette-burned carpet. A poster for an old French film is tacked to the wall. In a corner, a man sits on a green armchair picking out chords on an acoustic guitar, a cigarette dangling from his mouth as he sways slowly back and forth. In the corner of the room an old black and white television set flickers unattended. The lights are dim, but over in the other corner on an old armchair are a pair of male legs and a female back, blonde hair spilling over a pink

T-shirt, his hands pawing the small of her back, clutching at her buttocks through her jeans. *Josie.* Clytie quickly looks away.

Zack and Deb are in the kitchen, Deb squatting as she pulls a six-pack of beer out of the fridge. Clytie tells them about the man in the toilet.

Deb sighs, straightens. 'He'll be there for ages. Wish that cunt wouldn't do that. If he's going to shoot up, he can fucking well do it somewhere else. It's the only dunny in the house, as it is. You okay, Clytie?'

Clytie nods, less shaken now than she was.

'Go outside if you need to go,' says Zack. 'Out the back. I'll keep watch.'

'Needs a girl, Zack. She won't want you staring at her arse when she takes a piss.'

'Hey, I'll look away. I can be a gentleman.'

'That'll make a fucking start. Still needs a girl. Come on, Clytie.'

As Clytie squats down in a small patch of grass hidden from the house, jeans and undies about her thighs, she thinks, *If Mum finds out about this, I will be in so much trouble. And same if Josie's Mum finds out. So we'll make sure they don't. I'm seventeen in the new year. Welcome to the Eighties, Clytie.*

'Has she finished?' says Zack.

'Yes.' Clytie straightens her jeans as she stands. She laughs.

'What's funny?' says Deb.

'I never thought I'd end up somewhere like this. Josie and I were just going to see a band.'

'Is Josie the one in the front room with Sam?' says Zack.

'Pink top, blonde hair,' says Deb. 'She won't be going home anytime soon.'

They go further down the garden. The grass is worn bare in patches over dry hard brown earth. They sit on a low wall, Zack with his legs astride, Deb on the other end folding one leg over the other and tugging at the hem of her dress, Clytie in the middle. Zack passes a cigarette to her. Clytie takes it, though she knows it isn't tobacco.

'So what do you think, Clytie?' says Zack. 'We all live here, plus anyone who needs to crash here. Looks like that's what your mate'll be doing.'

'Not much sleep though,' says Deb. 'Look, Robyn's just arrived. See you. Nice to meet you, Clytie.'

Deb hurries back to the kitchen.

'That's her girlfriend,' says Zack. 'We'd better leave them be. Robyn's been away for a few days.' He turns to her. 'Having a good time?'

'Yes thank you.' The pot is making her lightheaded, but she is becoming more relaxed.

'Bet you never thought a good convent schoolgirl would end up in a place like this.'

Clytie laughs. 'Who says convent schoolgirls are good?'

'Oh, are they bad? I'd better meet some of your friends then.'

'They're not my friends. They call me...don't tell this to anyone...'

'I won't.'

'Please don't. Promise.'

'Promise.'

'Clitty.'

He laughs.

She thumps him on the arm. 'It's not funny!'

'No it's not. Sorry. Bunch of bitches.'

'Yes they are. It's Clytie. C-L-Y-T-I-E. That's my name. My middle name's Marina.'

'Nice name. Clytie's a nice name too.'

She wonders if she's simply trying to flatter her. Or if he's aiming to make a move on her. 'My brother's got a Greek name too – Theo. You can guess which parent named me.'

'So you'll both be giving your kids Greek names?'

'I doubt it.' Getting married, let alone having children, seems unconscionably far away. Theo doesn't have a girlfriend at the moment, nor does Clytie have a boyfriend. She can hear the girls at school now: *Who's that guy with Clitty?* Or even, *Who's that guy* rooting *Clitty?*

Zack shrugs, relaxes where he sits, takes a swig of his beer. 'So, do you think of yourself as Greek, Clytie, or just an Aussie sheila?'

'Just an Aussie girl.' She doesn't add *I think.*

She picks out the stars of the Southern Cross, low down in the south, visible through a gap in the clouds. Dad is a keen stargazer and from a young age she has often stood outside at night with him, taking turns with a pair of binoculars. They watched the Melbourne solar eclipse from their back garden three years ago; Clytie gazing up to see totality through a break in the clouds. 'Look, Zack,' she says, pointing upwards at two small fuzzy patches in the sky. 'The Magellanic Clouds.' She points out the constellations.

She feels quite small, the world suddenly much much larger.

*

At dawn, Zack goes with Clytie to the bus stop. There isn't a bus in sight, so Clytie walks home, taking her half an hour. She manages to stay awake during the ten o'clock mass. In another pew, Josie looks up and grins at her,

On Monday, Clytie takes a book out of the library and brings it with her to the hairdresser's. Inside is a still of Jean Seberg in *A bout de souffle,* which she shows to the hairdresser, a roundfaced, double-chinned woman in her forties who has cut her and Mum's hair for as long as Clytie can remember. 'Are you sure, Clytie?' she says.

'Yes, I'm sure.'

The woman holds a hank of Clytie's hair, as if in hesitancy, or regret.

'Cut it off, please,' says Clytie. 'Cut it all off.'

*

On the Thursday after Christmas, Clytie meets Josie in City Square, greeting her with a hug.

'Hey, Clyte, I almost didn't recognise you.' Her hand brushes the nape of her neck. 'Looks great.'

'It's Jean Seberg.' Clytie keeps tilting her head one way, then the other, expecting to feel the weight of the hair that's now missing. Every time there's a breeze she feels it on the nape of her neck. 'Mum hates it,' she says, hands resting on her cheeks. 'She says I look like a boy.'

They go to see *Alien* in a cinema in Bourke Street and afterwards have fried rice in Little Bourke Street in Chinatown.

'So, you and Zack, eh?' says Josie.

'You and Sam, eh?' It's a countermove, deflecting Josie from something that's a little too personal to share, except in outline.

Josie pouts, disguising it with chopsticks to her lips.

'Are you going to see him again?' says Clytie. *So who's the guy rooting Josie?* She can hear it now. Except Josie can shrug it off.

'Yeah. You?'

'I'm going to see a film with Zack in Carlton on Saturday. It's called *Pure S*. The censor wouldn't pass it when it was called *Pure Shit*.'

Josie giggles. 'Bet you won't be telling your Mum that.'

'It's got an R rating. Deb said to put on some makeup and say I'm eighteen.' She doesn't know what to expect. No doubt she'll find out. A tingle of anticipation.

They take the tram down to St Kilda and spend the rest of the afternoon on the beach, staking out their small part of the sand amongst the crowds. Changed back into their clothes after swimming, their hair drying in the heat, they sit and watch as the sun moves towards setting.

'Clyte...' says Josie. 'I haven't told anyone yet, but...we're moving to England at Easter. Dad's got a job in Manchester.'

Clytie doesn't say anything for a moment, a hollow feeling in her stomach.

'Clyte...we will keep in touch, won't we...? We'll write?'

'Of course we will.' Clytie lies back on her towel, gazing up at the darkening sky. 'Of course we'll write. Think of all the bands you could go and see.' All the ones she's read about, which she knows she hasn't a hope of seeing here in Australia, the ones she's read about in *New Musical Express*, which she and Theo take turns in buying, the issues over a month old by the time they arrive in the shops.

'You can tell me everything that's going on here, Clyte. I'll be on the other side of the world from you.'

Clytie leaves a pause. Sometime soon the stars will come out. They have different stars in England. What does their night sky look like? She imagines Josie there now, instead of several months in the future. She's looking up through Josie's eyes. It's mid-morning there now. Winter. Maybe there's snow on the ground, crunching underfoot.

'Are you looking forward to it?'

'It's scary, Clyte. I've hardly ever been out of Victoria before.' Josie turns her head away. 'I'll really miss you, Clytie.'

For a moment Clytie wonders if Josie is about to cry. But she doesn't. She's always been the confident one, the one who *brings Clytie out of her shell*, as they say when they don't think Clytie can hear. She'll have to stand up to the other girls on her own. *I'll have to. I will.*

'I've never been to England either, Josie.'

'Hey, one day you can come over to England and see me.'

'I'd like to one day.'

The sky is a deepening red-orange. Clytie lies as still as she can, trying not to breathe, but she knows the world is turning, spinning very fast, taking her and everyone around her into the future. If they stay here long enough, the stars will come up and the sky will be an upended transparent bowl extending far upwards, so high that she will be too small to see.

THE ROCK STAR

Richard Dellar

Rick was bored in his bedsit. He was fed up with being on the dole and living from day to day. His life seemed to be pointless. Going nowhere. He felt like a boat, randomly afloat, drifting haphazardly through waters uncharted yet which held no interest. 'What I need,' he said, 'is an anchor, an occupation that will bind me to the world and give me back my sense of self.' At the moment, he had no social function, no apparent worth, no identity, no achievements to let other people know he existed.

'What I really could do with,' he said to his fridge, 'is a career, one that would resurrect my humanity.' He thought deeply and silently for a few minutes, then said: 'I know. I'll become a rock star.'

Rick often spoke to the refrigerator. He didn't really know anyone. He wasn't much of a socialiser. But the fridge, whirring away day and night in the corner of the room, it was his companion, his friend, it comforted him. Its reliable, constant buzzing helped him to come to terms with the idea that he was really there. The fridge was Rick's confidant, his closest ally. He trusted it.

Rick thought about the things he was supposed to do to become a rock star. Learn to sing, play guitar, get a record deal, the usual hassle, and then he'd be on *Top Of The Pops*. He gave his guitar an exploratory strum. No sound came out. He looked down: the guitar just wasn't there. He didn't really have a guitar. It had been an imaginary one. But, he thought, if there really had been a guitar, I would have made one hell of a magic chord.

He glanced at his record collection. On top of the pile was *The Wall* by Pink Floyd. He no longer enjoyed behemoth concept albums, their excesses were no longer appropriate in these post-punk times, but he saw the lyrics printed on the sleeve, took a deep breath, and sang at the top of his voice.

He'd chosen the track, *Another Brick In The Wall*. The song was rubbish, he realised. But when he sang it, stripped it down, punked it up, it sounded so good, so cool, it was transformed. The fridge applauded. It was impressed. Rick was brilliant. He reached for his cassette machine, popped in a blank tape, pressed the record button, and sang it once more. Then he rewound it and played it back.

'Fuck me sideways!' said the fridge. 'It's a hit you've got there! What a debut! I can hardly believe it! It's a number one all the way! Ace!'

'Thanks,' said Rick modestly. He was already planning for the future. It was good that *Another Brick In The Wall* had been a hit, but he needed to consolidate the achievement to prove that it wasn't simply a one-off, novelty success. Rick wanted to be right up there forever with the greats, even if it meant being shoulder to shoulder with Eric Clapton. To do this he needed something special, exclusive to him. He peered at the sleeves of his records. Characters like Marc Bolan, Siouxsie Sioux, and David Bowie stared up at him, rock stars whose looks were entirely their own. Rick saw his reflection in the mirror. What a mess. He hadn't shaved or changed his clothes in weeks. His hair was long and ungroomed. His dress sense didn't exist, his clothes gathered according to chance, with no planned style. It might have been fine for the '77 punk scene, but music had got more sophisticated since then. What his competitors like Adam Ant had that he lacked was an image. 'I need a brand new look,' he said.

When his giro came he went to the hairdressers and had a rocker's quiff done with purple streaks in it. On the following giro day he bought a pair of tight black leather trousers. The one after that met with the purchase of pink pixie boots. On the next one he bought a selection of gothic jewellery, scarves, and other rock 'n' roll accoutrements, together with a T-shirt which he took home and slashed carefully with a razor blade so that it looked ripped, torn and terrific. On the fifth giro day he went to the tattooist and had *Born To Lose* inscribed on his arm. The purchases ate up most of his income, but at least he had the company of his fridge, and the pleasure of playing the tape of *Another Brick In The Wall* over and over each day. He could almost hear in the background the amazing chords from the invisible guitar that accompanied his singing.

He admired his reflection. He looked like a real rock star now. The follow-up to *Another Brick In The Wall* was taking its time to happen, but the wait would be worth it in the long run, because the next hit would coincide with the unveiling of his new image.

Rick decided to appoint his fridge as his manager, and spent long hours discussing his career with the whirring inanimate object. It was only fair that Rick's first and biggest fan should manage him. 'What should I do now, fridge?' he asked.

'What you need,' said the manager, 'is a decent addiction. Think about it. The one thing that the best rock stars – for example, Lou Reed, Johnny Thunders and Iggy Pop – have in common is that they all take vast quantities of drugs. Don't take the piss by saying 'oh yes, but what about Cliff Richard' or some talentless toerag like him. The fact is that if you want any credibility in this business you have to have a king-size habit.'

Rick knew drugs were expensive, so he drank several bottles of Jack Daniels over the next few days until his money ran out. Instead of getting the shakes he felt glad of the excuse to stop. Alcohol just wasn't addictive enough.

'How am I ever going to get hooked on anything, boss?' he asked his fridge despondently.

'You need to go for something more habit-forming,' it replied. 'Alcohol takes too long to get its claws in. Try heroin, it takes only about three weeks of continual use to get hooked to that. If you saved up money from your giro carefully you could buy enough smack in one go to develop a real problem!'

'That's a good idea!' said Rick, who spent the next few months saving. During this period he realised he had to produce a filler to bridge the gap between *Another Brick In The Wall* and the absolute classic he would record when he became a junkie. He discussed the situation with his manager, who suggested *Act Naturally* by the Beatles. He couldn't stand the band, but they had a track record, and they both agreed he ought to do one of the fab four numbers sung by Ringo. However, Rick preferred to knock out a more accessible one for the pop market. He stuck a tape into his machine, pressed record, and belted out *Yellow Submarine*.

The old family favourite was an obvious choice, he reflected. Novelty songs were big money. The Toy Dolls had just released *Nellie The Elephant* and punk stalwart Captain Sensible was doing his career every favour with *Happy Talk*. It was playing safe, treading water while he prepared for the big one. But he was still pleased with his second hit. He quite liked it. He kept playing it to himself and cackling dementedly. Really, the decision to do *Yellow Submarine* was a practical joke on his fans, a secret message to prove that he was smarter than they were. But deep down he knew that even his fillers were better than most rock and punk stars' heart and soul.

Rick became very frugal, parting with his money only to buy a minimum diet and to renew his hairstyle. Eventually he had enough cash to go out and buy lots of smack. By asking around in the local pubs he easily found a pusher, Ralph, who gave Rick a special discount for being a new customer and for buying so much at once. The rock star strolled happily back to his bedsit with the big scag bag. *Another Brick In The Wall*, a classical version with an imaginary orchestra, was getting a spin on the radio in his brain as he walked.

It took Rick some time to perfect his jacking-up technique. He acquired some pins from the needle exchange, but had difficulty in tying his arms so that the veins bulged out enough for him to slide the syringe in easily for a straightforward hit. The trouble was, he just didn't seem to have enough hands to get it right. Soon he had oozing septic sores all over his arms, which he welcomed as proof of his impending habit. He undertook research into the maximum amount he could safely inject without overdosing, and the proper rate to gradually increase his intake. He was on his way.

While becoming addicted he taped his new platinum hit. It wasn't quite the classic he'd expected to happen, but it was a number with appropriate relevance to the situation:

I'm Waiting For My Man.

Rick liked the references to dollars and Lexington in the song. As demonstrated by the tendency of most British bands to sing in American accents it was obvious that references like these made British rock authentically itself.

'What do I do now to consolidate the soaring success of *Waiting For My Man*?' asked Rick.

'For your next career move,' said the manager, 'you need to fuck lots of women, like all the other rock stars do. The way forward is plenty of groupies! They're yours by right – all you have to do is go out there and grab them! A reputation for pulling the chicks is a sure-fire ticket to eternal stardom!'

At first Rick found it difficult to pick up women. His social skills were limited, as was his experience of the opposite gender. His chat-up lines, which consisted of bragging about his musical talent and heroin addiction, failed to impress the grown women he encountered in the local pubs. When he discovered the Princess Margaret, a tavern frequented mostly by under-age drinkers, his luck changed. Adults had all met dozens of rock stars real and imaginary, and had learnt to avoid them. But adolescents were more gullible. The fifteen and sixteen year old girls at the Margaret were well impressed by Rick's rock 'n' roll junkie image. They were virtually queuing up to shag him. They thought Rick would introduce them to the dark, exciting, seedy side of life. He was much better than the boys at school, none of whom were wearing black leather trousers. Over the next few weeks Rick had a selection of the pubescent chicks. They were his pay-off, his royalties. Following the example set by the likes of Jim Morrison and Bill Wyman he took great pleasure in casually humiliating his conquests. Once he'd had his way they were thrown straight out the door.

Joanna was the fifth Margaret regular he'd got back to his bedsit in a week. She was completely won over by his chat-up talk of rock, drugs and stardom, and well impressed by his sores. But as soon as Rick had recovered his breath after the pair had made their own sweet music together, he shoved her violently out of the bed.

'Listen to this, Paula,' he said, confusing Joanna with the one he'd done the night before, 'You've just had the honour of shagging the greatest rock star that ever lived, and I expect you to be eternally grateful. I'll give you six out of ten. Now push off and go home.' There was no point in letting her outstay her welcome, he thought.

'You bastard!' said Joanna. 'Why aren't you being nice to me anymore?'

She was testing Rick's patience. 'Go on, get dressed and fuck off, quick. Vanish, slag; disappear!'

Humiliating women was a practice indelibly woven into rock's rich tapestry. It was what the fans wanted. It was all part of the show. Rick picked up a syringe and threw it at the groupie like a dart. It missed and hit the fridge, which squealed out in complaint. Joanna was scared. She didn't like people lobbing syringes at her. The fifteen year old climbed into her clothes and ran out.

'I'll get you back for this, you shitbag, just you wait!' she shouted. Her pride was hurt. She felt belitted.

All things considered, Rick thought alone in bed, you don't really need all the conventional stuff like guitars, amplifiers, agents and record deals to be a rock star. What you actually have to do is cut right through all that bullshit and get back to the generic kernel of rock, the fundamental elements of drugs and sex. Punk had stripped things back to basics, but even that hadn't gone far enough.

Rick's smack habit was coming on nicely. He was starting to really look forward to his fix every few hours. He liked the feeling it gave him more and more as the days passed. His intake was increasing steadily. Now he was a total rock star.

By the time his big bag ran out Rick had a huge habit. He'd put most of his dole aside for the next lot, but clearly his benefits weren't enough to cover what he needed for long. He sold most of his possessions to pay for smack, a procedure that kept him going for a while.

The more addicted he got, the lazier he became. He'd never been a very motivated sort of bloke, but now, with his monster habit, he could hardly be bothered to move. He gave up washing, shaving, changing his clothes, and leaving his bedsit except to score smack. He couldn't even get it together to go to the toilet when he wanted to piss or shit. Instead he pissed into empty bottles and crapped into carrier bags. Soon, he was surrounded by piss bottles and shit bags.

Finally he ran out of smack with no means of buying more. There was a week to go until giro day, he had nothing left worth selling, and no money. His withdrawal symptoms were horrific: spiders were crawling all over him and he kept having spasms and vomiting. He was desperate for a good jab. To make matters worse, he was falling out with his manager. It kept shouting abuse at him. 'You blew it, man!' said the fridge. 'If you'd released *Act Naturally* instead of *Yellow Submarine* you would have been all right.'

Rick couldn't deal with it any longer. He knew where Ralph, his dealer, lived. It was in a basement flat, where the dealer hid his stash in a flowerpot on the windowsill. Ralph went out every Tuesday morning to meet his probation officer. Its Tuesday morning now, thought Rick, he won't be in.

Rick staggered out of the bedsit and rushed through the streets. He needed a fix so badly that he ran all the way to Ralph's flat. The curtains were parted and Rick could see the pot of gold there on the sill, an open invitation. He took a brick and threw it at the window, which exploded into a beautiful cascade of shards and splinters of shattered glass. He grabbed the flowerpot and ran.

Ralph looked on in disbelief as his window was smashed and his drugs stolen. Rick had got his days muddled up. It was really Wednesday, and Ralph had been in his room all the time. The rock star had bolted with the extra-special smack that Ralph had scored in bulk the night before. This particular batch was to most smack what Tennants Super is to normal lager. Ralph ran angrily after the scarpering rocker, but it was to no avail. Rick's headstart was enough for him to quickly lose his man. He returned to his bedsit and had a nice big fix.

Not a bad batch of gear, this, thought Rick as he went on the nod. He was heading for an early burn-out, he was thinking. It was a shame, after only three smash hits. And even one of those, *Yellow Submarine,* had been a pisstake. But at least he had enough heroin to keep him going for a while. Maybe he'd even find some talent in reserve to create one last classic.

Ralph didn't know Rick's address. He spent the day touring all the pubs in town to find out. If, as he suspected, he wasn't able to recover his drugs he could still give Rick a good kicking. The rock star had never mixed much, and Ralph had difficulty locating the purple-quiffed, leather-trousered junkie. Eventually it was Rick's recent romantic rock raunches that gave the game away.

The rock star was pissed off. He wasn't getting on with his fridge, which had lost confidence in him ever since being struck by the flying hypodermic. It wasn't even talking to him anymore. Rick felt somehow abandoned and betrayed. He was well sorted, but he was alone, and his artistic talent seemed to have gone.

He took an old shitbag and looked inside. The excrement had hardened a little, but on closer inspection it was quite pliable. He started playing with it like plasticine, moulding it into funny shapes.

The Margaret was the tenth pub that Ralph investigated. As soon as he circulated the description he found that the under-age drinkers, several of the females of whom Rick had shagged, recognised it immediately. Ralph explained to the crowd that the rock star had stolen his stash, and that he wanted the bastard's address so he could go round and batter the living daylights out of him. It was Joanna who came up with the information, advising the pusher to give Rick not one, but two kickings, one on Ralph's account, the other on hers.

Rick enjoyed a satisfying hit, his third that day. He tossed the pin aside, and thought about his other three hits, the musical ones. They were shit, he decided. But the fourth would surpass all of them. His next hit would transcend the four dimensions of music. It would be a cosmic symphony, overturning the short sharp shock of punk and reaching to the very foundations of rock, to its concrete essence where all chords, voices and melodies melt away into space, into an irreducible, instinctive impulse. He didn't need a concept album, but a concept song. He'd had three triumphs, but needed another, better than the rest, if he were to achieve rock 'n' roll immortality. This is indeed good gear, he thought. He cooked up another as a special treat while he planned his masterpiece.

His loud bangs and shouts unanswered, the pusher kicked the bedsit door off its hinges in one go. He was waving a big plank of wood with nails sticking out of it, ready to give Rick a severe beating. But as the door fell to the floor Ralph was instantly overwhelmed by the nauseating stench. It was disgusting. It nearly made him puke. Flies were everywhere. He looked around, dazed, and saw a half-full Jack Daniels bottle. That's good, he thought, taking a swig, I could do with a drink. It tasted just like piss. He spat it out, his palate offended.

His sight drew itself to Rick's bed where the star's head poked out at the top, his body beneath blankets, leaving the purple hair and expressionless blue face visible. Beside the bed was the flowerpot, a tourniquet and a syringe. Ralph grabbed Rick by the shoulders and shook him a few times. He slapped one cheek, then the other, then he picked him up and chucked him against the fridge. Rick dropped lifelessly to the floor like a discarded rag doll, no sign of life in him at all.

Ralph's gaze drifted over to the fridge. Lying on top of it, fetid, nasty, was the dead junkie's fourth and final hit, his crowning achievement, composed with his last movements. A full-scale model of a guitar sat on the manager, sculpted out of the rock star's own shit. It might have been the buzzing of the flies, but Ralph swore he could almost hear a chord.

Punk Up Your Road Blues

Gio Clairval

Don't tell me my biggest problem is that my boyfriend, at twenty-one, has six years on me. He's also got a sodding driving license, and sometimes I think he wants to see me dead.

Luca has decided that it is my special task to plot each night's route, because I am his 'navigator.' I didn't ask for the job. I don't know anything about roads and I can't read a map without turning it in the right direction – which makes him crack up. He says any dumb chick can do it. A woman, I think to myself, is the natural navigator to her pilot man; he decides where to go and she plots the course.

This is what happens. As soon as I get in the car, he merrily goes: What's the route tonight?

If I don't have a special route planned – a scenic one, I mean – he makes faces. Ye disappoint me, baby.

I never know if I'm supposed to laugh or cringe. So I shut my gob, since it's the least risky thing to do. Often, I can't decide about the freaking itinerary at all. And when I suspect the route I've picked is shit and crap, I get a cold lump in my stomach.

If he doesn't like the landscape, he says, So *this* is yer favourite route?

Because it doesn't count if *I* like the road. And I don't send him packing because maybe it's my fault. Or maybe he's a dork – the thought crosses my mind sometimes. I know I shouldn't fall for his cheap mind tricks. I should give him two fingers and slam the door of the frigging car in his face.

Only I don't.

Every day that comes he picks me up from school for a ride in his souped-up Fiat 1300 fitted with a Pininfarina body – a storm-grey whale shark with curved tail fins and a lot of chrome, like an American car built twenty years ago. To rack up the fifties mood, Elvis screams from the cassette deck 'You ain't nothin' but a hound dog'. At this time of year, winter has swallowed the afternoon and shadows stretch across the streets like black rubber skid marks, and I get all lightheaded like a horror flick is about to begin.

We leave the Po River's plain in half an hour. It's like he thinks he's wheeling a Formula One.

I'm afraid of cars, seriously scared. Generally speaking, I don't enjoy going out. I'd rather stay in bed and read a book. I think I'd make a good paraplegic.

Every minute, we risk ending up in a mega crash. Cars leap at me. High beams burn round prints in my brain. Luca swerves and my stomach rolls to the side, trying to swing along with the wheels. A horn blares, drills my ears in a crescendo, fades behind me. My throat shrinks; a prune stone somehow just got stuck in there. I think: *Today I'm going to die. Maybe my heart will stop before the shock and I won't feel a thing. Do your job, heart. Stop. Now.*

Luca yells: Look at *that one*. We're gonna catch it right in our teeth!

That one is an articulated lorry.

I must be having fun without knowing it. If I weren't having fun, I wouldn't go out with him, right? This boyfriend may be the one that will want to marry me. See if I care. By the way, dunno whether a boy will ever want to marry his sweetheart since he expects to have sex outside wedlock, as Mrs. Devoti, my philosophy teacher, says. She says that the sexual revolution was men's idea and that now they're happy with throwaway love. Even so, marriage looks like a big bourgeois mistake to me. Let's consider the economic angle instead of the ideological, for a change. Marriage has just one advantage over prostitution: a husband costs you less than a pimp. And, all other things being equal, marriage is to freedom what chewing gum is to hair. Either I'll never marry or I'll marry three or four times, to prove it's not important.

Away from Milan, along one of the canals, the drenched road flickers under our headlights, neon signs pour out shavings of orange and green over the tarmac. Poplars run at our side, leaning at an angle. I eject the old timer and load my favourite. The Slits, a new all-female English band, sing about the typical girls that don't rebel and can't decide.

Boy, I say, I dig these chicks!

Luca smirks. Yer chicks can't even play, he says. They're just copying the real punks.

The car veers again and I can't speak. Not that hitting back comes naturally to me, unless it's about books and ideas. It's another big problem, I know.

In his car Luca has put long red rubber sticks on the headlight switches. He strikes them with the elegance of a pianist, a guy who knows where the keys are. He promised to teach me to drive, but he never lets me take the wheel.

Actually, the driving roles are inverted in my family. Greydad assigns the wheel to Greymum, but that's because she's the ballsy one, and he's the seriously short-sighted one. He comes from an old family, Greydad, and holds a Law degree signed by King Vittorio Emanuele, the third of the name, while Greymum, all she graduated from is the Red Cross nurse training during the war. Driving is the only thing Greydad delegates anyway. All the rest he keeps in his capable hands.

Now, I'm about to speak when Luca pulls on the handbrake to make the car skid sideways – oh, shit! – and I forget everything about *la condition féminine.*

On a straight road, I attack.

Look at the permissiveness toward women's fashion, I say.

Luca makes funny throat noises. My speech patterns annoy him a lot. He calls me Brainy.

I insist.

Why, in your opinion, does our culture prescribe serious or at least decent clothing for men but allows women to make up their faces (like war paint, right?), dress in colours and go about flaunting belly button and cleavage?

Luca grins. Coz ye're sex objects?

Yes, but that's not the half of it.

He sighs. Now ye're gonna tell me the other half, aren't you? Ah've got a headache already.

I survey the road ahead, in case a curve is about to ambush me.

Can't you see it? I say. Disguising oneself, showing skin and painting one's face is typical of those who are near to authenticity and Nature.

Ah see, he says. Except for the war paint. I don't get it.

Are you following? I yell. It's. About. SAVAGES.

Oh. Sounds like colonialist thinkin'. (I've briefed him a lot.)

Exactly! Our civilisation is tolerant of the primitive. Women are men's good savages. Which is why you offer us shiny necklaces and rings.

That's never gonna happen, he says. Ah promise.

He whistles. He's happy because we've been accepted by the massive of Porta Ticinese, where everyone wears chains and big signet rings, because being Society's bad savages is the point, here. They move around on motorbikes. Boy, bikes are scarier than cars. With these people, I feel like I never know if what I say is right.

Coz ye're middle class-ey, Luca volunteers.

I must learn to speak like them and I'm trying hard. (Not succeeding, I know.)

It's not that they are illiterate, the guys – not all of them. My man's got A levels. I've seen the diploma framed and fixed on the wall in his greymum's living room, but Luca is into his commoner deal so much that you'd think he'd been struck with illiteracy relapse. (That's when you forget for lack of practice.) His ambition is to become a professional thief. Yesterday, he took me along to steal a car. It was a Fiat Cinquecento, and the chick we stole it from was young, judging by the driver's license left in the glove compartment, and not loaded, judging by the state of the car.

I spoke my mind; he replied: Ye're so middle-classy. Look at the Pole. She's the smart kinda girl.

The Pole is his best-pal Franco's girlfriend, who puts it about for 10,000 lire. I don't think I have the makings of a princess of the underground, but if I did I'd like to be called Beauzieux.

Luca says: If ye're on the game, they'd still call ye Brainy and anyone hearing that name would get the droop right then.

He thinks my bum isn't sexy enough. It's true that I've got the buttocks of an 'eleven-year-old' (in his words), but my legs are fab. He ought to at least admit that.

Luca likes me in high heels. I prefer waterproof boots because they're comfy, but a true woman does not run and has corns on her toes. Look at Greymum. She's forever had sore feet because of her shoes. Look at the state she's in today. She's the embodiment of the idea of Life like a series of shoes too small to fit.

Most girls in the massive wear stiletto heels, poor cows. But, high heels or not, in this group the women have nothing to say on the important things, like planning the route for our rides.

Why? I asked the bikers' leader.

Because it's an art.

And my dorkish boyfriend has been telling me for weeks that nothing is easier than planning a route! I see now that if males take charge of a job, it is regarded as noble, but if women do the same thing, the activity is demoted.

Anyway, we've been riding about with the massive for two weeks now, and spring is here, in the Kingdom of Lombardy. The latest news is that we've decided to lend a hand to the organisers of this cool punk festival on Lake Como. So here we are. Ten thousand people have come, including hippies, anarchists, even a few pinkies, but not one police officer. The festival is self-managed.

A few of the 'No future!' hard-core blokes start to poke fun at my radical leftist utopianism until I go on stage to sing the Slits' song, just on my acoustic guitar, and it's delirious. When I get to the point that typical girls don't drive well, our men roar with laughter. Idiots. The guys of *Re Nudo*, the anarcho-punk magazine, will put me on the cover!

The drunkpunks are happy to hop and fall before the stage, and I really don't see the point of it. The gutterpunks, on the other hand, are having a behemoth of a time. Longhaired and covered with necklaces, the Grandchildren of the Flowers sit on the grassy slopes, puffing on their js and singing a song (the same for three days):

Come over the hill!
We're going to Lebanon.
The trip is guaranteed,
one month long.

It's all about an artificial paradise where you don't have to worry if you don't fit in. You always fit in because it's artificial, and you make it exactly your size.

Franco, Luca's best pal, has taken LSD. They've all been laughing at me since I said that drugs are snares set by the Establishment to divert our attention from the problems of capitalistic society. Instead of a nice 'spiral that turns and opens towards the others,' to quote the doltish folksinger who gave him LSD, the acid has plunged Franco into a state of felinity. To rescue him, two blokes climb the tree where the idiot is perching to greet *Ragnarok*, shouting, *Heil, Gotterdammerung!*

Our Franco is not even a Nazi, just German (his real given name is Werther but he's ashamed of it because of Gœthe's book on teenage depression).

Afterwards, waste papers on the lawn make a good white autumn in full summer. It takes us a day to pick up the rubbish. (You should have seen the hairy eye the field's owner was giving us as he surveyed our work.) Self-management has its drawbacks.

Most have driven up here in cars instead of bikes, to carry stuff. The Pininifarina is being repaired. We leave in Franco's old Lancia, commandeered by Luca after Franco's dad showed up to repossess his son. A poster of the festival stuck on the car bonnet, we come down the mountain making a rally on the curves. Given that I've been drinking a little bit of vodka, I am not scared. Until the coppers pinch us on a bend, motioning Luca to stop. We have no papers so we must follow the police to the station.

As soon as we get there, the rozzers make some phone calls.

Is it true, they ask Luca, that last year you took the train back from Rome at the government's expense because you didn't have coins? Does your father know about it?

Luca gets all pale and zips it. It's a first.

The coppers order him to take off shoes and socks. They intend to search him for drugs. There's nothing inside his shoes; so they order him to take off his shirt. Luca's fingers move like drinking straws with a bend, and he can't peel off his shirt.

In a flash, I see pictures of police torturing dissidents. I hear a crash-cling-bang sound in my head. Boiling over, I shout that they have no right to bloody body search us, 'coz we aren't on drugs.

They all stare at me. Luca's eyes are jutting out of their sockets, like the wolf's in the cartoons. The coppers stop Luca's striptease dead. I yelled very loud.

Unfortunately, they announce they need to 'make more inquiries'.

So I *do* it. I have to. If you found yourself in the same situation, you'd do the same. Yes, I drop Greydad's name. A shameful failure, I know.

After hearing the name of a barrister known across Lombardy, they call home. Shit! This is going to be an indelible stain on my badge of honour, and my morale is down in the third basement, but it was either that or a night spent in the Establishment's oubliettes, and revolutionary martyrdom.

But now Greymum is coming to pick me up. Hell. I need a way out. Some kind of miraculous escape.

I don't have time to come up with a breaking-out plan coz Greymum must have got into high gear to show up so quickly.

Instead of yelling at me, She of the Blond Ironed Hairdo plays the model mother in full battle gear (Aquascutum trench coat and trustworthy middle-class-ey eyes). She must have looked the same way – determined, dignified – when she was a nurse under the bombardments. You see, Greymum wants to save her daughter. As if parents could save their children.

She addresses the Chief Rozzer with restrained passion. *Signor commissario,* my daughter is unwell.

But out of the police station, she's all coldness and everything.

Now the car rolls on under a coat of fog. Greymum's eyes pierce me from the rear-view mirror. I'm riding on the back seat because back doors can be blocked.

What did I do to deserve a daughter like you? (Greymum herself doesn't unclench her teeth; it's the rear-view mirror that does the talking.) I really want to dump her and her Ford, which is sadness personified.

When I try to sleep, I can't because, changing tack, she starts blabbering.

Hold on. Did she just say I was grounded for six months?

It happens that someone speaks to me and I don't answer because I've gone some place where nobody's talking. It's a heavenly place, but it's not an artificial paradise because you were born with that place inside you.

Then it hits me, the inspiration. I feel like laughing but I don't. Greymum doesn't like it when I laugh for no reason. Yeah, it really gets on her wick. So I keep quiet, but, holy gums, am I happy: I'm going to give her the slip.

You know I get carsick. Wheels make me want to throw up, except when I'm scared, my mind being afraid of dying and all that. Here, what I'm afraid of is to go home with *her* – so there's no risk of puking. To reach the vomiting state, I need to put two fingers down my throat when she isn't looking.

I tell her, Stop the car *now*!

Greymum pulls over, gets off, opens the door for me, lets me out, a hand curled around my forearm. I throw up on her shoes just a little. She takes her hand off my arm to rummage in her handbag for a handkerchief.

My race down the hill does me good. I don't feel like vomiting anymore.

She yells and yells, jumping up and down, waving her arms like a windmill. I'm ashamed for her: she's the embarrassing kind of mother.

A motorbike is coming down the slope after me. The motorcyclist rides fast and steady. He cuts my path.

My daughter, Greymum cries. Bring her back! She's unwell.

What's going on? the biker asks. He looks twenty-something. I like him. I must have a thing for middle-aged men.

I give him the Marilyn glance, eyebrows up and eyes half-shut. D'you wanna run away with *me*, or d'you prefer my mother?

He laughs; so I get on behind him, ordering: Go!

The *Moto Guzzi* climbs back up on to the road and the biker sprints away.

I glance over my shoulder at the *mater dolorosa*. Greymum's face, I will never forget it.

Where are you heading? I ask the biker.

I was going home.

Can you help me?

Help you how? Where d'you want to go?

I squint at the mist-shrouded road. Half a kilometre away, on the side, I see a hole opening like a camera shutter in the fleecy texture of the fogbank. I glimpse a patch of murky blue inside the gap, like a pool, or a stretch of sky, and I know it's the beginning of the route I want to take.

I point. See that? Drive right into there.

You sure? I can't see a thing.

Oh, but I can.

WHAT USE OPTIMISM?

Adam Craig

Vision Thing

Stig wakes up this morning and decides to get his old band, The Child Molesters, back together. Sort of an anniversary thing. Show that the old times still matter, that Punk and that whole DIY thing's still relevant. You don't need publicity agents and record labels to make music. Music can be local, democratic, sustainable. What's more relevant than that?

Hands behind his head, he looks up at the ceiling and works out all he has to do. Get in contact with the guys, for a start. And then ... and then ...

It will all take care of itself. He knows it, lying there and looking up at the ceiling. He can see the band back together, see them projected across the ceiling. Just like they were when they were 15 and 16. He can see it.

Stig's pretty sure he can get in touch with Jake, and with Norman Normal and DDT, as well.

Thundering drums and crunching guitars filling the bedroom, he lets his eyes drift across the band as they pogo through 'Glad I'm Not Prince Charles'. What happened to X-Ray Sid is anyone's guess. And DC ...

DC died of an overdose when he was 24. Stig remembers the half inch-long column in the free newspaper. Bloody hell, that was over 25 years ago.

It's only as he thinks this that he realises the kid on the bass is faceless. Nothing there, just a blank. He plays well, though. Better than DC.

'You never did like me.' DC is sitting on the end of the bed, foot thumping on the floorboards more or less in time to the music.

'Don't say that.' Stig sits up in bed while, on the ceiling, the Molesters stumble into 'Some Bastard Pinched My Flying Car'. 'I always thought you did that bass riff really good.'

They both turn. Now Stig has his back propped against the wall, the band are playing on the opposite side of the room. Somehow the wardrobe has moved to one side and the wall pushed back far enough to make space for a microscopic stage. Two pokey spotlights push out from the coving. The faceless bass player gives it a bit of flash, noodling up and down the neck while pogoing almost high enough to bash his head on the ceiling.

'I never played it that well.' DC shakes his head, still a bit spotty despite being 24, despite having been 24 for the last 25 years. 'And don't give me that cobblers, Stig. You always wanted to get rid of me. Get someone else in, like Angie.'

'Hey – ' Stig leans forward and grips DC's skinny arm. The veins stand out, dark under the late bass player's ashen skin. From the corner of his eye, Stig checks for track marks. There aren't any. Pills, not H, killed DC ' – I mean it. I never wanted Angie in the band, alright? Never.'

'You married her though, didn't you, bastard? Even though you knew how much I fancied her.'

'I waited until after you were dead, didn't I?' He snatches his hand away, voice tight and loud even against the thrashing of the band. All the same, he can't quite meet DC's eye. 'What more do you want? And you hadn't seen her in six months. So who's the bastard, bastard?'

Up on the tiny stage, a teenage Stig mumbles something into the mic before the group plough into 'Cop Out'. Only to stop and start and stop again before giving up as Teen Stig makes a royal bollocks-up of the riff.

In the silence following a yowl of feedback, The Child Molesters plod off the stage in a hail of drinks cans and plastic glasses that materialise out of thin air just inside the cones of light from the two spots. This is the last gig for this line-up. It'll be over five months before the Molesters get on stage again. Teen Stig clouts Teen DC across the back of the head, screaming it's his fault the gig was a disaster.

'I'd still really like you to play in the reunion,' Grown-Up Stig tells Ghost DC.

*

Nostalgia's Cool

Stig is watching 4Music with his daughter, Suzie. He remembers when there were practically no music programmes on telly. Top of the Pops, Old Grey Whistle Test. So It Goes. He remembers So It Goes. That was great. Not that he wants to come on all Old Fart or anything. Okay, so he's turned 50. Don't rub it in. Not that he's bothered. Honestly. But this stuff on telly now ...

He's not mentioned the reunion yet. Not to Suzie or Angie. But it's on his mind.

As they sit together, sharing a large bag of Tyrell's, Stig watches Whispering Bob Harris appear on-screen as the current video ends. Bob looks just like he did back in the 70s.

'A fine band,' Whispering Bob whispers, 'if not quite to my taste.'

Bob nods, a sort of older-brother-knows-best nod. Stig remembers Bob doing that a lot. Remembers how bloody annoying it got. That said, just now –

'These bands these days.'

'Dad.' Suzie – sorry – Susan rolls her eyes, long-suffering. (She was christened 'Suzie'. Not the same spelling, no point making it obvious, but the reference was there. Until she decided she preferred 'Susan'. Stig sometimes forgets that she's nearly twice the age he was when Punk came around.) She takes another handful of crisps. 'Don't start.'

'I mean it.'

Whispering Bob nods in agreement. 'Fine.'

'They're all ... packaged. Manufactured. Corporate pop – ' Bob nods – 'McPop.'

'Dad.'

'I'm just saying, that's all. We did it different back then.'

*

Back Then

Inflation. Drought and heat wave. Legionnaires Disease. Irish Republican terrorism. Pakistani terrorism. Communist terrorism. The Cod War. Labour government. The Cold War. Notting Hill riots. Margaret Thatcher. The Queen. Respect for public institutions. Protecting public institutions. The ozone layer. Digital watches. Trade tariffs. Unemployment. Spaceships on Mars. The Bay City Rollers, Barry Manilow, Elton John, the Rolling Stones, Rod Stewart, ABBA. Doctor Who. Mary Whitehouse. Serial killers.

*

Progressing Enquiries

'He's on holiday with his daughter,' Jake's wife tells Stig when he phones later that evening. 'They won't be back for a fortnight.'

He didn't know Jake's daughter was talking to him.

'She isn't. This is his daughter from his second marriage.'

'Oh.' That must have happened around the time Stig tried moving to Manchester. 'Okay. No worries. But could you ask Rhett to give me a call when he comes back, please?'

'Who? Ask who?' asks Jake's third wife.

'Rhett Retard. I mean Ja – '

'Who did you say you was?'

'Stig Marshmallow.'

The line goes dead.

*

Cost Factors

'Don't you think this is all a bit ... 70s?'

'You're still making records.' Stig doesn't look up as he searches the Internet again for DDT's number. He turned the flat upside down last night without finding it.

'Yeah. But I've moved on, you know.' Viv Albertine is sitting on the other side of Stig's small dining table. She hasn't aged a day: tousled bleach-blonde hair and black leather jacket, just like he remembers, just like when Viv was in The Slits. Viv's feet're up on the table, bright pink leopardskin brothel creepers looking almost neon in the glow from Stig's genuine reproduction lava lamp. With a grunt, she opens a bag of Tyrell's crisps: beetroot, parsnip & carrot. 'We didn't have these in the 70s,' she crunches, as if this clinches the argument.

Stig finally gets DDT's answerphone.

'You have reached DD Twomlow, Plumber. There is no one here to service your call just now. Please use the following menu options to help us help supply you with all your plumbing and heating solutions ...'

He has more luck with Norman Normal, who is working as a school caretaker these days.

'I have to go soon,' says Norman (a.k.a. Gary Bilston), 'they've got a disco on and I have to close up.'

Tripping over his words, Stig hurriedly fills Norman in on the plan to get The Child Molesters rebooted. Viv snorts and chomps another fistful of crisps.

'Well, yeah, yeah,' Norman/Gary says, 'well, um, yeah.'

'So you're in, then?'

'Well ... maybe. But, like, doing a single and putting it out and that ... all costs, don't it?'

'No, no, no,' Stig shakes his head, 'well, yes. But it's even easier now than when we did our singles. With MP3s and websites for emerging bands. V – ' Stig looks at Viv crunching away and does a quick verbal sidestep – 'uh, someone showed me all about it.'

'Well, yeah. But you still need money. Don't you? To do it all proper like. That costs. I mean, I'm not doing that badly, Stig, don't get me wrong, not that bad, not like some people, you know how it is these days, but ... well, we'd still need money, wouldn't we? I already owe three grand on my credit card, you know? And my wife's got her heart set on another fitted kitchen – this one's already two years old and – '

'Look,' Stig interrupts, 'I'm hardly Starbucks or, or George Osborne myself. But it's not like we had any money back in the 70s, is it? We managed alright.' Stig feels the old DIY zeal flood over him. 'We didn't let having no money stop us then.'

'I know all that, Stig.' Gary (a.k.a. Norman) does at least sound upset. 'But everything costs so much more now, doesn't it?'

*

DIY

Stig isn't letting this beat him. If it comes to it, he'll get together a new lineup. But The Child Molesters are reforming no matter what.

It's that up-yours, DIY thing. That whole Punk thingy, ethos. He's not giving up.

Not without some sort of fight, anyway.

Stig makes a list, on the bus. Scribbled in the margin of a screwed up copy of the Daily Mail he finds abandoned on the seat. Basically, it all boils down to money and publicity, publicity and money.

Publicity sounds easiest ...

*

Media Savvy 0.0

'So, uh, Stig, would you like say that you don't believe in anything?'

The music journalist on the local paper is younger than Suzie by a good whack. But she has got spiky peroxide hair with pink tips. That seemed like a good sign. Until the young reporter mentioned how she had a teacher who used to like Punk ('he retired my last year of sixth form'), followed by things like: 'It's good to celebrate our traditional musical heritage, i'n' it?' and 'How big an influence are the Rolling Stones on you?' and 'It's a great look, Punk, i'n' it? Great lifestyle choice?'. Now she keeps banging on about not believing in anything, like it's the only thing she knows about the music.

'What,' Stig frowns, 'you mean nihilism? Well, I suppose there's an element of that in Punk. Doubting what – ' He bites off the rest of the sentence, brain fortunately running just ahead of his mouth and pulling an emergency stop before he can utter the words: 'Doubting what older people tell you'. Stig catches sight of himself in the large mirror, behind the reception desk taking up most of the newspaper's tiny entrance lobby. 'To be a bit sceptical,' he finishes lamely.

'So you don't believe in anything?'

'I ... s'pose. Yeah. Except the DIY thing. And Green politics. And Equality. And Fairness. And the Welfare State. And ...'

This isn't going the way he imagined. He's not making any impact. Stig thinks about swearing, but the young reporter has already dropped her pen twice and said, 'Fuck. Sorry,' each time, so that's not going to make an impression any more. Stig glances up at his reflection. Sid Vicious stares back, sneering and shaking his head in disgust. Popular Nihilism's cover boy.

Mercifully, the agony's cut short ten minutes later when the interview derails terminally. After thanking his interviewer, and her thanking him, and Stig thanking her again, he says:

'I always thought this'd be a great job, music journalism. Something to get really passionate about. Music's so important, isn't it? A part of everyone's life.'

'I s'pose. I mostly listen to whatever's on the radio or telly. To be honest,' the local paper's by-lined music correspondent whispers conspiratorially, 'I'm just waiting for an opening on the gossip desk.'

*

New Medial Landscape

He tells Angie all about the reunion the next day on the phone. When he gets to the end, Stig pauses. Waiting. When she doesn't say anything, he stammers:

'Better than buying a sports car. If you're going to have a mid-life crisis, I mean.'

'I suppose.' Angie sounds unimpressed.

They met at a Child Molesters' gig. She came to all of them from then on. Not that there were all that many to go to. Angie'd really had the look, the passion for Punk. She made all of her own clothes and started making clothes for the band. Stig'd fancied her from the first. Angie looked just like Viv Albertine. Same attitude, same spirit. But, when it became obvious she had a thing for DC, he'd hung back, waited. And waited. It'd been worth it, though. The wedding had been great. A real Punk wedding, as if it'd been '76 or '77 and not '85. Angie'd got out all her old gear: studs and safety pins, plenty of zips.

Now she looks like Hillary Clinton. Only thinner and a bit shorter. But the same determined look. Like she'd invade Venezuela all on her own.

'Yeah, well, I was just, just wondering, like, Angie ... Think of it as an investment. You know? An investment in our, um, musical heritage.' Angie earns so much more than Stig, she actually pays him alimony. 'What d'you think?'

'I think you should try looking out of the window sometime.'

He does right then.

The skyline isn't so different to the one he remembers from when he was a kid. All of the factories have gone, replaced by private housing estates. And nearly all the corner shops are gone, too. Replaced by All-Nite-Marts or yet more branches of Tesco or Sainsbury. And there's more traffic. And the road markings need painting, the weeds in the gutters chopping down. Otherwise, Stig isn't sure what Angie's driving at. All the same, he keeps looking out of the window.

Johnny Rotten, floating heavenwards on a ray of butter-yellow light, waves back.

*

<u>It's Only Business</u>

Suzie – sorry – Susan is the manager of the largest fashion store on the retail park. Stig looks at the racks of Made-in-India tartan bondage trousers, the Made-in-China Sex Pistols T-shirts, and wonders if this was what Angie was driving at.

'I could do a personal appearance. Maybe get some T-shirts printed-up. Do a signing, yeah? I'm going to be in the paper.'

'I don't think that'll make you a big enough celebrity, Dad.' Susan pauses to look at a tablet one of her staff has handed her. She taps the screen, has a brief conversation about unit throughput, or unit markup, or unit something, and turns back to Stig. 'Why not go on YouTube or Facebook? Create a platform? That's how you do it these days, Dad. Network, build a tribe. I mean, what's your USP?'

'My ...? Isn't that one of the plug holes on my laptop?'

'Unique Selling Point. Every business needs one.'

'This isn't a business, Suz – Susan.'

'Everything's a business these days, Dad.'

*

Sponsorship

Stig wakes up next morning saying, 'Sponsorship.'

'You say the dirtiest things,' Viv mumbles, turning over. (They're sleeping head-to-toe, her head invisible under the covers at the foot of the bed, so it almost seems as though it's her leopardskin creepers talking.)

'Shurrup,' DC grunts from the camp bed in the corner, 'tryin' sleep.'

Collecting his clothes, Stig tiptoes off to get dressed in the bog.

'You sure about this, man?' Joe Strummer is sitting in the shower cubicle, legs sticking out under the half-open curtain. A single droplet of water falls from the showerhead and plips onto his DA. 'It'll be like selling out. Michael Jackson Land. Every time you drink, gargle, brush your teeth, it'll have to be in fizzy brown sugar water. You know what I'm saying?'

'You're going a bit over the top, aren't you?' Stig looks at the loo, at Joe, and plaits his legs as he brushes his teeth. 'It isn't like I'm,' he says through a mouthful of foam, pausing to spit, 'signing a pact with some Corporate Satan or something. But The Child Molesters need seed money, investment capital, to get up and running again.'

'Yeah, Stig, but you start in telling yourself it's all in a good cause and before you know it they think they own you, you know? They reckon they can buy everyone in the end.' Joe clambers out of the shower stall, somehow managing to appear cool as he does so (no mean feat) and ambles out of the bog just in time to let Stig take care of some pressing business. Before he goes, Joe glances back. 'They reckon everyone's up for sale, Stig.'

So saying, Joe Strummer slings his designed-in-cooperation-with-the-estate, Fender *Joe Strummer* Telecaster® over his shoulder and closes the lav door.

*

Negotiations

Philco Wilco (a.k.a. Mr Five-To-Twenty-Percent, after the mark-up he places on every single deal he ever makes) gives Stig something in the vicinity of a welcoming smile: Jabba the Hut leer cross-fertilised with halitosis.

'You alright, Stig, like?' Philco lifts a hand from the untamed frontier of his midriff, to wave vaguely. 'Going to buy summat?'

The hand takes in Philco's retail empire, a dynamic range of tat, some of it new(-ish), more of it ancient, most of it dubious.

'I've some Romanian designer bathrobes. Just like them in *The Times* colour supplement last Saturday, like, but loads cheappa. Do ya a great deal on a dozen, Stig.'

Stig eyes the white, er, off-white, um, garments hanging from a rack like something from an abattoir's closing down sale. Sid Vicious, shrunk to the size of a neurotic leprechaun, swings wildly from the hem of one of the, um, garments. Expecting to hear the sound of tearing seams any second, Stig blurts:

'I always use shower gel.'

Blundering over the *non sequitur*, Stig outlines his idea that Philco Wilco should sponsor the re-formed Child Molesters, ignoring any inner voices of doubt or good sense bellowing softly inside his skull.

'Well ...' Philco ponders, grudgingly conceding: 'That's a interesting business proposition, that is ...'

In the following silence, Stig's inner voices helpfully remind him that the road to hell is paved with good intentions. As if to back them up, Philco Wilco finally tables a sum of money a good five to seventy-five percent less than Stig imagined in even his wildest and most optimistic fantasies.

'We're going to have, you know, overheads,' he argues. 'Have you seen the price of things lately?' Just look at your own stall, Stig adds silently.

'What you'm on about?' Philco holds up a newspaper, podgy finger stroking the headline. 'Inflation's going down, like.'

Stig opens his mouth. Closes it again. Thinks. 'That just means prices aren't going up as quick. They're still going up.'

Philco stares, eyes peeking over the top of bulging cheeks.

'You really talk bollocks, you,' he tells Stig finally.

*

Over on BBC Four

Paul Morley is on telly. Talking about music. Talking about Punk.

'It was really ...' Paul considers carefully, 'it was so ... punk. The whole thing, the ethos. The whole ethos. Punk. Very punk.'

Stig frowns. Surely, Paul could make a better argument than this. He used to write all those really great, really insightful reviews. That's what people always said.

'It's like,' Paul is saying in that soft Lancastrian accent of his, so down-to-earth, 'George Formby. Look at George's career. What George did. He was really punk.'

Brushing crumbs off his T-shirt, Stig puts the bag of Tyrell's on the floor, positive it's the crisp crunching that's making him mishear.

On-screen, the camera moves in close, so Paul Morley's face fills the screen. In living HD.

'His whole ethos. Using the ukelele. So simple, so basic. George was the Jimi Hendrix of the ukelele. Really punk.'

'That's true. He was just like Frank,' Tony Parsons drawls.

'Frank Sinatra?' Paul asks.

'That's right,' Tony nods. The picture on the telly slews. Stretching so both journalists are in the same shot. Not quite in close-up, not exactly a medium-shot. 'Frank had tremendous cool – '

'Timeless poise,' Paul nods.

' – a gravitas all the really timeless artists have.'

'And he was really punk,' laughs Paul.

'Entirely.' Tony laughs too. 'Frank and all the Rat Pack. Proto-punk. The real thing. Just like George.'

'Real punk,' agrees Paul. Only it's not that Paul any more. It's Sir Paul. Liverpudlian instead of Lancastrian but still in warped two-shot with Tony. 'Like us. Back in Hamburg. We were punk. We invented it, you could say. John would say that if he was here. And George. Punk.'

'Punk,' says Tony.

'Punk,' they say together.

*

And Now

Austerity. Droughts and heatwaves. Bird flu. Inflation. Muslim terrorism. Cyber terrorism. Banking crises. Eco-terrorism. The War on Terror. Coalition government. The New Cold War. Riots all over the place. Margaret Thatcher. William & Kate & the Queen. Demanding respect for public institutions. Privatising public institutions. Global warming. Cloud computing. Globalisation. Unemployment. Spaceships on Mars. The Bay City Rollers tribute bands, Barry Manilow, Sir Elton John, the Rolling Stones, Rod Stewart, ABBA tribute bands. Doctor Who. Boris Johnson. Serial killers.

*

Media Savvy 0.5

Friday: Thing In the Paper Day.

They're all gathered outside the newsagents. Viv (blonde spikes starting to grow out a bit), DC (really getting that cool gaunt-

&-sickly look now), Joe (Sandinista sash tied around his head), Stig in the middle, paging through adverts for houses, cars, car boot sales, raffles, farmers' markets, and used-once-sale-forced-thro-financial-hardship jacuzzis.

(A knocking on the newsagent's window: Sid, open mouth pressed against the glass, bug-eyed before going back to sifting through the scratch-&-sniff lottery cards.)

'It's not here.' Stig starts working back from the sports pages. 'They haven't printed it. It's not – '

It was. Only not what he'd imagined.

The headline reads: *Local Simon Cowell.* Apparently, some guy called Fitz, from Birmingham or someplace, was promoting an evening of 'genuine Punk tribute' at the Assembly Rooms in a couple of weeks.

'I asked Fitz what he thought of the DIY issue associated with the music back in the day,' Stig reads aloud. *"Music is an industry,' Fitz told me, 'just like the stock market, washing machines or meals-on-wheels. You've got to be professional. There isn't room for people without business plans in the contemporary music scene.'* – ' Stig looks at the others. 'What's he on about?'

DC shrugs. 'Who is he?'

'... well respected in the heritage music scene, apparently – '

'There!' Viv and Joe both point to the same paragraph, crammed in underneath a large picture of this Fitz posing with a cardboard cut-out Goth and captioned, *Bringing back genuine rebellion.*

The paragraph reads: *Also timing their comeback to coincide with all this free publicity are former New Wave wannabes,* The Child Molesters, *led by Stick Malmo (56). 'I don't mind anyone trying to cash in on the wave we're creating,' says Fitz, generously.*

Silence ... eventually broken (so to speak) by the sound of Sid farting ...

Later, at Suzie – bugger – Susan's fashion store, Stig is still furious.

"Cashing in'? What do they mean? I didn't know anything about this pillock, Fitz. First I've heard of him. And that reporter never said anything, either, and I bet she ...'

Susan, having shown Viv around the shop, comes back behind the counter to offer appropriate soothing noises. Angie, there on a late lunch break, has given up trying to calm Stig down and is persuading Viv she'll look great in an up-to-the-minute, very-latest-thing, early-70s style maxi-dress.

'And they got my age wrong!'

Stig's yelp falls into the microsecond gap following the end of a techno cover version of 'Shakin' All Over'. It feels as though every customer is looking at him. Luckily, an acid folk rendition of 'Saturday Night Fever' blares out the sound system to cover up his embarrassment.

'They got it all wrong,' Stig mumbles.

'Yes, Dad.'

'It's not right. Doing that.'

'No, Dad.'

'I mean, they should take it seriously. I do.'

'Yes, Dad.'

'It's nothing to do with money, or cashing in. It's not about money.'

'No, Dad.' Susan pats his hand and then rockets from behind the till.

'All of these – ' she pats a rack of bright, polka dot dresses with massively flared skirts ' – are guaranteed to be just like the ones you see in Oxford Street or New York,' Susan tells Viv, smiling and giving her best patter, smooth and confident. Angie smiles, the proud mother.

'And,' Susan adds, 'they're so much cheaper. Take this one. A bargain at £99.95. Why pay more to be on the edge of fashion?'

*

Kenny Ball

No one wants to drive with him. Even DC refuses to come, saying he doesn't want to take his afterlife in his hands. Stig's still smarting about that. Okay, so he hasn't been behind a wheel in three years and this van of his mate's is hardly state-of-the-art (instead of sat nav it's got a magnifying glass on a loop of wire, bobbling over a yellowed copy of the *A-Z* bungee-corded to the dash), all the same Stig's smarting. It's only a short trip to pick up a few boxes of T-shirts. Genuine vintage-style reproductions of The Child Molesters' *What's the Fuckin' Point of Optimism?* tour shirt. Identical. Apart from the added notice. Just on the back beneath the list of the dozen or so local dates they'd played back in '78. In not as small letters as Stig had hoped. The legend: 'A pop music stravaganza brung to you by Wilco International.Com'. It's not far to the printers. Anyone'd think it was the other side of the planet, that Stig didn't observe the speed limits (these days) – was it this turning he wanted? – didn't know how to drive safely – no, probably not, although he could've taken it, perhaps the next – doesn't watch the road properly – no, no, maybe go straight across at this island, after all – couldn't be trusted to –

A horn bellows. An elderly bloke who really looked as though he shouldn't know that sort of language, flicks the Vs at Stig, shaking his fist and creating. The bloke's black Vauxhall is a quarter of the way over the stop line, nose pushed firmly into the flow of traffic around the roundabout.

Stig jumps on the brakes in plenty of time to definitely almost avoid colliding with the front of the Vauxhall.

The bloke carries on creating, fist shaking and V-flicking as he yells out the open window.

Funny bugger, Stig thinks, *doesn't he know he's supposed to give way to oncoming traffic? I was signalling ... wasn't I?*

Ignoring the cacophony of horns from behind, the elderly chap continues violently threatening and abusing Stig.

Perhaps he *doesn't* know he's supposed to give way to oncoming traffic and he's embarrassed about his mistake. That's why he's going on so ...

Stig's eyes are drawn towards the road island. Kenny Ball and his Jazzmen have set up on the top of the grassy mound, hemmed-in by signs advertising the local companies sponsoring this particular island. Kenny's in mid-solo, trumpet tone sharp and clear enough to cut over the traffic. The drummer does a fill and the whole band come in on the melody in time-honoured, family-friendly, English Trad style.

A couple of bars go by before Stig realises they're playing 'Anarchy in the UK'.

*

Visionary Thing

Stig wakes up this morning and imagines all sorts of things. Time going backwards. Time going forwards. Time going around, like an LP on a turntable. If DIY means not having to wait for permission but being free to tackle anything, Stig reckons he should be able to make up a decent end to this story himself. One of those thingy ... epiphany type endings. Doesn't have to wrap up. No. Doesn't have to conclude, end definitively or anything. Just show that things have changed. Yeah, that's what it should do.

So, waking up this morning, Stig imagines a proper end to this story. What he imagines is something like:

Stig wakes up this morning and decides to get his old band, The Child Molesters, back together ...

Starfire

Richard Mosses

My Sword emerged from the Chalice bloodied. I knelt between the legs of the Goddess and received the sacred Starfire; salt and copper, I struggled to swallow it.

The temple peeled back. I walked amongst the stars, in the light from a thousand suns. I walked through the first eleven gates of the Duat with ease, having already overcome the guardians and learned their passwords. The twelfth and final gate remained barred, something was missing. Perhaps it was wrong to do this to get the score draws for the Pools.

I came back to the room. Soror Fiat Et Lux continued to lie on the altar. The opal inlaid talisman of Mercury jabbed into my chest. I pulled it outside of my scarlet robes and wrapped them round my cold body. I did the same for the Soror, who sat up and climbed off the table with a slight smile. We closed the watchtowers and were free to step outside the circle to join the other members of the order.

'That mass was sublime,' said Frater Detesta Matribus.

I thanked him. We had taken over his family home. It was good that he was happy.

'I was wondering,' said Soror Adeste Fideles, 'if I could be considered for the role of the Goddess next time? I'd do anything for the opportunity.'

'I'll discuss it with the higher grades,' I said. It would give her good experience, but she was still relatively new to the group.

'Perhaps I might have a moment of your time, Frater Lux Ex Tenebris,' said Frater Per Aspera Ad Astra. 'I've been studying the Book of the Hierophant and have some questions about the New Aeon. I'd welcome the chance to discuss them with you.'

'Perhaps we could do it later?' I said. Sr. Adeste Fideles had been spending too much time with engineering students. While her popularity on campus had brought in some new recruits I was concerned that her steps on the path of the sacred whore would lead to trouble.

I went upstairs to change. When I came down everyone was in the living room. Food and drink sat on the sideboard. Someone had brought moussaka and there was stroganoff with rice. A bottle of Riesling was chilling in the wine bucket. I joined the others on the floor. The food was good, the wine refreshing, and despite my frustration I began to get my groove back.

'We're going to the Green Man after,' said Sr. Adeste Fideles. 'There's a band on. You're welcome to join us.'

I was going to say no, spending too much time with the lower orders took away some of the mystique, but something in her smile made me change my mind. 'Okay,' I said. 'What's the band called?' I picked up a vibe from Fr. Ad Astra and knew my instincts had been right. Trouble was brewing. I had long ago learned that I should only have ritual relationships with order members, but my earnest Brother didn't know that.

'Fish Fingers,' said Fr. Ad Astra. 'You won't like them. They're ripping up the rules, man.'

'I thought Tet Offensive were playing?' said Sr. Adeste Fideles.

'Al and Synthia had a row with their drummer and bassist. They found some replacements and kept the gig, but it still says Tet on the posters and flyers.'

I had grown up on the Beatles and the Stones, but my mum had been more upset when the Beatles split than I was. 'I'll go in with an open mind,' I said. 'Are they like Zeppelin or Black Sabbath?'

Fr. Ad Astra just laughed. I stared at him until he looked away and hung his head.

*

The Green Man was a Bitter and pork scratchings place. Tonight it was hot and crowded. There must have been fifty people in the bar with the regulars shifted into the lounge. A few amps were set up. The mike stands looked forlorn without someone behind them.

The crowd was different to what I'd expected. There were small knots where people were selling seven inch singles out of cardboard boxes. No flares, tie-dyes or hippy tresses, these people had short spiky hair or shaved heads, drain-pipe jeans, ripped vests. It felt like they could kick off at any moment.

The band came on to wolf whistles and booing. The singer had dyed her hair red. 'One, two, three, four,' the drummer called out as he clacked his sticks together. No one was in time, none of them seemed to know a chord and the singer was out of tune and in the wrong key. But they were fast, loud and the song was short. Half the room pogoed along with them and without delay they collapsed into another song which sounded the same as the first.

After half an hour we were all dripping with sweat, my ears were ringing and the singer taunted the crowd. 'You're all a bunch of fuckin posers. You've no fuckin taste. We're shit, you're shit. You're all sheep following the fuckin crowd.' We yelled back at her, someone gobbed green phlegm on her face. She reached under her skirt, pulled out a tampon, and threw it straight at the crowd. Blood splattered across my face, hot and tangy. We went mental. The band was showered in spit and beer. The lead guitarist shoved his fingers down his throat and sprayed puke over the crowd. We roared back. The tension broke as two guys with flecks of vomit in their hair started to swing for each other. The fighting spread and the barman jumped across the counter with a cricket bat and began laying into everyone. There was a crush for the doors and we were ejected out into the night, sirens getting closer.

I'd never seen anything like it. I was buzzing. I expected sparks to crackle from my fingertips. Sr. Adeste Fideles caught up with me in the street, streaks of blood on her face, hair corded with sweat and her thin shirt stuck to her skin. She was like an angel after the fall. Her eyes were bright, she was charged too. With all this pent up energy I was about to offer to take her there and then but Fr. Ad Astra ran up and saved me from myself.

'Let's run riot,' said Sr. Adeste Fideles. 'I want to start a fire. Burn this town down.'

'The Man here will just call the plod,' said Fr. Ad Astra. 'You hated it, right? Told you.'

'The singer was right,' I said. 'They can't play for shit.'

'She's called Synthia,' said Fr. Ad Astra.

I wiped my hand across his face and showed it to him. 'Can't have been that close to her -- you're clean.'

'We'll see you on Saturday,' said Fr. Ad Astra, leading Sr. Adeste Fideles away.

I went back to my room in Fr. Detesta Matribus' house.

*

In the dole queue, remembering the night before, I was illuminated. All this order stuff was like prog rock – all costumes and pomp and guitar solo masturbation. It was layers of bullshit blotting out the real music beneath. The band had made their own rules, done their own thing and it worked. They had nothing but contempt for people who weren't doing it themselves.

I found Fr. Detesta Matribus in his kitchen making breakfast. 'I'm leaving the order,' I said.

He dropped his spoon into his cornflakes. 'Who will run things? Who will teach us?'

I shrugged. 'You need to find your own path. Any path. Actually, that's wrong. Get off the path, walk in the woods. Lions, tigers, and bears oh my!' I smiled. 'Unless following the yellow brick road works for you.'

'I'll do that then,' said Fr. Detesta Matribus.

'Don't do it cos I said so, do whatever you want. Use whatever tools you need. Don't listen to me, there's no-one behind the curtain. Nothing is true, everything is permitted,' I said. 'I better pack my stuff.'

I had a lot of crap. Most of it would be of use to the order, so I could leave that behind. I picked up a book at random. It was about the Norse gods. The book fell open to the chapter on Loki. A real slippery character. Sometimes a god, sometimes a giant, sometimes male, sometimes a mare. No fixed form, no fixed shape. Loki was anything he needed to be. This was exactly the essence of what this new direction would be about, the magic of disorder and dismay. Playing a role to get things done. Although I had some reservations about giving birth to eight-legged spider-horses.

I met Sr. Adeste Fideles at the front gate. 'You're leaving?' she said.

'I realised this morning that the order's way of doing magic is complete bollocks. I'm not a hypocrite.' I shrugged. 'I hadn't expected to see you again.'

'I came to apologise for Alfie being such a nob last night.'

'That's his responsibility, not yours.'

'I'm just not cut out to be a sacred whore.'

'Why did you choose it in the first place?'

'I thought it would be good for me.'

'At least you were trying to find your own way. Try something new until it works.'

'Where are you going?'

'Where my feet take me,' I said.

'You could stay at my place.'

'What about Fr. Ad Astra?'

'We had a difficult talk.'

It was time to throw away all the rules. Then I could do anything I wanted.

*

If I knew then what it would do to my life then maybe I wouldn't have created a mock religion around Loki, dedicated to discord and mischief. I would have chosen Aphrodite or something like that. Love might have been a better choice. But I cut the discordian knot, and life didn't so much unravel as become truly chaotic. It was always fun, in unexpected ways.

I gave up doing magic a couple of years ago. I was sitting at my kitchen table and I turned bread into gold. No one else was there. Afterwards I went outside and sat in the sun for a while.

I'm a Buddhist now. I've seen through the illusion so what else was there to do?

QUANTUM PUNK

Sarah Crabtree

'And I thought to myself, And the men don't know what the little girls understand.'
Steve Harris, p.81, 'Please Kill Me'

Attitude. Think about that word for a moment. (By the way, I never introduce myself – what's the point?) Here I imagine tutoring my nursery pupils with teenage brains inside their toddler heads. Attitude. You can say it several ways. Said quickly, it means the way somebody deals with an unpleasant problem; i.e. with something they don't really want to do. I remember my mother – product of a bankrupt father and jealous mother - despatching me to do my homework when I showed a negative attitude towards helping with the washing up, when what I really wanted to do was find my space. Her take was that if you didn't have a willing attitude towards doing something, then she didn't want you around. We have to disagree on that. We all have parts of our lives that we don't want to deal with; if it's an unpleasant job, up the ante, get it done as quickly and efficiently as possible. By all means get it done properly; otherwise it becomes a chore because you end up having to do it all over again.

Some things need to be done over and over. I have heard it said that creative people such as Danny have a tendency to want to reach closure with difficult things because that's how they function when playing music. It's rather like playing with dolls as a child: you take them out, play house with them, and then pack them back in the box when you are tired of them. A genius controlling the conflict. Real life isn't like that. You can bet your bottom dollar that if one problem resolves itself, then another will quickly spring up to take its place.

Attitude. Say it slowly, enunciating the first letter. Try it again. There. That's the way the cool people say it. A-tti-tude. Attitude is who *you are; how you choose to think. It's often the first thing children display when they are rebelling against their parents. It's a mark of self-respect. If we don't have attitude, then we become the puppet of others. They pull the strings and we perform to their desires. If we display the wrong attitude, in another person's eyes, then he can use that as a weapon against us.*[*]

Danny is waiting for me to dismiss him, rather like, I think, the children in my nursery class await my permission to go and play in the sandpit. I can't make him visit Mum, but I still have a little hold over him.

'I feel, sometimes, that I abandoned you, B-Tanny.' He was about to call me Baby Sham again, and corrects himself, thank God.

*

Lover, Mother, soon-to-be Holy Ghost...Mum doesn't know it's my birthday. She doesn't know it's me anymore. Still, there is sunlight on the bed. I sit like a mime holding her hand in the care home; together in silence, embroiled in our own fantasyland. Mine was once chasing the handsome prince through every continent; now I keep dreaming of searching for a clean loo through a labyrinth of hotels. There's something Freudian in that but I cannot be bothered to find it. Once I dreamt I was driving along the Tottenham Court Road in an odd kind of apocalypse: Boris to the left of me and Ed to the right; both shouting for votes. I dodged the bullets, woke up, ran to the bathroom and vomited. There was something Mieville-esque about it all. And one day I really will bother to find out what that means.

For now, shadows from the past flit just out of my vision. Even though I am unable to see them, I know they are always around us along with shades of the unknown unknown.

On a good day, Mum will tell me how she danced in the rain when the sauna summer broke in '76. She smiles a slack smile. It has taken me a long time to share the joy of that moment when the heat

---

* 'Attitude' adapted from 'A Princess Dies' from 'Zombies, Novellas and Rookie Writers'

© Sarah Crabtree 2013

was washed away bringing England back to its customary freshness. I stare at my mother's form and try to picture her from way back. It's hard to get my head around that this is the same woman. She used to be so vital, so funny, so popular with the guys. She wore long bright Indian cotton dresses. Cool for the heat. Now, where the rain stuck the cloth to her body, it's sweat; yet as before it hurts to see the revealing shapes of her form. I realise the feeling I had then was jealousy of being the B side to their Double A side. I knew I would never be beautiful like her and Danny. Already my blonde hair was turning mouse-brown and my facial features were sharpening into a female semblance of my estranged father, I can only assume. 'Blotchy,' I think I heard her describe me once. It's incredible how much she used to tell me; and not that long ago. Then she began forgetting it all. I swear some of these memory lapses were selective. I would remind her pathetically without the back-up of a video re-run. 'No, no, no,' she would say.

I give the bed clothes a well-meaning fiddle around the edges. There's currently a lot of talk about the five regrets of the dying. How about the five regrets of the living? Right now I wish I'd given a shit less, worked a little harder on my career, owned at least one puppy from cradle to grave, or even a kitten or an iguana, learned to play guitar or the keyboards more than passably, and my last wish...being careful what I wish for...been better able to know when it's time to let go. Now she wants me to leave.

Earlier I opened my cards at home. It's not the home we all shared when we were young. Not quite. It's a mirror image of the old townhouse. After Danny moved out, Mum and I drifted for a while between residences, constantly reinventing our culture. We were always happiest in places that had a washing line. Where we had to dry our stuff indoors, the condensation would drip off the walls and ceilings and the mould would spread its evil. We stayed for a month or so in a town in the South East. I cannot remember its name, only that it had no washing line and an annual regatta. I waited until the last of the fireworks had been lit, and as Mum and I walked back to our bedsit, reminiscing about the summer when the reservoirs cracked and a tropical storm exploded the night skies, I pleaded with her to take me home.

There was one more step to take: Mum secured a temporary Christmas job in a town closer to London in an old department store with a vintage money tube. The townspeople were kind and funny in a down-to-earth manner and it was almost-but-not-quite like home. We watched the pennies and saved up for our train fare back to our beloved City for New Year. I guess we were always meant to return to Chilcombe Street, because when we were house hunting again the property three doors along came up for rental. All it needed was a washing line to run the length and breadth of its tidy stone-paved and gravelled back yard.

John never forgets my birthday. This year he sent me a CD with a photoshopped cover of Danny's band: the original photo was shot in Hamburg in the summer of '76. Danny had just turned sixteen; John a year older; and there are two other teenage musicians I don't recognise. But then there were so many line-up and name changes that I guess it doesn't matter. There's only one track on the CD: 'quantum punk.' I smirk at the memory: its original title was 'dont let the barsterds grind u down' using the punk book of grammar with no capitals, punctuation and the obligatory misspellings. Sadly another punk band had already decided to issue a single with that title and after a punch-up in a car park, John backed down and went for the more succinct 'quantum punk' just to keep everybody happy. I'm not sure if John wrote it for Danny or me. Maybe both. Maybe neither. Maybe John wrote it about himself. All I know for sure is that John penned the lyrics the day after our beach excursion to celebrate Danny finishing his O'levels. I slot it into the player and turn up the volume. Not bad. A remix. It sounds like he's been working with Pet Shop Boys. (John hates being reminded of his brief yet brave PSB tribute band, It's A Grin, but hey that's another tale for another time.) The former angry sound has been ameliorated and charged up with high-energy. It's a new voice. But the lyrics are the same. Like the story.

Danny. Sunglasses, black leather jacket and a Brad Pitt smile. Yesterday, he told me our father had died: the vacuum in my life now filled with ashes. Even the DNA is gone. I swear for a micro-second I wonder if our father passed his genes on to anybody else. In a parallel universe – dystopia/utopia - there might be another Danny and Tanny living out their own version of a fucked up dreamworld. Do they ever consider our existence a possibility? Do they share any traits? Is there a cell or two that yearns to meet us? I don't fool myself we would be running into open arms. This is not a Disney movie.

I fashion my lips to enquire about a funeral, a legacy, maybe even a little money to share between Danny and me. Before I make a twat of myself, I realise he and I will be lucky to get away with not having to pay off the old boy's debts. In a strange, twisted way that would be kind of funny. Danny offers no details of how, where or when the father died. Maybe he heard it on the urban grapevine. Intuitively I keep schtum: the less I know the safer I feel. Whilst I don't know Danny's exact financial standing, I know Mum's and mine is just about manageable and selfishly I'd like to keep it that way. My brother and I spent the afternoon walking through London. As we wandered back and forth over bridges, he relived the rows, slaps and screams; the relief when this vicious man finally left his pregnant wife and eight-year-old son in peace, and Danny didn't have to listen to his mummy crying anymore. Mum and Danny shared so many secrets then. Now she knows nothing about the people he and I have become. I notice one of the bridges is peppered with insect corpses. Danny clocks them and explains they are mayflies that only live a few hours after hatching. He told me he wrote a poem about them once at school and how they dance away their short lives over the river.

Just as we part, Danny is distracted by a tall, slender woman in a midsummer skirt (Boho chic?) stepping briskly into a BMW. I clock the navy designer handbag she's carrying. I swear it's the one all the fashionistas are raving about that retails at four hundred and fifty pounds. It's gorgeous but, even if I could afford it and I cannot, I think I would rather kill myself than spend that amount on a handbag. It's probably worth more than my car. No. Scrub that. It *is* worth more than my car. I ask him if he knows her but he pretends not to hear. She doesn't acknowledge him, so I guess he's mistaking her for somebody he once knew. Or maybe just maybe she's one of those astonishing creatures on form, who knows that *being seen* with him is actually better than the bourgeois concept of *being with* him. It's all bullshit in the grander scheme of things. I should know. I am his sister, after all.

I ask him to accompany me to visit Mum, so we can be a family again for my birthday. Birthdays. Christmas. Easter. Another anniversary. It's the way we hold on to our family ties. Without them we would be unleashed to follow our dreams and only crawl back to the nest when broken-hearted. I wish I could remember the day I stopped crying for my big brother. Was it that time he returned once and I was so pleased to see him but he hardly spoke a word to me? I remember feeling hurt that I looked forward so much to seeing him again but it was like I wasn't important to him anymore. It's at this point he hands me the CD John has made and apologises for having to dash back to the studio.

'Couldn't you have just emailed me a download?' Even as I hear myself say this, the knowledge that I am way too old to be snide is almost enough to slice through my tongue.

'You're a really strong person now, Baby Sham.' I still wince when he calls me this, and I see a one-all in his eyes. Does he know about the restraining order my ex threatened me with?

He thinks I don't see through his attempts to make amends: like the time he wanted to help by offering to get Mum this apple cider vinegar with *mother* in. It was just before she went totally incapable of living on her own. Danny had read that this special type of vinegar might make her better. So he'd trawled the streets of London – allegedly – asking for this precise vinegar which had to include the mother. I have visions of him going into the first Tesco Express and being fobbed off with Daddie's Sauce. Because that's what he came back with, deciding en route - presumably - that his kid sister bypassed the ironic phase and slipped straight into seriousness; but for old times' sake is still the innocent hiding behind the blare of the music. Genius. Chaos. Control.

It's entirely likely I have completely misread the situation. It's hard enough for me to see our beautiful mother looking so drawn and dried out despite sleeping so much of the time. For him it must be easier to cope with the sadness in my eyes when he cries off yet again. I really don't mind that as much as him refusing to open up about his real relationship with John. I want him to stop treating me like an innocent. I suspected his orientations when the girls kept getting younger, prettier and more frequent. He was trying to kid himself about his feelings for John. And poor John had to play the waiting game for so long. At least that's what I talked myself into thinking until...when? When was that precise moment I realised with a double-edged sword of sadness and relief that it was never going to happen? Danny and me. Me and John. John and Danny. No. Delete those unsatisfactory pairings. We were destined to stay in our polyamorous perfection.

'I guess I can't persuade you to come and visit her with me tomorrow?'

I'm expecting him to say 'Nah' just like he always does. The true Danny would now be out of sight. But today is a red letter day: 'Do you really remember what happened that day?'

'What day?' I say, knowing damn well...

Life is very beautiful and gets better everyday. Having a brother eight years older and in a band was always an interesting crowd-puller. Most of the local kids walked to school with siblings either in the year or two above or year or two below. My big brother was the biggest brother of them all. At least in our little neck of the city. So nobody beat me up in the playground or nicked my dinner money because I'd get my big brother to sort them out after school. Just like he sorted out the bully who ordered me to ask the dinner lady to give him a triple gigantic pudding when I was on dinner duty and I was too afraid to do so 'cos the headmaster was eavesdropping, so I asked for a medium and the bully went mental at me for bringing back a less-than-triple-gigantic portion and made me cry. Once upon a time I was that little girl who wanted to be the cute singer in Danny and John's band. Danny on lead guitar and John on bass. We would audition for the drummer, who would be handpicked by me. My own little rock family, posing for our album cover: the cute one, the talented one, the funny one and the nutter.

I played all of these roles at least in my head. But I'm still here so I must have been doing something right.

For the first eight years of my life Danny looked out for me. Always at the school gate, sometimes with a girlfriend in tow, and they all liked me too, 'cos I was little and cute and blonde. Plus I never told when Danny left me downstairs with my Barbies and Sindies while he nipped upstairs with his Jennies and Lindas. Capital Radio would drown out all the other sounds I was too innocent to know about and too preoccupied with changing dolls' outfits to care about.

With Mum out working, Danny took over the chores. It was a tidy arrangement. We weren't exactly skint but we couldn't afford the school trips and foreign holidays some of the other kids went on. Mum wouldn't let us play in our narrow, echoey hall, even though we pleaded that the high notes bouncing off the walls sounded like a real record. Instead, Danny would take me along to listen to him rehearsing with John in his dad's garage, leaving the guitars by the amps for feedback fury. I hated their early stuff and then grew to love the music. I have the tinnitus to prove it. We were happy then. I can't really think of it any other way, and like most little kids I just expected it to go on and on like that long hot summer of '76. The summer Danny hit sixteen.

People talk about punk like it happened overnight. I liken it to menstruation: the first time it's a shock however well prepared you are; yet at the same time you knew something was going to happen to your body; you sensed it even before they started leaving little booklets lying around. They say it's all in the timing; but the right time for somebody can be the wrong one for somebody else. Life is short for some; long for others. Some people crave change; others have change thrust upon them. I'm not sure even now which category my brother slots into. He just decided to go off and form a punk band with John after they caught the Ramones at the Roundhouse. Or maybe it was when an ex-girlfriend saw the Pistols playing in Brighton. On a bad day I prefer to think it all started with Mum dragging along Danny to watch Cliff at the Palladium. That reminds me. I must pick up that Hello Kitty pencil case I promised to buy for one of the helpers who's leaving to go back to Uni.

Danny finished his O'levels and left school. Mum told me later that she nagged him to stay on into the sixth form. All I can remember was a feeling of change in the air. Electric. Exciting. A wobbly feeling in my tummy like when it's the day before my birthday or I'm trying to get to sleep when Father Christmas is going to come. The morning after Danny finished his last exam, he took me along with a group of his mates down to the seaside to celebrate. I was so excited. I got to sit on the back of his mate, John's motorbike, Danny's girlfriend on the back of his, and we whizzed down to Hayling Island for fish and chips on the sand. I got a bit burnt and my white sandals got wet. I cried a little, so John hugged me and found me a shell and bought me a red lolly and I got it all down my white sundress. Danny's then girlfriend whose name escapes me cleaned me up as best she could. She kept getting me to lick this hankie so she could clean the sticky stuff off my mouth and hands. The sun was hurting my eyes and I kept blinking. I had long eyelashes and they curled back into my eyes where I would rub them and see rainbow spirals and flashes. It was then I spotted something that made me rub my eyes again. My brother and John closing in, the razor cuts, wrists touching, together at the edge of the water and it looked like they kissed. When I opened my eyes again, the guys were running into the sea. I was tired now and the next time I opened my eyes, somebody must have carried me on to the ghost train, for I remember the spider webs brushing my face; the long drive back home when John's motorbike broke down.

The next day Mum got really, really mad at Danny, and he stormed out. I started crying and Mum gave me a strange look, like she didn't know I was her little girl; yelled at me to shut up 'cos I was too big to cry like a baby anymore. I was crying 'cos I wanted my big brother to hug me. I wanted my mummy to hug me. Even John was gone. Everything was too angry and sad and broken and confusing and my tummy hurt with the horridness of it.

Everyday before the heat got too much, I'd run to John's dad's garage and hang around waiting for them to get back. John's mum and dad handed me a bottle of coke the first time and said the boys had gone away for the summer. After that it was a glass of water.

I guess Mum must have quit her job because we ended up taking a bus journey to somewhere outside London and then on a ferry to the Isle of Wight. I asked her years later what this place was but she said she couldn't remember anything about that summer when Danny left, except dancing in the rain when the weather broke. The only reason I was able to confirm it was the Isle of Wight was because I bumped into a guy, a bearded history lecturer at Brighton College, who remembered us, 'the beautiful bohemian with blonde kid in tow,' from that 'crazy, crazy seventy-six summer.' Mum was working at a holiday camp and he shared spliffs with her in one of the abandoned chalets. It was a weird way of confirming it, but I already knew I didn't imagine it because I hung out with a bunch of other kids. We played hide and seek in this woodland bit where the shade of the trees blocked out the sun, and this old lady with a bad leg used to keep us going with trays of lemonade and ginger nuts. I could never have conjured up a memory as precious as this: I still remember the beach, the bleached pebbles and the white heat. As I watched Mum dance in the rain, my fingers curled round the shell John found on the beach. He placed it to my ear and whispered in the other that if I wanted to hear the sea, I could listen to it there. That even on the wettest, coldest day inland, the sea was never far away if I held the shell up close. The summer wave of punk rolling back and forth along the shore.

*

I want to scream: 'Of course you sodding abandoned me, you selfish prick. You left me with *her*. And now guess what? You're doing the same.' Was it so unbearable? Her sanity gradually unravelling as she lost her looks and self-esteem; her fear of falling; her fear of me falling; her refusal to leave her flat; her gradual caving-in to the stiffness of joints. I tried. God knows I tried. For years I refused to allow her to give in. But on the day she gave herself away, I quit trying to coax her into going out again. That day she called me a good girl I realised how she had been playing me for a fool and had been watching me become bitter and resentful because I was trying too hard to be a good person by being too good to her.

But it wasn't her fault over that mindfucking business to do with the overhanging threat of the one hundred and twenty-five quid fine – her share of the sum – for carrying the garbage can of blame for the resident who kept sticking rubbish sacks in the communal recycling bin. For years this dragged on. Couldn't people bloody well read? Or did they just not give a shit about destroying the planet with their carelessness? You didn't have to worry about us, Danny. I managed to rescue her from all that.

For years I was angry at him for leaving me despite knowing one day he really would take off for good. Christ knows he was always saying he was going to go one day. And Hayling Island is no substitute for Sunset Boulevard. I'm still piecing together the places he played and the people he met.

Other than brief unannounced visits, I got just one lousy postcard from NYC: 'Dear Baby Sham, Just hanging around. Keeping it real. Luv Bruvx.' I carried that card around in my school satchel right until a bully from the third form ripped it away from me. I got the satchel and the postcard back; the bully got a scratch down the face. We were all getting the message: Punk helped us to deconstruct people more easily.

I don't think I'll ever tell Danny this. Unless, of course, this story gets published and he bothers to read it. In my head I rehearse his reaction: 'You were always too much, Baby Sham. Each day with you was always just...a question.' He will pause for thought as he paraphrases one of his idols, Warhol, Reed, Iggy...I don't know which one; there were so many in Danny's crowded life; and one day I'll get tired of re-writing the script like the pop video I helped Danny with when he jumped on the Fifty Shades bandwagon. He wanted to fill the Oracle with a flash mob of gorgeous young girls fitted with remote controlled vibrators riding the escalators.

His mansplanation had them climaxing simultaneously when he pressed a button. John's input was a young rapper and some boy dancers who would strut their stuff against a throbbing beat. I pacify the security department when the buzzing orchestra of fifty vibrators sets off the mall's burglar alarm.

My nightmare afterwards consists of running up and down staircases cut into the house with a thousand corridors (The Exorcist, The Shining and Vertigo, but not necessarily in that order), doors opening and closing but I never get to meet the person or thing that's heading my way. This version cites the theory that Danny didn't hang around any longer to answer my questions because I simply hadn't suffered enough to be worth his while listening to. Spitting and safety pins. I could tot up the number of years gone by...Maybe next time.

It's the oddest thing but as I watch Danny slip away in one of those rare moments when he is not living for the applause, it seems he really isn't as big as I thought he was. Shorten and fly. There. Now. If I stretch out my hand and measure his outline between my thumb and forefinger, I can shrink him to the size of a Polly Pocket and drop him into my afternoon cuppa. The one I enjoy the most after a particularly hectic session at the school. I think he's ready to explain it all now. Simple really. Good old Grandfather Hindsight has paid him a call.

I jump into my black Fiat and just as I'm indicating to move over into the right hand lane, the BMW bitch appears from nowhere and cuts across me. I watch as she smoothes her blonde hair in the mirror like she's got 'Princess' tattooed on her arse. Reacting to my verbal abuse, she sticks one finger up. At the next row of traffic lights I manage to pull alongside her, wind down the window, lean across and give her both fingers.

My analytical side kicks in: good or bad. Nobody is completely one or the other. So far I succeed where others have failed in dropping the eff-bomb in front of the kids. The little angels are only three and four years old and yet they are light years ahead of the adults who tend to their needs. I don't blame the mothers for hanging on to their shitty jobs by dumping the little darlings on us five days a week from eight 'til six. Is it really only one in five women remains childless? It's more likely that one in five women actually plans to have a baby during that particular period of ovulation and achieves that objective; another changes her mind; another is coerced; yet another does it as a career change; and the last one has the courage of her convictions. Not that I give a shit about all that personally. We had a staff meeting the other month about maintaining discipline, and we brainstormed this idea of one of us wearing a robot mask and sitting in the broom cupboard so that when one of the kids was being so totally bad that we couldn't control him/her, we would send him/her to 'speak to the 'droid.' I thought it was just a joke, but after returning to work after a week's holiday and being collared by an angry parent who screamed that her kid was now in therapy because he kept having nightmares about the 'droid, I realised the staff, in obvious desperation, had launched the project.

Only the other week a new recruit – a Directioner no less who tweets throughout the day to her two fellow Directioners - was fired on the spot for using the c-word when one of the little darlings bit through her thumb. We were doing a seaside themed arts and crafts session with old milk bottle tops (so rare these days, therefore hard to get hold of, so please do send some in/stick them on eBay), toilet roll tubes and empty cereal packets. We seem to have defaulted to the old stuff, i.e. cardboard and foil. (We were involved in a project some years ago called Plastic Fantastic but the kids hated it, probably because it's nigh on impossible to safety-glue plastic onto card.) I took in John's shell to show. The little darling snatched it and my colleague grabbed it and rugby passed it back to me. I am no Spitfire pilot or man on the moon but this is my version of fantastic. As the child bit home, I swept the shell up to my ear, and beneath the sea sound I swore I heard John sing, 'Goddamn dive smells just like a piss factory...'

'The ultimate rock star is a child.'
Danny Fields, from 'Please Kill Me'

JESTER PUNK FUFFERY

Douglas J. Ogurek

'Three young men stood in a field beside a subdivision street. One wore earphones and chewed his hair, while another threw rocks at passing birds. The third and oldest, dressed as a jester, limped to a box. 'Subjects, I have something that will fuff Gavel Guy beyond recognition.'

The thrower picked up a rock. 'Poosh. What smells like shit? You take a dump in your pants, Loot?'

Loot removed the hair and bowed before the jester. 'Your Brilliance, prithee fuff this knave, perhaps.' He returned the hair to his mouth.

Your Brilliance held up a checkered flag and a toy race car. 'Behold: the fuffernalia that will fuff Gavel Guy. Agreed, Cheers With Farts?'

Cheers With Farts threw the rock, but missed a bird. 'Shove Gavel Guy's daughter's cello up his bung.'

On the street, a man — he walked wobblingly on his toes — pushed a wheeled music stand. He read the large book it held.

Cheers With Farts stomped. 'Chugga-chugga Ball Boy.'

Your Brilliance put on a pair of mirrored sunglasses, then raised one hand and spoke confidently. 'I, Gavel Guy, shall use my Gavel to take my daughter to the flopera, for one day, she will be a famous cellist.'

'Poosh, Gavel Guy, can I have a ride in your Gavel? We can wear cool glasses and listen to flopera and floor it.'

Your Brilliance sang operatically. 'My boss drives a Gavel as well, / my boss who takes credit for my work. / Perhaps I will see my boss in hell.'

Ball Boy let go of the stand, and then, holding his hands at awkward angles, lurched toward the threesome. He wore a Redbirds basketball jersey over a T-shirt and rolled a rubber band ball against his stubble.

When he was married, Your Brilliance had a Lab named Sorcerer. Sorce loved to play with big rubber bands.

Ball Boy addressed Cheers With Farts. 'Sir, will you please stop that? With the rocks?'

Cheers With Farts imitated the man's posture and lisped. 'Stop, stop. You're such a bad boy, tossing those rocks. You might hurt the special bird.'

Loot cavorted and sang, shifting from falsetto to growl.

This drug will fix the misbehaving child.

This drug will make him obedient and mild.

We the university professors substantiate it.

Now what was it that you said about a stipend?

Cheers With Farts flipped up a rock, then caught it. 'Ball Boy's a Redbirds fan, and Ball Boy's got a special relationship with the special birds.'

Your Brilliance took off the sunglasses, then pointed toward a woman pushing a stroller. 'Behold: Wobemo approacheth.'

Cheers With Farts hurled the rock, but missed three birds. 'Oo, it's a booby trap.'

'Sir, will you please not throw that?'

'Pooshy pooshy. Come here, Ball Boy, and I can paint your fingernails a special color and you'll be pretty just like your special bird.'

Ball Boy, clutching his ball, tottered to Your Brilliance. 'He might hurt a bird.'

Sorce should have lived longer.

Your Brilliance scowled at Cheers With Farts, then squinted at Ball Boy. 'Subjects, the time to fuff has arrived.'

Loot took off his earphones. 'Inspired.' Cheers With Farts dropped a rock, then pretended to steer. 'Oh Your Brilliance, let's fuff him up.'

Your Brilliance shook the bells on his shoes. 'Ball Boy is concerned, Cheers With Farts, that you might injure a bird.'

Cheers With Farts bent his hand and grunted as he thumbed his phone. Loot took a globe from the box.

Your Brilliance put a plastic pipe in his mouth. 'I suppose, Ball Boy, that you've never hurt a bird?'

Ball Boy picked at his rubber band ball. 'No.'

'At Thanksgiving, for instance?' Bubbles rose from the pipe. 'Did you think your entrée grew on a tree?'

Cheers With Farts's phone made a flatulence sound and he yelled 'Choo choo.' Loot chewed his hair and tossed sparkling confetti from the globe.

'And when your beloved Redbirds built the practice facility, they destroyed that forest. How many trees, I wonder, did your cherished team destroy?'

Ball Boy clutched his jersey and scratched his bristles.

'And subjects, are you ready for this? How many hundreds of birds lived in those trees?'

Loot spit out the hair. 'Galvanic.' Cheers With Farts picked up a rock.

'Subjects, subjects, watch this.' Your Brilliance placed one foot before the other and extended his arms. 'I hereby propose that we change the name of Ball Boy's Redbirds...to the Deadbirds.'

More flatulence noises and confetti, then Cheers With Farts threw the rock, but missed the birds. 'What smells like poo? You poo your pants, Ball Boy?'

Ball Boy took off the jersey, then plodded back to his stand.

*

Wobemo pushed her stroller and texted.

From his box Your Brilliance took a bottle of baby powder, which he limped to Loot. "Mooncalf' means fool, and most women are concerned about their weight. Especially this one. Sweet Loot, I'd like a fuff puff each time I use the word 'mooncalf.' Or with any variation of the word 'weight."

Your Brilliance gave Cheers With Farts a baby rattle, then flourished his bubble pipe. 'Pardon, my lady.'

Wobemo put her phone in a purse branded with a zigzag symbol. 'What's wrong with you?'

'The pleasure's all yours.' Your Brilliance bowed. 'My lady, my subjects and I are composing a book, and I thought you might like to contribute. It's about...' He put his hand on Loot's shoulder. '...mooncalves.'

Powder puffed from Loot's bottle and Cheers With Farts pretended the rattle was a gearshift. 'Poosh. Fuff this milf.'

Wobemo retrieved her phone. 'What's wrong with you?'

'I'm all rainbows and butterflies.' Your Brilliance watched bubbles ascend. 'What do these clouds remind you of, my lady?'

The sky was clear. She shook her head and thumbed her cell phone.

Your Brilliance placed a hand beside his mouth and whispered to his followers. 'Doesn't the sky remind you of her head?'

Cheers With Farts shook the rattle and stomped. 'Bullllldoze this bitch.'

Your Brilliance pretended to text on his palm, then raised his voice. 'OMG. Here's a pic of baby blinking. Facebook. Alert the universe. She's a prodigy.'

The zigzag on Wobemo's purse flashed. 'My daughter was in tears because of you.'

'They must have been tears of admiration.' Your Brilliance spun around and reached upward.

'You're a rock music loser.'

Cheers With Farts pretended to slam down the brakes.

'Au contraire, my lady.' Your Brilliance hopped. 'I listen to jester punk. Jester punk is to rock music as Gucci is to, well, some inferior brand. Like ShroudStone.' Bubbles rose from his pipe. 'Oh, I'm sorry. Isn't that a ShroudStone?'

'Fine. You're a pop punk loser.'

'I'm afraid that's erroneous as well. Jester punk is to pop punk as butterflies are to bubblegum.'

Loot crossed one leg over the other and bowed. 'Exploding butterflies, that is.'

'Only idiots listen to that.'

'Oh, you and your rocket scientist family must listen to what? Classical?' Your Brilliance popped a bubble. 'Are you aware of the research that reveals that pregnancy decreases brain size? If what you say about those who listen to jester punk is true, my lady, then perhaps I can interest you in some samples?'

'You're a monster. Telling my daughter about Audrey Quick's perfume.'

Cheers With Farts watched approaching birds, and shook the rattle. 'Steam... roll... this... bitch.'

Your Brilliance rang the bells on his wrists. 'You mean the cherished teenage musical star? America's darling? It turns out that her perfume — the one that all the little girls want? — is tested on animals, sprayed in rabbits' eyes. So, my lady, *who's* the monster?'

As Cheers With Farts shook the rattle, Loot removed his hair. He sang softly, then roared. 'Your lips shimmer, your face gleams, and your skin's ambrosial, /Thanks to the suffering of thousands of lab animals.'

Wobemo shoved her phone into her purse, then hurried forward.

Ball Boy sat on the street. He bounced his ball and read his big book.

Before the opera that night, Your Brilliance's wife applied a ruthless shade of lipstick. 'That stuff you listen to is so silly. It's embarrassing.'

Wobemo stopped, then flipped her hair. 'Aren't you kind of old to be dressed like that?'

'Wait...wait.' Your Brilliance flicked a bell on his cap and leaned toward Loot, who puffed more powder. 'I was thinking the same about you, my lady. But wait. Well, maybe you're on your way to an Audrey Quick concert? I'll bet you can't wait.'

While Loot puffed, Cheers With Farts pretended the rattle was a microphone and sang in falsetto. 'The earth gets greener when you are near. /The sun gets brighter when you are here.'

'Cheers With Farts, stop. You're turning me into a girl.' Your Brilliance pretended to brush one of the arms on his cap. 'A girl who tortures rabbits.'

'What's wrong with you? I should call the cops on you.'

Your Brilliance pretended his bubble pipe was a phone. 'Officer, officer, come quick. There are three people in my neighborhood committing an atrocious crime: they're standing. You might need to call reinforcements.' The rattle shook and Your Brilliance leaned back. 'My lady, I saw you texting while driving. Should I call the cops on you?'

'Asshole.' She huffed and started to walk away.

'Did you know a texter killed my entire family?'

'Liar.'

'I've also seen you speeding and talking on a cell phone, which is comparable to driving drunk. May I speed and talk on the phone whilst your prodigies are out playing?'

'You're an asshole.'

'Words of wisdom, spoken by World's Best Mommy. Mommy mooncalf.'

She strode past Ball Boy, who stretched a rubber band.

As Your Brilliance and his wife prepared to leave the house for the opera that night, Sorce was not there to see them off.

'Poosh. I think you made milfy cry.' Cheers With Farts picked up a rock and studied advancing birds. 'What smells like shit?'

Your Brilliance retrieved the toy race car. 'Subjects, hey, subjects. Are you ready for this?' He pressed a button and the car made a racing sound. 'Alert the masses: Gavel Guy will get fuffed out of his mirrored sunglasses.'

*

Blue smoke streamed from a smoke bomb amid the threesome. Near them, a bird squealed and skipped frenziedly over the grass.

Ball Boy, who'd stood over the downed bird, plodded back to his mobile music stand.

Cheers With Farts nudged Your Brilliance. 'Hey Ball Boy, I think I can get you a few more special friends.'

The night of the opera, Your Brilliance's wife took her keys from her purse. Gucci. 'It got out. The thing almost knocked me over.' 'Well let's go find him.' 'No, we have to go. This is too important. I can't let this client down.'

An older man wearing an orange safety vest waved away smoke. 'What's this tomfoolery?'

Your Brilliance tiptoed to the smoke bomb. 'Is it okay for me to cross now, Betsy?'

Cheers With Farts stomped and rubbed a balloon he'd halfway inflated.

'What kinda guy dresses like that?'

Your Brilliance spun in the smoke. 'An *inconsiderent* guy?'

Loot chewed his hair and sprayed an 'Earth Scents' aerosol can.

The man rubbed a plum on his vest. 'Now I see this and I say, 'Gosh, you guys are absolute nutcases.''

The smoke bomb finished, and Your Brilliance gave the man a black plastic bag. 'Betsy, I receive you bearing gifts.'

'What...' Betsy dropped it. 'You're absolutely unconscionable.'

'Not long ago, you accused me of not picking up after my dog.'

'The thing's an abomination.'

'So I wanted to absolve myself of any *flault*.'

Loot sprayed again, and the scent of roses blended with the odors of smoke and excrement. Blunderingly, a cello played in the distance.

Your Brilliance put on his mirrored sunglasses and pretended to conduct. 'Moreover, Betsy, I believe that your turn signal's broken.'

'Bunch of ne'er-do-wells. Lighting off that smoke shit.'

'I saw you turn yesterday, and your signal didn't work. Don't the *rules* of driving say that you're supposed to signal?'

Cheers With Farts released the balloon. It squiggled around them, then landed near the struggling bird.

A red sports car sped by. Betsy yelled, 'Slow down, for Christ's sake. Nutcase.'

Loot sang softly. 'You warn against pride and chastise avarice.' His voice dropped to a quiet rumble. 'But then you get into your Gavels and your Lexuses?'

Betsy slurped at the plum. 'What about your sound pollution? Ya drive by and I hear that music and I say, 'Gosh, that's dark. That's like satanic or something."

'Alas, jester punk isn't dark, or satanic. It's playful. And its practitioners wear bright, lively colors.' Your Brilliance pointed at Betsy's vest. 'Now I'm thinking, 'Gosh, are you a jester punk fan?"

The cello screeched, and Cheers With Farts pinched a partially inflated balloon. 'Poosh. I can't keep up with this fuff.'

Ball Boy paused on the street, looked back at the field, and then lumbered out of sight.

Your Brilliance pleaded with his wife that night. 'You go. I'll stay and look for Sorce. Please.' 'No, you're coming, Matt.' 'He could get hurt.' 'Serve him right for running out.'

Betsy used the back of his hand to wipe his mouth. 'What kind of guy does this? Tearing up the environment like that. That smoke shit.'

'Yes, I am at *flault*, I am at *flault* for celebrating the early career of the future best cellist in the world. By the way, may I borrow a cigarette?'

Cheers With Farts released a second balloon, and Loot sprayed. 'Inspired.'

'*Flault*. What's with this *flault*? It's *fault*.'

'Not according to your most recent association newsletter.' Your Brilliance puffed his bubble pipe. 'In your diatribe against pit bulls, you said that owning pit bulls is *inconsiderent* to neighbors. You also said that whoever's at *flault* for not picking up their dog droppings — 'pit bull-sized droppings,' you said — will be fined if caught.'

'I'll tell you what's dangerous. That dog of yours is dangerous.' Betsy took a bite and leaned forward to avoid dripping on his vest.

'You nutcases know, kids have been attacked. Attacked. By them pit bulls. Kids have been killed.'

'Alert the universe: I think little league baseball should be banned.'

'Poosh, poosh.'

'That is absolutely ridiculous.'

'A boy got nailed with a line drive, right over there in Veerville. He died. And nobody's ever been killed by a pit bull around here. So if they ban pit bulls, they should ban baseball, right Betsy?'

'My name's not Betsy.'

'Oh, I assumed it was, because not long ago, you told me not to walk my dog down your street.' Your Brilliance tapped his glasses and whispered to his subjects. 'It's Elizabeth Street.'

Cheers With Farts released another balloon. 'Your Brilliance, Your Brilliance, fuffing Your Brillance.'

Ball Boy, his Redbirds jersey puffing from his pocket, reappeared on the street. He did not have his music stand.

On the night that Sorce got out, Your Brilliance decided to leave with his wife without first looking for his dog.

Betsy spit out his plum pit, then walked away.

The cellist played a cadenza stumblingly, and Cheers With Farts, watching two birds, grabbed a handful of rocks.

Your Brilliance distracted him. 'I assume college resumes quite soon?'

'You envious, old man?'

'Older equals wiser.'

Ball Boy — he had a shoebox — touched his ball to his stubble and trudged toward the felled bird.

Your Brilliance thought about Sorce throughout the opera. When he got home, he went out looking.

Cheers With Farts pinched an inflated balloon in one hand, and shook the rocks in the other.

The cadenza, slightly less awkward, played again. Your Brilliance sat cross-legged in the grass, and yelled. 'Betsy, I've heard that the number one cause of death nationwide is heart disease. Therefore, if we ban pit bulls, shouldn't we also ban hearts?'

The balloon zipped and blubbered, then landed at the feet of an approaching man. He wore mirrored sunglasses.

Loot spit out his hair. 'Gavel Guy approacheth. Prithee, Fuff this knave.'

Cheers With Farts squinted at a tree. 'Chugga-chugga Gavel Guy.'

Your Brilliance hopped up, limped to his box, and then took out the checkered flag and the race car.

Ball Boy gathered the bird into the shoebox, and then, holding the box and cradling his ball beneath his arm, walked gawkily back to the street.

The cellist's third attempt improved.

Your Brilliance found Sorce lying beside the road, then carried his dog, wheezing and whimpering, back toward the house, but halfway back, Sorce stopped wheezing and whimpering.

Your Brilliance took off the sunglasses.

He admired the way that the birds, their peculiar bodies gleaming, bowed then rose above him. They belonged up there.

He dropped the items back into his box.

OUT OF THE BOX

Douglas Thompson

It took me 35 years to find him. The kid I saw jump from one of the boxes at Glasgow's Apollo in 1979, a daredevil feat that briefly landed him in the limelight with the band he loved. It had taken me 25 of those years just to find out his name. These days Jimmy Jessop lived off the grid, which certainly accounted for some of the tracing difficulties. I'd had to ask around in local pubs before I found a rough location for him. He didn't just not pay the Poll Tax, or its contemporary incarnation the charmingly named Community Tax, he didn't pay any tax. Fair's fair if you don't vote I suppose. Except technically you can never enter a NHS hospital or use a refuse bin or walk across a municipal park either. When I finally met him however, I would find I doubted if he ever did any of those things.

His address officially did not exist, not as a residential flat anyway. It was the upper storey of a former glaziers' showroom, long boarded up, which he had acquired in cash through some relative whose name went on the deeds rather than his. The number, '66b' was pretty much his own (logical) invention, and scrawled on his solid steel door in chalk. I'd sent word ahead through a contact of his in the pub that I would be calling. Otherwise, legend had it, he would just play dead inside for hours in case you were *The Social* or some other form of dangerous snooper. I wondered what the guy had to hide, or if he was just a common-or-garden whacko.

As I stood on the doorstep and drummed my toes, I found some old punk anthem had wormed its way into my head as I gazed back across the dreary afternoon traffic towards a distant horizon of green hills. Stiff Little Fingers: *They wanna waste my life... and they've stolen it away.* I took a few steps back and gazed at the façade above me. A waste of time of course, no windows to the street, no peepholes, the perfect hideaway for a crazy bird man. I hoped this wouldn't be a waste of time, actually. I had walked right across town from the office, rather than risk trying to park my shiny materialistic sports car among the draconian traffic restrictions of student bedsit land in this district. Returning my eyes to the steel door, I found the tune in my head had transmuted, like some kind of spooky automatic update into something closer to recent: Save me from the nothing I've become, by Evanescence. Suddenly, I nearly jumped. Keys were turning at last on the other side of the door.

*

A LEAP IN THE DARK: OUR EDITOR'S REFLECTIONS ON A PUNK YOUTH

Once upon a time my own editor set me a research challenge as a rookie reporter, after I was foolish enough to tell her my fondest punk concert anecdote. Now that I've finally completed my mission she is retired and I find myself in her shoes, exactly the kind of establishment figure, perhaps, that I considered myself an enemy of, back in the days of punk.

He must have leapt a distance of 15 to 20 feet in order to clutch the enormous fire curtain and continue his sliding trajectory, so as to land like a latter-day Errol Flynn almost in the centre of the stage. The crowd, already in joyous uproar at the live rendition of Nice n' Sleazy, went ballistic. Hugh Cornwell and JJ Burnel to their credit, seeing that neither themselves nor the teenager had been harmed, played on good-naturedly. But the infamous Apollo bouncers took another view and descended upon their prey like hyenas, ejecting him into the alleyway through the backstage fire exit in less than a minute.

What happened next summarises my enduring memory of punk rock, and forms a defining metaphor for me of what the movement was about. JJ Burnel, in many ways the unelected leader of the band, stopped playing, closely followed by Hugh and the others. JJ nodded to Hugh and, seemingly telepathically, their course of action was agreed. Hugh announced into the shocked silence of their discontinued set in that laconic north London accent of his (which to us sounded very John Peel): 'That's it. We're not playing another note until that kid gets let back in...' And it was clear they weren't joking.

*

The inside of Jimmy's house could not have been imagined in advance. You simply had to see it. Rather than throw out the leftover bric-a-brac from the space's previous incarnation as a shop store (it had been a drapers and god knows what all else before a glaziers), he had kept and incorporated the weirdest of it. Tailor's dummies held up his clothes, such as they were (hardly an extensive wardrobe), their elegant plastic fingers holding coats and shirts aloft. One with a hollowed-out stomach incorporated what he called his 'sound system', little more than a reconditioned ghetto blaster from a flea market. His television set (I was surprised he had one) was a black-and-white portable circa 1978, balanced on top of the lower half of an elegant pair of plastic female legs with painted toenails: as if the whole thing might strut off any minute if the news turned boring. A wall of exposed white glazed brick had been spray-painted with elaborate graffiti during some previous period of dereliction and vandalism. On the other walls he had hung old beat-up oil paintings in elaborate gold frames. Edwardian chests of drawers and armoires lay round about, all charred and smashed to varying degrees. It occurred to me for the first time that perhaps punk had been Britain's answer to Europe's Dada and Surrealism, just 50 years late, and made myself a note to research the concept.

Jimmy's shower was a hole in the roof which he let rainwater fall through now and again by removing festoons of polythene from above it, into an ancient (and cracked) claw-foot bathtub rescued from a skip. For heat and power he had an industrial gas burner and a mobile generator, both obviously pilfered from building sites. Naked bulbs swung from wires on the ceiling, but now and again one would find a charming or quirky detail: a pair of antlers on the wall, a Victorian hobby-horse in the corner with a batman costume hanging over it, or a trio of wooden ducks flying across the wall. In pride of place over a stolen marble fire surround hung a framed portrait of Margaret Thatcher, with a Hitler moustache drawn on and various pieces of newspaper text papered across her features, *God Save The Queen* style.

The man himself I think I had half-imagined to be wearing punk garb, a ridiculous notion of course. He favoured black jeans these days it seemed, trousers, shirt and jacket, black Doc Martens (a touch of continuation there at least!) and his hair was in long rat-like grey dreadlocks swept back, as his hair receded from the front. Maybe I expected him to smell of tobacco, cheap spirits or worse, but he gave off nothing, neutral like his hidden life, a shadow-man. He laughed nervously but infectiously, like a man who indeed hadn't got out much, an astronaut exiled to his own orbit. But when his darting blue eyes finally met your gaze they pinned you with a certain penetrating insight, as unsettling as it was unexpected.

*

The Stranglers had come late to punk, being classed almost against their will as part of a movement most of whose exponents were a little younger than themselves, but like all true artists their heads were thoroughly well-tuned into the zeitgeist of those heady days. Disregard of the young by the old was a declaration of war within the context of punk, and the bulk of the Stranglers fans were young alright, a fact doubtless not lost on the band nor indeed their record company. Police and arrests had followed a recent Stranglers gig in London at which strippers had been deployed on stage. They were not strangers to controversy, but the opposite: eager embracers of it. Silence reigned on stage.

The Apollo would be closed in 1985 and demolished in 1987 after a fire. A blessing in a way. I can still clearly remember the way the entire building shook like a ship when the crowds began stamping the floor in unison. It was a death-trap by anyone's standards. The rats probably wore safety vests. The clever Victorian engineers had certainly designed for many eventualities, but I seriously doubt if the point-loads caused by pogo-ing Doc Martens had been among their considerations.

That night, the foot-stopping and slow-clapping took hold to deafening proportions, and the atmosphere quickly became oppressive. The bouncers were big hard guys, but they were outnumbered by a ratio well-beyond their likely command of arithmetic. They looked worried. They backed away against the fire exits, just in case they might need them themselves soon. Remarkably quickly, as if they had been expecting something of this nature (they quite possibly had if they read the music press), police appeared at the rear of the theatre, blocking every aisle. In brilliant and uncanny unison, the entire crowd began to whistle the theme from 'Dixon of Dock Green'. This was very Glasgow: a city where withering and all-levelling ridicule is traditionally the base ingredient of most humour, and proven through long experience to be always mightier than the flick-knife. Sure enough, in no time at all, the backstage fire door was opened, the dishevelled kid located and returned unharmed to the theatre. It was our own little terrorist hostage situation. The insurgents had triumphed.

*

I sat back and relaxed as best I could, in one of Jimmy's flea-eaten sofas, I recognised it vaguely as something by Le Corbusier, probably tipped by (or nicked from) an architect's office over the road in Park Circus. I asked him to tell me about his life, not from the start necessarily, but from that night, the night of the long leap in the dark, out of the box and onto centre stage, to the present day. He lit a cigarette and poured me a whisky in a plastic cup, made himself a double.

'You liked it then?' he smiled wryly, baring an intermittent set of teeth that reminded me of partially demolished tenements, 'Ma wee acrobatic feat?'

'God, yeah…' I encouraged him, 'It looked dangerous. You could have broken your neck, surely? What the hell made you do it?'

'Och, ah wiz oot ma box, man. Been drinking for oors beforehand, and snorting speed. I thought ah wiz superman, invincible, ya ken? Every cunt diz when they're that age. Did you no?'

'Yeah...' I nodded, 'I suppose, when I was pished, certainly.'

'Ma mates an' me hud done a loat o' tree climbin' in all when we were younger... I remember that. Daft games we used to play, swingin' aboot in trees, playin' at Tarzan in the woods up behind oor hooses. Did you no?'

I shook my ahead. 'Not flying through space for 20 feet horizontally, 25 feet vertically. You could have gone into the circus, mate. What did you do?'

'Efter ah left school, like?' Jimmy looked shy now suddenly. 'Dinnae laugh like, but ah pal o' ma dah's goat me a joab in an accountants furm.'

I laughed.

*

It wasn't about spitting on old ladies. We were bored with that by the time Punk came around. Just joking. You might find it hard to believe now, but back in seventy six I had the torn and spray-painted jeans and T-shirts, the safety pins, the spiked hair. Well, when I went to concerts anyway, not when I went to school. I was still in secondary. But my brother and his mates bought all the albums, The Sex Pistols, Crass, The Ruts, The Vibrators, The Clash, The Stranglers. The Stranglers were actually seriously skilled musicians by today's dismal standards. The Clash weren't of course… every song on their first album consists of about three chords if I remember correctly, but they must have learned to play as they went along because by their third album (London Calling) they were actually technically talented, not just spirited. That was very much the attraction of punk you see, anyone could have a go, it wasn't about skill and patience, it was about energy and anger. Anger above all. Back to the spitting on old ladies thing: a misconception.

The anger was directed at Thatcher's government, the way it looked from where I grew up anyway. But not just at her and her loathsome cabinet who so closely resembled Hitler's inner circle (Tebbit as Goebbels, the unelected Lord Young as Göring), it was directed also at an entire older generation who seemed to have taken leave of their senses and voted that fascist woman into power. In that sense, Punk was a war between the young and the old, with a real urgency to it that I don't think we've seen before or since. I know there'd been all that hippie stuff in the sixties and seventies, where a youth movement became disenchanted with their parents, but that was milder. Vietnam notwithstanding, flower power had been about your parents being square, about there still being a chance you could convert them if you dropped a pill or two in their coffee. Punk, if it was any kind of a successor to that (though its proponents didn't think in such terms), represented a kind of point of no return. Maybe the constant threat of nuclear annihilation at the hands of the Soviets had played a part in this, wearing us down as we grew up with a television diet of apocalypse and societal breakdown, but our mindset was not that our parents were to be negotiated with; they were to be overthrown. I suppose many of us were attracted to the idea of that overthrow as nothing more than an orgy of mindless violence (when you're a fourteen-year old male those hold a great appeal), but as the product of a highly political household I also dimly grasped it as a means with which to re-make the world order and re-build our society along different lines.

*

It seemed that Jimmy, to everyone's surprise (not least himself), had turned out to be a pretty good accountant. Passed his exams, risen through the ranks all through the eighties. So the punk boy that had swung through the air that night like a monkey in his hour of glory, had 'sold out' like everyone else, The Pistols, The Damned, and ended up wearing a suit and carrying a briefcase, cosying up to rich clients, hoping that some of it might rub off on himself. Got tired of waiting, doing all his bosses work for them, letting them take the credit. So he'd seen his chance and started his own business, took some of the client's with him. Yeah, his accent and his style had seemed a bit rough and ready for some tastes, but some of the clientele had liked that... a particular kind of clientele. The nightclub owners, the 'respectable' gangsters turned property developers. Self-made men like him. Glasgow excels at producing those kind of businessmen. In Edinburgh you might need a good school and a posh voice, but in Glasgow sheer balls can go pretty far. Then a recession had hit. Jimmy seemed to be starting to get tipsy by this part of his story. My sense of time and what particular recession he was referring to was hazy. And his wife left him. Now he began to really unburden himself:

'Ahh wiz daft like. It wis ma ain fault. Ah hud a wee daughter, eight year auld, and a wife an a loast the pair o' them. Ma oan fuckin' fault so it wiz. There wiz this crackin' wee burd working fur me, gein' me the eye every day. Ah wisnae a bad lookin' bloke back in those days, ye know, but she was ten years ma junior. Ah right wee shag. Beautiful girl, lang blonde hair, figure like...' Jimmy put his bottle down and stood up in order to perform an elaborate mime performance worthy of Marcel Marceau, a flurry of arms and hands outlining sumptuous curves in empty space. Getting into the swing of it, he went over and swept one of his tailor's dummies off her feet and wheeled her around the room while singing some kind of execrable disco number from the late eighties. It wasn't punk at any rate.

He flumped down into his armchair at last, expelling a cloud of dust and fleas from the torn lining at the back of it. 'So ya get the picture. You married? You never been tempted yoursel'? JJ Burnel, wasn't he supposed tae huv slept wi' a different burd every night fur a year? Ahh wiz bored as hell wi' the wife by then. No spark left in the thing at all. Just her nippin' ma heid every night, telling me do this and do that aboot the hoose, like I was her wean or somethin'. Reminded me too much o' ma auld dear and the auld man, the way they used to treat me like shite. What ah rebelled against, as a punk. What ah...' He lifted his arms up before him in space and I nodded, getting the metaphor. What he had leapt through space for, trying to escape, to think outside the box.

'We goat caught in the end, and ah hud tae leave the wife. She turned ma ain daughter against me. My wee girl. She never forgave her daddy. Never seen her in a' these years. Disnae read ma letters, disnae take ma calls. The bitch o' a wife I could live without, but ma wee girl... that hurts like.'

Unexpected silence reigned suddenly, and Jimmy stared into space over my shoulder, his eyes glazed. I remembered a Stranglers lyric suddenly: *Broken down TV sits in the corner, picture's standing still, standing still.* 'What about the girl you had the affair with? Did you not team up with her?' I asked quietly.

Jimmy's eyes slowly came back into focus, until he looked at me perplexed, as if I had only just arrived there. 'Aye.' He nodded his head then tilted it to one side as if weighing his life in the scales, adding up sums, making his accounts balance. 'For a wee while, until ma money ran oot and the business folded, then nae cunt wanted anythin' to do with me. Come tae think o' it your aboot the first fucker tae gie a shite in fifteen year.'

*

Anger can be a very positive force you see. Pogo-ing up and down at a Stranglers concert (the dance had the great advantage over all others that anybody could do it well), what you felt in the thick of it was not threat but a great sense of belonging, of warmth, of being amongst people who shared your passion and anger and were directing it towards exactly the same targets. Punk gave me my first sense of belonging as a teenager, an emotion one feels strangely short of at that age. It also gave my first sense that social change was possible. It was Martin Luther King who said that a riot was the language of the unheard, and in 1977 we were the unheard and punk was our riot.

It's hard to believe now, but in a sense punk did win. Thatcher's Poll Tax was finally defeated, three miserable political terms later, and the woman herself duly dispatched. But by that time, most of the punks were wearing suits and getting married or taking the kids to school, and contemplating nothing more rebellious and dangerous than voting Labour. Steel plants and mines and all kinds of heavy industry were gone forever by then. Thatcher had reshaped us all like little wax voodoo dolls, with or without our permission, made us the stewards of a post-industrial husk of a nation, slippery entrepreneurs and managers where before we might have been craftsmen and grafters. Using the hot air in our lungs rather than our sweat and muscle. Flimsy somehow, no longer solid. It was a pity that Thatcher seemed to escape blame for the bank crash of 2008. It was her denouement really, just a long time in the coming. The moment at which we realised that the entire edifice of our nation's supposed financial strength was built on nothing any stronger than a mirage, a cheap salesman's empty rhetoric. Nations ought to produce things you see. Make things, real physical things and export them. It's called manufacturing, and it makes useful products out of your natural resources, and that's what any nation's wealth should ultimately rest on. It's as if Britain got the idea from somewhere, back in the eighties, that it could just be the world's manager, a useless git in a suit that lived off everybody else's efforts while it sailed around pontificating, not really doing any work itself. That's called the financial and services industries. And at the end of the day, bullshitters like that always get caught out. You can probably tell by now that the anger of punk has never left me. I hope it never will.

*

The lyric in my head had was still running: *Duch of the Terrace never grew up, I hope she never will.* So now this was Jimmy's idea of adventure, and having a good time these days. He had lured me out through one of his many velux windows, taken me up several rusting fire escape stairs, and now the two of us sat side by side, perched precariously, legs dangling over the A-Listed ornate stone façade of Charing Cross mansions. His training shoes were kicking a carved angel in the face. He passed me a joint, and after a few puffs of that I found myself sharing his bottle of Italian brandy, swigging it straight from the neck, an incongruous choice of tipple in its ornate circular bottle. The stars were out overhead, the traffic whizzing by, four storeys below in streaks of red and yellow, the first Friday night party-goers parading the streets with their territorial catcalls and overcooked laughter. But soon I was laughing myself, at Jimmy's infectiously anarchic view of the universe. I liked the guy. He was honest. He'd learned the value of that the hard way.

'It's all shite, man...' He marvelled, bottle in hand, eyes wide, shaking his head but grinning like a deranged demon. 'Men and women, rich and poor, the whole big fuckin' pantomime. You'd think it mattered. Whazzit say in the old testament? My ma' used to quote it... *vanity, all is vanity.* We take credit fur oorsels and oor so-called achievements but we're ah jist chess pieces, tossed aboot by the gods...'

'Hubris...' I said.

'Whit?' His eyes narrowed, as he drew on his joint.

'A good Greek word for it. Pride before a fall.'

'Sounds like sandwich spread. But yeah...' he laughed, 'Those fucking Greeks eh? Every way you jump they goat there first.'

'Jimmy...' I said, relaxing, leaning back on the slate roof, putting my hands behind my head and trying to find the North Star. 'Do you ever think your life was a mistake? That you made an error back there somewhere? And that if you'd chosen differently then everything would have turned out better?' I was talking about myself of course, my lost dreams of being a real writer rather a hack, the moral squalor I sometimes found my office at the centre of, but maybe I should have chosen my words more carefully.

I listened to the long sighs of the traffic, the gentle babbling of the city as I waited for his reply. I thought maybe he was taking a particularly long drag on his joint before he answered. But when I opened my eyes a few moments later, he was gone. I sat up rigid, shook my head, pinched myself, tried to sober up. I'd have heard him go past me if he'd climbed back in through the skylight. Sick suddenly, and shit scared, I edged towards the parapet and looked over. Nothing, no disturbance below. I looked up and along the roof from side to side, top to bottom. Empty. Silent.

As if Jimmy Jessop had remembered how to fly.

THE GOD FEARING CRACK DEALERS' SONGBOOK

Jude Orlando Enjolras

1. Angels & Anarchists

Stumble into the Morningstar, down four flights of stairs sticky with what you can only hope is sweat and alcohol. Exchange your coat for a token; raise an eyebrow at the cloakroom boy, his neck a hickey-fest of teeth marks, this healing, that one scratched open, yet another still fresh. Watch him smile brightly as he chirps, 'Snacks are extra. I can get you a loyalty card if you like?'

Tempting as the offer is, hit the bar, where the pretty young sparks coil around each other, the edges of their bodies melting into the black light. Rightly oblivious to the sorrow swimming - not drowning - in your glass, they saturate the air with smoke and the smell of promised sex.

Emboldened by gin, you find yourself hollering song suggestions. The DJ ignores you, hands hovering over his vinyl stash, blending hoarse screamer with smooth ballad, power anthem with demo EP gem. Watch him work his magic until school night curfew hits, and the slivers of wildlife vanish with a swearword and a sigh. An inchoate mob of older kids replaces them; a thousand safety pins pierce the silence.

Just in time, the DJ emerges from the ladies', wiping a speck of blood off his lips. A crimson violin flies into his extended hand. The crowd - vocal, restless - splits to let him pass. He climbs onstage, flicks on the lights, and reveals the night's entertainment: Dylan on keys and synth, mohawk soft, skin like an illuminated manuscript;

pinstriped Joe on rhythm guitar (shoes: two-toned, immaculate); Johnny Q. on bass and wearing little but a guitar strap of dead animals dyed pink; Frank, drummer boy you wouldn't want to meet in a dark alley; and, under a foot of rainbow liberty spikes, Cam on lead guitar.

'We are The God Fearing Crack Dealers,' the singer screams. He is just a scrawny kid, baby-faced, black nails flying over a black guitar. Yet his eyes aren't his. 'I am Lazlo Farkash, and I hope for your sake you're all having a good night - I know where you live.' A-ha, yes. Eyes on timeshare; a lovechild between an Angel, a time machine, and a bottle of whiskey.

*

On the other side of town, Anghel Farkash stood at his office window, Lazlo's eyes staring out of his skull into the darkness. Around him, the Misfits Motel slumbered, haven to the slightly weird, and home sweet home. Angie squinted as the shadows coalesced into a large lumbering figure, shuffling up his driveway. It was a strange apparition, even by the rather relaxed standards of someone who took in the dispossessed for a living.

'What the hell is *that*?'

That, it turned out when Angie opened the door, was a skeleton, bony wings and sword trailing on the steps behind.

Angie found the sword a place among the fireplace pokers, and his guest a comfy chair. It looked like a long story. *Might as well start at the beginning.* 'What's your name?'

The skeleton raised their head, displaying teeth that could not choose but to smile. 'I don't have a name. My maker didn't see it fit to give me one.'

'Your maker?' Angie asked.

'Yes, and yours; He's everybody's maker.'

O-kay. A longer story than I thought.

'He made me to be His soldier - the one true God. There used to be others, many worlds ago, but my kind killed them all, war after holy war. There are no more enemies now; just light as far as the eye can see, light and gold and marble, forever, for no good reason. It very nearly drove me mad...'

Angie had closed his eyes, to better keep his mind open. He'd had faith once, in the vague way that children do; then Lazlo had flown away from him - in the literal way that bloodsuckers do. By the time the twins met again, Angie had grown the fuck up, and stopped praying. *It's all nonsense,* present Angie told himself sternly. *Except, there's an angel in my house, all bones and fucking bleeding on my carpet.*

'... until one night, as I guarded His sleep, I overheard my God remember His only son, who at the dawn of the last creation, vanished without a trace - escaped to dwell with mortals. Traitor, my God called him; but to my mind, he became a symbol of salvation...'

*

Joe, mod demigod, always smiled to see the Theatre d'Anarchists, its big bold murals melting doors into walls. Sickest anarchoparty that ever was seen, run on rye and the Dewey Decimal System. Dylan had found the place years ago, tucked down the unfashionable end of town, just another playhouse forgotten by the arts council. What had started as a squat soon acquired a sheer veneer of legality, and a reputation for rabble-rousing on a shoestring.

In a world where so much as a lip-ring could get you lip, the Theatre was a sanctuary to pirates and outlaws of the brave new world; dregs to society which, just like dregs, threw shapes on the shape of things to come. Artists, visionaries, prophets, satirical pens and boys with ukes. Alcohol and conversation ran in intertwined streams, minds and bodies communing in various states of heightened perception and undress, everyone equal under the blanket statement of neon throws and damask rugs.

The Theatre could have been a temple in Joe's image, except it was much more than that. A spring in his step and *The Back Of Beyond* blaring in his ears, Joe pushed open the stage door, expertly navigated a tangle of wires and legs, and skipped down through the trapdoor steps, all the way to the hollowed out hell Dylan and Cam called home. *A hell for a home. Funny.* A bunch of godless second wave nihilists, his most successful creation. That was quite funny, too.

The flat was already full with the catcall of guitars tuning. 'Morning lads,' Joe said, 'and hello sunshine.' Frank was too busy getting the beers in to take any notice.

'Anyone seen Cam? The lazy sod's late. Again,' Dylan asked, rolling his eyes at the teeth marks on his bottle cap. *Lovely.*

*

By a staggering coincidence, *Lovely* was also Cam's thought of the moment. Jem Q. always had a way of brightening up his sheets. Then, without warning, she wriggled out of his arms. 'Aw. Where're you going?'

'I was never here, remember? Johnny would kill me.' She thought about this. 'Nah, I've changed my mind. He's far likelier to kill you.'

Cam looked genuinely horrified by the very idea. 'Why would he want to kill me?'

Jem shook her head. *Bless.* Just as well she didn't love him for his brains. 'Don't you see?' she said, coaxing dreads back into their respective ponytails.

Cam didn't see. God only knew where his contacts had got to. With myopic ardour, he ran his hand along Jem's leopard-print body.

'Oi. That's how we got into this mess.'

'Mess, what mess?'

'What else do you call this?' she said, pulling his hand out of her jeans and onto her belly. 'Lucky for you, there is no one I'd rather be in this mess with. Johnny will deal.'

The penny dropped. Cam grinned up at the love of his life. Jem grinned back, kissed him goodbye and was gone, a technicolor caterpillar inching towards the trapdoor. Cam sighed happily, and went on a hunt for his trousers. *Lucky me indeed.*

*

'Ah, here we go. One lazy sod, coming right up.'

'Hello to you too, Laz,' Cam said.

'I wouldn't 'Hello Laz' him quite yet, son,' Dylan said.

Lazlo smiled a broad, fanged smile. 'I haven't had breakfast yet.'

'You really shouldn't be allowed in civilised company unless you've eaten,' Frank said. 'A bloody menace, you are.'

'Flatterer. But just so we're clear, it's my bloody menacing the girls come to see.'

'Keep 'em.'

'Thank you. I will.'

'Er,' Cam said, pointing at Johnny. 'What's the deal with him?'

'Away with the fairies,' Dylan said.

'Seriously,' Lazlo said, 'some people are just so unprofessional.'

'Ah, leave the man alone.' Joe scratched Johnny's chin and he purred, flailed a bit, then went back to tripping balls in his sleep. 'He'll wipe the floor with us all the day the rock'n'roll revolution comes.'

'Yes, yes,' Cam said, 'now what do you say those of us in our right minds get down to work? We haven't got all day.'

2. The Original Songwriter

Among the Theatre regulars, there was one Nicholas Chasteington. Art schooled, every bit as posh as his name suggested, Nicky was used to being branded a poser, but Dylan would have none of it. A firm believer in equal opportunity social distortion, he offered the man a sleeping bag on the Anarchist boards - after all, Nicky was as much of an embarrassment to his parents as the rest of them.

By day, Nicky set up his easel by the riverside. It was the oldest pick-up trick in the world, and little did it matter that he had little talent to speak of; he was reasonably good-looking, and just decadent enough to be completely unsuitable. Therefore, he was perfect. *This is living,* he thought, as a group of girls walked by, whispering so loudly you could hear them from the other side of the Streamline. It was then he saw the kid, cross-legged on the pavement, drawing. He leaned over to take a look.

The kid's pencil surfed on the paper, conjuring a badly trimmed beard, capturing the tremulous gait of an old man making his way up the bridge. In the picture, the bridge was a rainbow, stretched out across a river of molten gold. From that gold merfolk carved a kingdom, and swam about their lives in such dizzying detail Nicky could have sworn he'd seen them move. 'Wow,' he said eventually. 'You're good.'

'Thanks. I try,' the kid answered, staining the glass on the merfolk's windows with visions of dry land.

'I'm Nicky.'

'Ezekiel.' Daisies now dotted the miniature pastoral idylls. The mind boggled. This drawing seemed to have infinite depth, and counting.

'That's a bit of a mouthful for someone your size,' Nicky said.

'Friends call me Zeke.'

Nicky clocked the ragged pyjamas. 'What about your parents?'

Zeke started drawing faster. 'I don't have any. My mother worried sick about me. Then she died.' Faster. 'My father didn't like me much after that.'

'My god. I'm so - '

'Sorry? Don't be. Father didn't hold much truck with all this... creative nonsense, he called it. And this nonsense makes me happy.'

'Good for you,' Nicky said. 'Still, everyone needs a family. Coincidence is, I know just the one. Now, let's hit the dangerous streets of my mother's nightmares, shall we?'

So it was that the Anarchists acquired their first official mascot. Of all the artists and visionaries to pass through and pass out in their Theatre, no one was quite as artistic, nor half as visionary as little Zeke Vanderplow. His pencil moved so fast, it could scarcely have been said to move at all - you just assumed that it moved because, if you stared long enough, the paper would fill with a game of light and shadow like a chess match for the soul of mankind. *And this is black and white,* Nicky thought. *Is there anything he couldn't do, given colours?*

So it was that with a newly fattened wallet, Nicky strolled into an art shop that had his face on the walls, above the word: WANTED. *Don't I look dashing.* Best present ever under his arm, he sauntered into the next bakery - it would have looked dodgy, returning from a shopping trip minus the shopping. Back at the Theatre, he found Zeke in front row, sketching scenes from plays yet to be written. 'Lunch,' he announced. 'What kind of sandwich do you want? Bacon, bacon, or bacon?'

Zeke held out his free hand. 'Bacon.'

*

The night after his fourteenth and best birthday ever, Zeke dreamed of nothing. Soft, soothing nothing that embraced and carried him, until a bit of void shifted from where the horizon should have been, to reveal a huge canvas. The nothing set Zeke down and lingered, to see what he would do. What Zeke did was take up a brush and paint around the canvas, giving it a context in three-dimensional space, and himself a universe. Colours flowed, dimensions sprung forth; lines came to life, and Zeke with them.

From then on, he dreamed in colour. The colours of his universe called and he answered, running barefoot through the oozing oils, fingertips following the brush strokes like roads to be departed from. He befriended a pheasant once, the main course on a sumptuous spread; like a stage magician, Zeke whipped off the tablecloth, swished it around to reveal a bird newborn, alive and well and waving *thank you* with its wing.

One early morning, Lazlo saw Zeke struggle against bedtime, drawing sleepy circles in a quiet corner of the main Theatre stage.

He was holding no pencil or oil stick, just an index swirling, dipping into the wood like butter, going against the natural grain.

'Hey, kiddo.'

''ello.'

'What are you doing?'

'You know. I heard the wood's voice in my head, telling me stories of its home, of being uprooted from friends and family - like, literally - and I wanted to help. So I told it I could re-write the stories if it wanted. Not put it back in the wood of course, a bit late for that, but let it say goodbye at least. Put affairs in order. That kind of thing.'

A re-write, Lazlo thought, as the kid re-assembled reality under his feet. *Now, who do I know who could do with one of those?* He thought of the angel then, all bones and fucking bleeding on Angie's carpet. *God I'm clever.*

*

To the angel, the Theatre d'Anarchists was a glorious kind of nonsense. The colour scheme was pretty repetitive where they came from, and as for freedom... last time they'd dared dream of freedom, the one true God had broken their wings and skinned them alive, just in case any of their siblings got any fancy ideas. So yeah, freedom. Not really a thing, way up in heaven.

Here, no two mortals looked alike. The angel's eyes were everywhere, wide, understanding little, dying to understand everything. Music surrounded them, nothing at all like the swan song of dead spheres; rather, a raucous hymn to the pain and ecstasy of being alive.

Awed, they almost sleepwalked in Lazlo's wake, through a stage and into a living room, stripped to make space for a minimalist pop-up studio, contents: an eager-beaver wunderkind, and exactly one fold-out chair. In the far corner, the sorta-grown-ups sat on a sofa. They'd been told to stay there, and not one of them was about to argue with the young master painter.

Zeke sat the angel down and got to work, paintbrush darting over nerve and sinew, wrapping bones in stripes of muscle like marble. This distressed the angel, to whom marble meant the wrong kind of heaven. Nightmares flashed through their skull - Zeke could see them shimmer, right there in the infinite void between eye and socket.

'What's wrong?'

'This new skin, so white - it burns.'

'Sorry,' Zeke said. 'Not to worry, though; this is just a base coat. When that's dry, I can make you any colour, hell, any *colours* you like. I'm that good.'

The angel glanced around the room, on the hunt for inspiration. Before that, they found something - someone else. 'Who's that?'

'Hey Joe,' Zeke shouted towards the sofa, which now housed a heated debate regarding the Oppressive Structures of Feminism's third album, *Non-Trad Rad Femmes*: inspired post-punk deconstruction of a politicised aesthetic, or over-produced major label drivel? 'Come over here a sec, will you?'

Joe came over there. Under the trilby, nevermind the suit, the angel saw him for what he was: the son of the one true God. Instinctively, they knelt; the brush of their wing sent Zeke flying, oils and all. 'My...' the hyperbole melted in the reverent angel's mouth.

... what? Joe thought, *liege? No, thanks. I don't do leadership. I haven't done in a long time.*

And that is precisely why I'll follow you to the end of all possible worlds.

I know.

'Do you mind?' Zeke said, removing Joe's hand from the angel's skull, piloting his model back in their chair, 'I've got a project to finish.'

Joe laughed. 'Did you really just call an angel a project?'

Zeke waved at him impatiently. 'Details, details. Now could you just move over,' the kid thought for a second, 'there. Visually pleasing as you are, you are not transparent.'

'No such thing,' came a voice from the Oppressive Structures side of the room.

'Hm?' Joe said.

'There's no such thing as angels,' Frank said. 'Now get your arse back down here, I need your memory for lyrics. How's that line from *Tarts in Tartan* go again?'

Joe got his arse back down there, his mind stuck like a record. 'What do you mean, no such thing as angels? What do you think they are?'

Frank shrugged. 'Don't know, don't really care. No offence,' he called towards an angel too high on existential exhilaration to take any. 'But, c'mon. You might as well tell me you believe in fairies.'

'Oh, I believe in fairies.' Joe said, grinning, waiting for Frankie to do the math. He ducked. 'Now, now, we've been through this - violence doesn't solve anything.' The grin vanished as Joe had second, third, fourteenth thoughts about what came next. Was this a good time? Was it ever going to be a good time to have The Talk, the one that went, 'Hey man, I'm a demigod, sorry I didn't tell you before, it just kinda never came up?' *Probably not. Oh well. Here goes.* 'Angels are not a question of faith, Frankie. They're as real as heaven is, and that's pretty damn real. That's where I was born.'

Frank knew Joe's kidding face well enough. This wasn't it.

'You always call this the worst of all possible worlds,' Joe continued. 'Truth is, it's just the latest in a long list of worlds. Creation begets strife begets apocalypse, rinse and repeat. It always begins with us - me and my dad. The one true god, he likes to call himself. I suppose he is, now he's gone and had all the others killed.' Joe shook his head. 'Megalomaniac git. We're not really on speaking terms, you understand; I left him and that life behind, at the dawn of this time. Been down here ever since, on the fringes mostly, but then... then I met you guys.'

Frank stood up, slowly, as if sudden movement might break him. 'I've got to go.'

'Frankie...'

The trapdoor swung shut. In the deafening silence that followed, Zeke said, 'He'll be back. He just needs some space.'

Joe considered the kid, who hadn't, in all this time, taken his eyes off his angelic project. 'You seem pretty chill.'

'Yeah, well,' Zeke said, sandpapering the excess gesso off his walking, flying canvas. 'I'm not the one fucking you, am I? It's hardly a big deal if you lie to me.'

Lazlo poked his head through the trapdoor then, cheerful as someone who this time has had breakfast enough. He raised an eyebrow at where Zeke was preparing to colour the angel by numbers, in shades of violet and green. 'Huh. Interesting colour choices you've got going on there, kid. What's it all mean, anyway?'

'This,' Zeke said, brushing hair out of his eyes, leaving a trail of pine across his forehead, 'is what a rainbow looks like once you've taken away anything that reminds us of fire. Because some memories are where madness lies, and we can't have that.' He said this not to Lazlo but to the angel, with a serious smile that said, *I get that I don't get it.*

Lazlo had stopped listening by now, and was headed straight for the sofa where Joe still sat, stunned. 'Frank's in a right state, you know,' Lazlo told him. 'Whatever you've done, you probably want to go after him some time this decade.'

Joe gave him a look of utter misery.

'Whatever, mate. Not my business,' Lazlo said. Without missing a beat, he continued, 'and yet, you want to know what I think? Of course you do. Life's too short to spend apart from yourself. And I say that as an immortal.' Lazlo thought of Angie as he said this; his brain and better half. Pride and circumstance had kept the twins apart for too many years. He was going to be damned again if he'd let Joe make the same mistake.

Joe, meanwhile, seemed amused. 'You, immortal? Oh, Laz. You goddamn amateur.'

'You really should be careful how you talk, you know. Never know who might be listening.'

Joe blinked. '... you knew?'

'I'm insightful like that,' Lazlo said. 'Frankie... he just needs a little push.' He shrugged. 'Or maybe a kick in the teeth. Who can tell? But I'd try the little push first, if I were you. And ain't no one but you can give him that.'

Joe unglued himself from the sofa; sadly, he ran out of steam shortly after. 'The fuck am I meant to tell him?'

'Haven't the foggiest,' Lazlo said. 'You're the weaver of worlds. The bloody original songwriter. You'll figure it out.'

3. Just Snuffed It

Fast-forward to summer, and a hospital playground full of Dealers - those not allergic to senseless sunshine, at any rate. It was big smiles all around. They could not wait to dress baby Bambi up in tiny tartan tees and darling doc booties. It was going to be epic. Screw letting the poor lad breathe; how big was she, who did she look like, when could they bring her home? They had to know everything, and they had to know it now.

Joe was the first to realise that Cam was just standing there, like some grotesque puppet built in the image of himself. 'Cam, what's wrong? Is Bambi alright? How's Jem?'

'There's no Bambi to be ok,' Cam said, his voice hollow. 'No Jem either - Doc says she died of grief. What'd she do that for, dying of anything? Selfish bitch.'

The word barely left his lips before Johnny punched him in the stomach. As Cam curled towards the paving, Johnny joined him there, first into a wrestle, then a lock, and finally a frantic, desperate hug. Eventually, Johnny got to his feet. In a cheery tone which must have made sense in his head, he offered to take Cam home - home to the good stuff.

'I think Cam's alright as he is.'

'Did I ask you, D? Sod off. You're not family.'

Dylan was used to emotionally barren bastards, but that hurt. 'No need.'

'Know what I don't need? Sermons the day I lose a sister.'

Dylan nodded to Frank and Joe; their hands brushed on Cam's back. By the time Johnny clocked what had happened, the trio had turned the corner, destination: home, sure; but not Johnny's home. 'What are you doing?' he asked Dylan.

'Looking out for Cam.'

'Cute.' A thought occurred to Johnny. 'D?'

'Yeah.'

'Why aren't you looking out for me?'

It was a good question, and not one Dylan had a good answer for. He thought of the last time he'd tried to save Johnny from himself, and realised he couldn't remember.

'You've given up on me.'

'Johnny...'

'Don't you 'Johnny' me. I can look after myself, even if you won't.' He shrugged off Dylan's hand, and slunk away. He could have stormed, he might have marched; Johnny did neither, every muscle in his back screaming to Dylan to run after him.

Dylan didn't dare call after the friend he had little right to call so; he settled for strangled screaming, forgiveness he would have begged if the sound had not moored in his chest, making him sway like a paper ship stapled to a swelling sea.

Nothing? Ah, well. Johnny took a step towards home, to the good stuff. *You lose some, you lose some.*

*

The Q. family home had never been so quiet. Johnny's siblings were, presumably, in kindergarten, school, or prison; his stepdad, teaching suitably wrist-cutting poetry at the university. As for Madame, Johnny's mum, she sat stock-still, surrounded by cups of over-brewed tea. Moving would have meant accepting the touch of the world on her skin. Reality beckoned, and Madame resolved to ignore it. The Dealers stared at unmatched doilies, dust bunnies at play, anywhere but at each other. When Cam spoke, he knocked over some nearby nail polish. Acid green spread on the plastic wipe-clean tablecloth. Madame Q. let it lie. 'Of course you can see him.'

In his room, Johnny sat up in bed, head in the crook of walls that leant upon one another for comfort. Cam sat next to him, and examined the photographs on the wall. *All the close family.* Frank in front of the Palace of Justice, fresh from bounding the steps two at a time, chanting, 'Free of all charges, free of all charges!' Dylan deep in literary conversation with Johnny's stepdad. Joe asleep under his beloved trilby, skinny legs climbing the window of a bus. Jem, striving to be sultry, while her hair did things to itself that should have probably been illegal. To her right, Cam had been cut out by a less than steady hand. Johnny, it turned out, had exceeded all expectation in being difficult about it all. What was he thinking, getting his baby sister pregnant? An uncle's pride had in time overwritten wounded honour, however, and Cam's head had found its way back onto the wall, stuck onto the squat body of a bulldog. *Hilarious,* he thought, shoulders coming to nestle in Johnny's extended arm.

'Cam.'

Cam's eyes stayed soldered shut. 'Hm.'

Frank sighed. 'I said, I'm not standing for this. This is not the way it goes.'

'How's it go, then?'

'We,' Frank said, joining them on the bed, 'are going to have a party. You want a party, don't you Johnny?' Johnny's hands clapped together in excitement. ''course I want a party. I'm more fun than some.' A limp hand swatted Cam's cheek.

Cam's eyes slammed open. 'Ow.'

'Got your attention now. So what d'you think?'

Dylan turned from the window, which overlooked the sewer-end of the river Streamline. The paper ship had set sail, and he felt free. 'I think it's a brilliant idea.'

'It's bloody genius,' Frank beamed.

'What do you have in mind?' Joe asked from a kiddie swivel-chair.

'Your horses, hold them,' Frank winked. 'You'll see. You'll all see. Just give me until,' he checked his watch, 'call it nine? We reconvene here, and no one get ideas. The dead boy stays here until then.'

That said, Frank left the others to fend off the clammy nothingness. *Now what?* The words hung about them, tight as cling-film; no need to speak them out loud. They sure needed other words, but for the minstrels of a lost generation, it was amazing how speechless they became with no strings beneath their fingers. Joe reached for Johnny's bass and started playing. Nothing fancy, just enough of a soundtrack to breathe again. Crack the odd joke, even. When Joe and Dylan next checked, they found Cam asleep on Johnny's shoulder. Elastic still clung to Johnny's other arm.

*

They reacquired Frank at 9 o'clock sharp, to the sound of a car horn blaring from the street. Leaning out of the window, Dylan shook his head in awe. Frank had really outdone himself this time.

Madame hadn't shifted from the mess of tea and polish, by now equally congealed. It was hard to think of what to say to a twice grieving mother while making off with her son's dead body, so none of them said anything. Dylan made a mental note to check in on her, though he couldn't help feeling she must have been relieved to have them out of the house. All of them.

'A cop car,' Cam said. 'Really.'

'Really,' Frank replied, as Johnny and his wingmen clambered inside. 'Bit of an ugly cow, isn't she?' He crushed a beer can and tossed it in the growing pile at his feet. Dylan bit his lip. This was Johnny's party, and they were going to do this the Q. way, driving smashed off your face included. No tomorrow - for today at least. He'd re-evaluate that statement tomorrow. 'Also understands nothing about music,' Frank was saying a block down the road, 'Tried feeding it some Depressive Missionaries on the way, chewed the tape right up. Still. You've gotta admit the girl has style.' They admitted, but Frank wasn't finished. 'So,' he said while turning a corner on what felt suspiciously like a single wheel, 'Who's feeling artistic?'

So it was spray-paint that had been in the way of their legs all this time. Should have known. 'I'm feeling artistic,' Joe volunteered, waiting for a relatively pedestrian-free stretch of street to roll down the window, and climb onto the roof. He wiggled his fingers for supplies, and had to smile at what Dylan passed him. Acid green. Frankie could be a real poet when he wanted to.

Hanging onto the side of the car with one hand, Joe let his eyes wander along the avenue's exuberant expanse of retail opportunities for the discerning gentlefolk. A bridal shop caught his eye. Chubby cherubs gravitated uncertainly above an even split of fluffy, feathery tents, and skirts so short no self-respecting priest would have ever allowed them in their little branch of the great house of God. Not without some encouragement, anyway.

This got Joe thinking. Unholy dresses, dirty bridesmaids, getaway tricked cars trailing streamers and homemade 'JUST MARRIED' signs... bingo. An askew halo and a broken pair of wings were the first to mar the sleek patched surface of the Ugly Cow™. Below them, Joe traced the words 'JUST SNUFFED IT.' After some thought, he added two needles for crossbones. *Johnny, you tit.*

Joe climbed back into the car, and Frank sped on. They zoomed past - and in one case dangerously close to over - passers-by who seemed not so much at a loss, but downright offended by the sight of them. And sound; Cam had persuaded the stereo to collaborate at last. To the soothing synths of the Mirthless Skirts, they raced through town and into a sunset too picture-perfect to bode any good.

Defying the day to get any worse, they made for the hills. Here at last they rested, tired and giggly. A bonfire spluttered into the mist of twilight, taking with it the sides of a son a mother should never have to see. They sang - of innocence lost and found, of blood and brotherhood, of anarchic spark and sweet cynicism and zest for bad taste.

When the flames burnt low in their eyes and their throats ran out of songs, Frank produced a banner, from the good old days when the earth was green and they still answered to Johnny & The Crack Dealers. He draped it around the party boy - after all, it was his funeral. A toast raised, Frank poured the last of his beer over Johnny. The others followed suit.

A shower of sparks and a good strong kick later, they stood shoulder to shoulder as the body of Johnny Q. floated down the river, like an oversized cherry atop a fancy-drink-flambé.

Real Reggae

Joe Briggs

Pasigu was inside listening to the opening bands and I was leaning on a railing outside the venue watching the traffic and intermittently taking swigs from a can of very cheap cider when Mittens walked up to me. He had a black eye.

'The fuck happened to you?' I said.

'Got punched in the face last night.'

'Who by?'

'Dunno. May have been a friend. Still hurts though.' He shrugged.

Mittens was a friend of mine. He was a rangy red-faced kid with a quiff kept up by dirt and the permanent uniform of a Queers t-shirt thin as an old banknote. And he was a cunt. A drunken fuck with a sharp left and plenty of reach. A tendency to cut the bullshit a little too fine and stray into tender areas of conversation that he knew would fizzle and burn inside people, to light fuses, provoke response just to prove he was alive, just to see it explode, even if people fucking hated him. To sculpt the ground somehow even if he knew it would only leave a crater rather than mighty earthworks. He was an arsehole and everyone loved him except the people who fucking hated him and even the people who loved him were the people who fucking hated him half the time. Everyone I knew had some of him in them, but he always took it one step over the line and then started running with it. It was that desire to prod and probe because you can, to search out minefields in unlikely places and dance upon them. So I loved Mittens but I'm not benevolent, no-one is, he swung punches and we did not indulge his shit indefinitely. We had enough to deal with ourselves. Love. Loss. Lack. The future bearing down on us. Friends slipping away into acquaintances. All the usual. Careworn clichés that are always ready to spring up and take our heads at any time, skitting about like pondlife in your skull. Anyway, that was Mittens. Sometimes sort of an avatar for all that careless itching fury we wanted to stretch for and avoid at the same time, but more than that, a mate. I handed him a cider from the plastic bag at my feet.

'Cheers. Why you standing out here?' Mittens asked.

'Someone booked a fucking cod reggae band as the opener.' I said with disgust.

'Shit. I thought they outlawed that in the wake of the horrendous events of the last ska revival.'

'They opened a song by announcing *'Let's get this party started'* which I thought was just shit stage banter but turned out to be the title of the song and about 80% of the lyrics.'

He laughed and pulled at his shirt distractedly. 'Man, I hope it's a good one tonight.' He said. 'I could use it.'

I nodded. Because we could always use it. We could always use the shakedown that comes with throwing yourself about in a dark pit of slipshod souls to the sound of the guitars flayed and vocal chords stripped and left hanging. Crushes of bodies and the choral emetic. Songs of terrible dayjobs and wasted hours that make those meaningless trudges into an armour, a communion. A reason. We keep going like this. Hating our lives and feeling alone and finding a rough camaraderie and power in tumbledown anthems of how we hate our lives and feel alone. One more song about dying today so you don't wanna die today, one more show where you go down flailing on a beer-wet floor and crack your head and don't care and get dragged up by strangers. A tattoo in sharpie script that reads MINIMUM WAGE IS A GATEWAY DRUG. It's all just a vicious circle that we cling onto as it spins and squeal like kids on a roundabout. We could always use it. If we couldn't we wouldn't be here. Talking shit by the roadside and checking our phones to see if it's safe to enter. It wasn't, yet.

'So why's Pasigu inside.' Mittens asked. 'He's usually got better taste than... than that.'

'Was hitting on the merch girl for the cod reggae band. Had to show face.'

'Ah.'

'Man's never met a merch girl he couldn't hit on.'

A bunch of the punx had acquired a football and were standing around on the little patch of pavement kicking it about amongst themselves, cheering and laughing, as the ball squirted about, coming haphazardly off hefty boots not designed for the optimum ball control. Every now and then it shot into the air heading towards the road and there was a quick scramble to stop it bouncing into traffic. Then it did bounce into traffic and some white van screeched to a halt and the driver shouted out the window 'FUCKIN TWATS' at the punx and the punx as one did their best to look sheepish in their ratty jeans and military jackets proclaiming FUCK NAZI SYMPATHY or THEY EAT SCUM on the back as someone went to get the ball. They booted it back towards the punx. It went high and wide and towards the door of the venue where it struck Pasigu on the arm as he was coming out. He flinched and looked around wildly for what happened. When he'd properly assessed the situation he kicked the ball back and came over to us.

'Jock bullshit,' he said. Pas was a shorter guy, wearing a shirt that said WHAT WOULD HENRY ROLLINS DO? and a jacket patched out of need rather than fashion. Pas had the unerringly ability to acquire free drugs.

'How's it going, Pas,' Mittens said.

'Alright. You?'

'Alright. How's the merch girl?'

'Got a boyfriend.'

'That's never stopped you before,' I said.

'That's stopped me plenty of times before,' he said. 'It's just usually not stopped me before someone threatened to hit me, or hit me. But, you know, I'm tryna grow as a person. He shrugged. Tryna respect some more boundaries and shit.' He looked around, he looked twitchy.

'Sellout,' said Mittens.

'Ever try growing as a person, Mittens?' I asked.

'What? Like working out? Hulking up? Jock bullshit?'

'No, like, being less of a cunt? Ever been like 'Yo I'm gonna be less of a cunt'.'

'I dunno. Not deliberately. Ever spit on a cop? Ever look at a flower and be like 'That is a shit flower'? Who gives a fuck?'

'Ever get punched in the face?' Pas said, looking at Mittens face blankly.

'Yeah. Couple times.'

'How is it?' Pas asked.

'Fine. Hurts,' said Mittens.

'You got it from hitting on a merch girl?' Pas asked.

'I dunno, maybe.' Mittens said. 'Maybe a merch girl hit me. Maybe she hit me or her boyfriend hit me. Or the merch girl's girlfriend hit me. Maybe a merch girl hit me with some fucking merch. I dunno. Something happened.' He twirled around as he said this, taken balletically by the moment, by the fluttering possibilities. It wasn't much of a moment, but he wasn't much of a dancer.

'Yo, I have heard the word merch girl so many times in this conversation it is losing all meaning,' I said. 'Stop saying merch girl.'

'Is there a band called the Merch Girls?' Pas asked, realising he wasn't gonna get shit from Mitten.

'Merch girl, merch girl, merch girl,' I said.

'I bet there is a band called the Merch Girls,' said Mittens. 'I bet there is and I bet it's all fucking dudes, cos dudes are lame like that. That is the lamest shit ever. Bands fulla dudes with names like The Girls, or The Cool Girls or whatever.'

'Cheap Girls,' I said.

'Yeah, them,' he said.

'Yeah, if you went in expecting badass all-female rock and roll like Girl School, you'd be bummed,' Pas said.

'Girl School fucking rocked,' Mittens said. 'Man, they were the best.'

'I read the other day there's a punk band out of Portland or somewhere called Bitch School. Girl School's their main influence,' I said.

'Fuck, man. I know nothing about that band. I do not know that band. But I already know that that band is the greatest band in the world,' Mittens said. 'Bitch School. They got any releases?'

'A demo, maybe,' I said.

'Guess we're stuck with fucking Clorox Girls or whatever still then,' he took a long swig of his cider and continued, 'It's like the cheapest easiest gender fuckery ever. Oh ho ho. We're all dudes but our band name is girls. How radical. All on the stage being boring, wearing flannel. Pffft.'

'Yeah, flannel,' Pas said, chuckling a little.

'They always fucking wear flannel. It's like, you're gonna do that, gonna name your band that, go up in drag. Do something more. Blow a dude on stage. I want to see a dude get blown by another dude on stage. That is what I want to see.' He mimed sucking a dick.

'You know, there are places you can just go see that. Like, without the danger of getting hit by someone, without the threat of shit whiteboy reggae bands opening,' I said, getting out my phone. 'I'll just search for some places in the vicinity.'

'Yeah, whatever band's on next'll probably suck. Let's fuck it off and go watch some gay sex.'

'Reggae band's probably finished by now,' Pas said.

'Let's start a non-reggae band called Reggae. That'll work,' Mittens said.

'You know there's a Japanese hardcore band called Real Reggae,' I said.

'There's a Japanese hardcore band called everything,' Pas said.

'Got an 8-inch flexi comp with their songs on it. They're like halfway Gauze or, like, uh, Jellyroll Rockheads, that style of Japanese hardcore, real noisy thrashy stuff, like the nuclear burn stuff, half that and half Steel Pulse or something.'

'Like Bad Brains?'

'Yeah but Bad Brains were like: hardcore song, hardcore song, reggae song, hardcore song. Real reggae are like 'Hey you think this is a hardcore song NOPE it is a reggae song, fooled you!"

'Wow, that sounds awful,' Mittens said.

'It's pretty bad but in its way it's pretty good,' I said. 'It's pretty fun.'

'Whatever you say, man.'

'Let's head in,' I said.

'Alright, I guess we're seeing whatever shitty punk band this is, guess we're doing something totally straight and boring like dancing around in a sweaty darkened room full of dudes,' Mittens said, sighing overdramatically.

'Let's get this party started, as Pas would say,' I said.

'Ha. Ha. Ha,' Pas said, flatly.

I finished my cider and Mittens finished his and we headed in. We passed the bouncer. Mittens paid his fiver and me and Pas waved a stamped hand. The sound guy was playing Doug Mulray's I'm a Punk. I'm a Punk is a parody punk song where the lyrics consist mainly of the singer saying that they want to take drugs, and get drunk, over and over again. It was an attempt to highlight the faux-rebelliousness and the shortsighted nihilism of dumb punks, and, naturally, punks love it and the whole room was engaged in various levels of singalong, some just kinda mumbling the words, I was mouthing them under my breath, shimmying a little bit, a couple groups of people were going full tilt, arm in arm like terrace crowds, doing weird old man dances and spilling their pints. Probably never been possible to write a fake punk song that portrays punks as so dumb that they won't appropriate for themselves, shout it back at you as a weapon. Yeah, we're that dumb. Yeah, we're that silly. Twist the mockery into a celebration. I once tried making a fake punk comp, of bands like FU2, a shameless cash-in from a 60s r&b band called Downliners Sect who changed their name and released a punk album, or the song I Hate You from Star Trek IV where Kirk and Spock visit the 1980s and Spock does a Vulcan Death Grip on a guy with a mohawk.

'I like this song,' Mittens said, bouncing up and down on the balls of his feet.

'You would,' I said.

'Yeah, it really speaks to me,' Pas said. 'It's like a beautiful ray of light, shining from within.'

'Like a warming log fire after a hard day in the cold, like a salve upon the soul,' I said.

'You got any drugs,' Mittens asked Pas.

'Yeah but I took them.'

'Greedy prick. Share the wealth, man.'

'Only had a couple pills. I was outside earlier and some guy I know gave me them and I looked around and there was a cop looking at me so I was like, I'd better do these drugs so this cop doesn't think I'm a pussy.'

We laughed at that and I asked, 'How you feeling?'

'Eh. Alright. They're not doing much,' Pas said. 'Take drugs, get drunk.'

'I'm gonna fucking go nuts first chords. I don't give a shit,' Mittens said, getting excited, looking at the guitarist tuning, teasing the strings. 'Y'all in?'

'I'm in,' said Pas.

'I'll punch you in the face if it makes you feel better,' I said.

'Will it hurt?' he replied.

'Not til tomorrow,' said Mittens.

'Man, I guess that's the best you can do,' Pas said. We were silent for a little while as Doug Mulray told us about taking drugs and getting drunk.

'Real Reggae, man. That is some weird bullshit,' Mittens said.

'I'll send you a link,' I said.

What It Is

Terry Grimwood

I

And then we were in her bedsitter, a place that was a thousand times more untidy than even my own flat. But that didn't matter, not at that moment. That moment was a sweat-slicked, wet moment, a hot-breath, biting and scratching moment. A wild fuck moment.

Skin, the girl I rutted in her cramped lair of discarded clothes and unwashed crockery, had told me nothing, other than that she sang in a punk band called The Shout.

Afterwards she knelt on the bed and looked down at me and said, 'Do you always shag the people you interview?'

'Hardly ever.'

Never in fact. I was freelance, part time (my real job involved a warehouse and fork lift trucks) and writing for a struggling new music rag like Noise didn't bring you into contact with many Big Names. Well, not often. I had been told to piss-off by more than one Big Name at the stage door. Does that count?

But perhaps it was comeuppance time, because back then, in the tail end of that long hot summer of 1976, people had stopped listening to the pomp and strut of those Big Names. People were starting to tell them to piss-off.

'Your clothes are down there,' Skin said.

'I don't want them.'

'Going home naked are you?'

'I thought I'd stay here a bit longer.'

She got off the bed and went to the tiny little fridge. She pulled out a couple of beers and threw one to me.

'Anything softer?'

'What?'

'Squash, Coke, with cola, not, you know...'

'Got water, or some coffee, no milk.'

'Water's okay.' I needed coffee, but I didn't want her distracted by the mundane.

She went to the sink, rinsed a mug and filled it. She was naked, tall, skinny, pale-fleshed. Her hair was dyed platinum, her make-up vivid pink rather than black, de rigueur for the new punk damsel. There was a cross-hatch of time-whitened scars on her left forearm.

'Aren't you going to ask?' I said when she handed me the mug.

'Ask what?'

'Why I don't want beer?'

She shrugged.

Her absence of curiosity irritated me, odd, because normally I was sick of explaining myself.

'Stay if you want,' she said.

She sat on the bed. I sat against the pillow. There was no bed head, just the wall and its covering of vile wallpaper. I touched her face.

'Pink punk,' I muttered. I liked the phrase. I'd use it in my next article.

'What's Pink Punk?'

'You are.'

'Fuck you.' She wasn't joking. 'Punk isn't pink or black or fucking green. It's what it is.'

'Pure, yeah.' Was it? Christ knows, but I didn't want to see those angry eyes again. I raised my mug in a toast; 'Three chords, proud and straight. No pomp, no pretension.'

'Is that all you think it is?'

'Well no...' Wrong again, and panicked. One fucking session and I was frightened of losing her. 'So what is it?'

'What it *is*.' She sniffed, contemptuous. 'I'm hungry.'

*

We found a late night café. Skin sported a surprisingly conventional outfit for our adventure in fine dining; jeans, tee shirt and cardigan. 'So?' she said when I was stupid enough to comment. 'Am I supposed to wear a fucking bin liner all the time?'

The food was greasy, the tea, strong. It was the best meal I'd ever had.

Afterwards, we went back to her bedsitter. I didn't leave it for another three days, except to go to the day job. I was supposed to write a review for Noise, but I didn't go out to see any bands, and besides the typewriter was in my flat. Perhaps that was a sign, time to jack it in. Writing had become a way to fill the empty spaces. Skin filled them now.

Skin was usually at home. There was a television, which she watched most of the time.

'When do you rehearse?' I asked her on the third night.

'We don't.'

'But - '

'We just play.'

II

I'd never actually seen Skin's band. The interview had been a favour for a badly hung-over colleague. The next Shout gig was on the Saturday night after we met, the fourth day. I'd never been the boyfriend in the audience before. I had fantasies of secret glances, of lyrics given new meaning by the intensity of our love.

'Where is it?' I asked. We were taking an afternoon stroll-and-smoke in the local rec.

'Where's what?'

'The gig.'

No, I didn't know where it was and she hadn't told me there *was* a gig until that morning.

'Hammer and Nails.'

'Where's that?'

'Near St Paul's Cathedral somewhere.'

'I hope you know where *somewhere* is or we're going to get lost.'

'What do you mean *we*?'

'Don't you want me to see you play?'

She shrugged.

'Fuck's sake. I'm your...' Her what exactly? 'I want to see your band.'

'We're at the Hammer and Nails, on at nine.' She turned to walk away.

I grabbed her arm. 'Don't you care if I come?'

'It's nothing to do with me.'

'What is it to do with?'

'What it is.'

'I'm sick of your riddles - '

'I'm sick of your questions. I'll see you later.'

'What questions? I never ask you any questions because you never want to answer them.'

She walked away and tossed a weary 'Fuck you' over her shoulder.

'Bitch!'

She didn't look back.

*

My flat. Fifteen floors up the flank of a 1960s tower block, with a big expanse of sitting room window that gave stunning views of the other identical towers on the estate. For all its faults, it felt infinitely spacious after being cooped up in Skin's bedsitter. I could breathe here. I sat on the floor and stared at my music collection; countless LPs, spines outwards in their second-hand, wood-effect shelf unit. I selected one, at random; *Made in Japan;* Deep Purple live.

I slid the first of the album's two big, black, vinyl discs from its bronze sleeve and laid it carefully on my hi-fi turntable. A few moments later Jon Lord was leading the way into *Highway Star*. I closed my eyes and let the rock-roar enfold me. There was momentary comfort here. Realities shut out, lids closed. Gillan's scream, Blackmore's virtuosity.

Punk didn't belong to me.

Skin didn't belong to me.

I opened my eyes, shattered by the thought, just as *Child in Time* moved abruptly from quiet-and-menacing to loud-and-terrifying.

The music was suddenly bloated and self-regarding, the flat, dusty, tatty and empty; a stale den for a twenty-five year-old teenager who should have grown-up when he did possess the accoutrements of adulthood; a wife, a child and a career.

I did a good job of chasing them all away. I was a serious writer then, a journalist, newly moved from fete-and-wedding local rags to the lower ranks of the *Evening Standard*, as well as some nom de plume moonlighting for the music heavies such as *NME* and *Sounds*. I chased them away while fighting in bars, throwing-up in the street, or at best, sleeping it off while exiled to the sofa.

I didn't hit Sarah, or our child. Never. Wouldn't. Couldn't. But I was the maggot that rotted our marriage from the inside. The useless toe-rag who loved a drink, was entitled to a drink and was going to bloody well have a drink because He Worked Hard And Deserved It.

I don't know where Sarah escaped to. She hadn't contacted me since she walked out. My son was two now. They were better off without me.

Child in Time finished, the crowd cheered. Then the turntable arm lifted, silence.

I hated silence. It was the soundtrack of solitude.

III

The Hammer and Nails function room was upstairs. Its ceiling was low, its walls closing in. The place was packed, everyone in newly-minted punk uniform and tanking-up as fast as their throats and bellies would allow. A scuffle broke out, a punch was thrown. It came to nothing, just the usual dynamics of a tribe waiting for its music.

The performance area, more rostrum than stage, was already kitted out with amps and mikes. I had seen Skin in the bar downstairs, surrounded by a bunch of male punks. They were laughing, having a party. I stayed out of it. I was nervous for Skin. She, on the other hand, hadn't seemed at all anxious.

A stir in the crowd, and then a procession pushed through, stage-bound. I glimpsed Skin, walking beside a huge guy with a shaved head and fearsome looking Mohican. The big guy stripped to the waist then sat down behind the drumkit. A tall, lanky streak of piss plugged in a bass. Beside him, a slight-built, sullen-looking character with sticky, messed-up hair tuned his Strat. Skin said something. There were nods all round. She spun about, grabbed the mike in both hands and screamed. The sound ripped through the room and bent my eardrums inwards until they hurt. There was an answering howl.

The band erupted into life. The crowd surged, swirled, pogoed, more mob than audience. I clung to my Coke bottle. The music was loud, unrelenting, a solid wall of blazing white. Song merged into song, each one too loud to reveal any melodic landscape it might have possessed. It was effect. It was energy, sweat and noise, the soundtrack to a half-lit sub-world of violent, staccato movement and barely-contained aggression.

Afterwards, the band went back downstairs to continue their party. Ears ringing, consumed by an ill-defined sense of dread, I followed. Once down in the bar, I stood on the edge and watched Skin get drunk. Someone, I think it was the bass player, asked me who the fuck I was. Skin said nothing, just carried on flirting with some fat little punk who had more metalwork in his face than Sabbath's Iron Man.

I walked out, went back to the bedsitter and waited outside.

I was still waiting when she came home.

'Didn't you want me there?' I said.

She shrugged as she unlocked the front door. 'Up to you.'

'I don't want it to be up to me.'

'I'm not your mother.' This was tossed down to me as we ascended the narrow, ill-lit staircase.

'I just want you to...I don't know...to let me in.'

'Let you into what?'

'Your life, your self. *You*.'

She shook her head. 'No one goes there. *I* don't go there.'

'I don't know you - '

'Yes you do. I'm here. This is it.' Into the bedsitter now, light on, her jacket off, thrown towards the bed but ending up on the floor.

'No one is just what you see.'

'Well find someone else who *will* let you in, or whatever it is you want.'

'I don't want anyone else.' I grabbed at her, tried to pull her to myself.

'Fuck off...'

She struggled and managed to squirm out of my grasp. In one fluid motion she snatched up a knife from the pile of dirty cutlery in the tiny sink. It was a sharp, short-bladed thing, crusted with food. She spun round to face me and slashed the knife across her left forearm. The cut bubbled, thickened and leaked blood.

'For Christ's sake Skin - '

'See it do you?' she yelled. 'What's inside? There's nothing, fucking nothing!'

Blood ran down her arm, dripped onto the threadbare carpet.

She backed away and stood in the middle of the room. Her injured arm hung by her side, almost unheeded. 'Nothing...' She bowed her head. It took me several seconds to realise that she was crying.

I went to her and this time she let me hold her.

*

The next day, Sunday, neither of us mentioned what had happened. The cut wasn't serious, easily remedied by a plaster. I cleaned the bedsitter. Skin watched me. Bemused, I think. Perhaps it was scorn.

I didn't care. I cleaned up, took the sheets and our clothes to the launderette. I fetched my typewriter and some more clothes from my flat then spent the afternoon typing my column; 'Punk; What is it? What it is'.

Skin sat on the bed and wrote a song. She slept, stared out of the window, drank beer, watched me, then watched television; a Western, 'Songs of Praise'. I moulded myself around the quietness of her existence. I wanted to be here. I didn't want to be alone. The day exhausted me.

IV

A few days later I came home from my job at the warehouse to find the bedsitter empty. No sign of Skin. No note, no message, just the crumpled bed, mouldering discarded clothes and a sink full of dirty mugs. Things had settled down, almost into routine. Skin hadn't asked me to stay, but she hadn't asked me to leave either. So here I was.

Only tonight, here she wasn't.

It had happened before, even living a life of *what it was*, required food, toothpaste and toilet rolls, even Skin needed to go to the corner shop every now and then. I sighed, disappointed to be alone, and filled the kettle. While it heated I switched on the television and cleared up Skin's mess-of-the-day. *Blue Peter* was coming to an end, Noakes, Judd and Purves, on the sofa, saying good night. A little shock of nostalgia made me stop. I wanted to be a kid again, safe at home, no worries except getting my homework done so I could play.

Nostalgia faded, my disappointment turned to irritation. How could Skin live like this? I wasn't exactly Mr Clean and Tidy, but compared to her I was the Jack Lemmon half of the Odd Couple.

The kettle boiled. I made coffee, using the last of the milk in the process. Hopefully Skin would bring a replacement from her shopping expedition. I sat down and waited for the News.

It came and went. I sat through *Nationwide*, not paying it much attention. I grew restless. Still no sign of Skin. I stood, went to the fridge in search of food. Cheese, bread. Perhaps I should walk to the café. But I wanted to be here when Skin got home. I made a sandwich. I tried to watch *Top of the Pops*, but all it did was add to my irritation. Mimed crap most of it, fronted by DJs who were too ancient for the job. Dear God, when were they going to put that bloody programme out of its misery?

I was up again, wandering to the fridge. Door open. A tub of marge, a half used tin of evaporated milk, bacon, a few eggs. And four bottles of Newcastle Brown. I slammed the door shut.

I deserved it though didn't I? How did that song go? *The poor sod is entitled to a drink and is going to bloody well have a drink because He Works Hard And Deserves It.* Yeah, that was the one.

Off with the television, on with the radio. No, too lonely, too depressing. Cassette player then. A rage of noise, someone telling me he's the Anti-Christ. Suddenly punk was pissing me off. What the hell was so special about rock and roll played at twice the speed by people who couldn't play it in the first place?

Television back on.

Fridge.

Come on, a little reward for your heartache...

Fuck it, a walk, the cafe. Skin had lost her chance of a Hollywood homecoming I had to get out of there.

She wasn't there when I came back to the bedsitter three hours later. She wasn't there until one in the morning.

She was gone too long.

I didn't say it, didn't ask the question, not at that moment. How could I? What moral high ground did I hold now? I was sitting on the bed, television off, no music, no radio. Alone with the dazed, grind of my failure. I watched her throw her jacket onto the floor then go to the fridge.

There were, of course, no bottles left. I think I chuckled, giggled maybe.

She sat on the bed, by my feet. She smelled of sweat, cigarettes and stale alcohol, and was wearing her stage costume; torn sweater and ripped jeans.

She stared at me, a little puzzled perhaps, but with no recrimination. I reached out to touch her, nervous of rejection, the movement, booze clumsy. She took my hand and pressed it to her lips and licked my fingers. I grabbed at her and drew her down beside me. I ground my mouth hard against hers and tasted beer, cigarettes and the scorching heat of her breath. I fumbled and tore at her clothes and she at mine. And for a moment, everything was Skin again.

V

For a moment.

The next evening, after work, I went back to my own flat. How could I not? I made a shopping detour on the way. Once indoors I placed my purchase on the kitchen worktop. It was in a plain brown paper bag. I stood as far away from the thing as was possible within the cramped confines of the room. Then I forced myself to turn my back on it and fill the kettle.

Buying the scotch was as much a self-inflicted wound as those caused by Skin's knife.

It was a battle I needed to win, because after last night the war was no longer going my way.

Nursing a freshly-filled coffee mug between my hands, I walked past the bottle and into the sitting room. I selected an LP. *Watcher of the Skies* hammered through the flat's stale air.

You couldn't get further from punk than Genesis.

I sat on the floor, drowned by the music, *my* music, drinking strong cheap coffee and fighting the urge to run into the kitchen to snatch the bottle from the worktop.

If I did, the tenuous umbilical that joined me to Skin would snap.

And if that happened, I would bleed to death.

*

'Crone?' I said into the phone's sticky, grubby mouthpiece once the coin had silenced the pips.

'Fuck's sake Baz, it's two in the morning.' Cronin was a friend from my serious music press days, Scottish, soft accent, hard-nosed attitude. He managed bands, successful ones.

'The Shout, one hell of a band.' I talked fast, no more ten pence pieces.

'Yeah, them and a thousand others.'

'They're at the Hammer and Nails, tomorrow...no, no, it's tonight. Please come, for me, please Crone...' The pips sounded. The line went dead.

I hung up and stumbled out of the phone box. I didn't want to go home, so I walked, miraculously still sober. Cronin would come to the gig and sign-up The Shout. And I would have made my grand gesture, like Romeo shouting love poems up to Juliet's balcony. Doors would finally open, literal ones and emotional ones.

He had to sign them. Christ, he had to.

VI

Time always passes, no matter how slow and torturous its passage might be. I abandoned any thought of work. Not a problem though, the union would make sure I kept my job. I returned to my flat, made coffee and placed *Houses of the Holy* on the turntable. The day would be measured by the forty-minute segments denoted by each album in my collection, played for the last time then snapped over my knee. Each forty-minute slice was a battle through which I only had to stay dry from Track One to the end.

VII

Lights down. The compere for the evening took to the mike. He shouted something incomprehensible. The crowd howled back at him. Someone threw a bottle which shattered at his feet.

No sign of Cronin.

The band once more made their way through the tight-packed crowd like ring-bound boxers. I strained to see Skin, caught a glimpse. She was laughing, hand on the drummer's shoulder. He spoke to her, mouth close to her ear. Panic drove me into the press, trying to tear my way through, to show her I was here.

Someone hit me, not hard, but enough to throw me back. The crowd seemed to give beneath the impact of my body, then pushed me forward and back onto my feet. Hands grabbed at me, pushed, shoved. I fought back, wild in my anger and fear.

'This is all that matters,' Skin yelled. She never usually talked to the crowd. They roared back at her and I was forgotten, flotsam, driven forward by the band-wards surge. A whine of feedback then it started, that relentless wall of sound, distortion, energy and Skin's screeched vocals.

Cronin you bastard, where are you...

When it was over the band simply unplugged and left the stage, No goodbye-and-thank-you, no love-you-all, it was done.

I swam through the crowd, trying intercept Skin.

Someone else beat me to it; big man, out-of-date leather jacket, receding hairline, bulldog jowls.

Cronin put his arm about Skin's shoulders and led her towards the stairs.

VIII

Her light was on but she wouldn't answer her buzzer. So I used the spare key. Both doors opened. No chain, thank Christ. I went in.

Skin was sitting on the bed, still dressed in her stage gear: torn sweater and jeans.

'Cronin, I told him about you,' I tried not to sound breathless.

'Fuck you.'

'Jesus Skin, didn't he want - '

'He was all over me.' She looked up, eyes as dead as her voice. 'He said he wanted me, and Sledge, but not the others.'

Sledge, I had discovered a few days ago, was her drummer.

'That's the business Skin. It's hard but - '

'Sledge is joining one of Cronin's bands. He's got them a recording contract, but their drummer quit.'

'What about you?'

'Cronin'll put a band together for me, session musicians. What the fuck do session musicians know about punk?'

'They're pros, Skin, they can play anything.'

'No they can't, they fuckin can't. He's killed The Shout, you bastard. They walked out on me when they heard.'

'Something dies, something's born.' Very fucking profound.

'The Shout was mine.' She had the knife. I hadn't noticed it until that moment. She drew it across her arm as she spoke, unflinching, as if unaware of its bite.

'Skin, don't, we can make it right, we can get your band back, Cronin's my mate, I'll phone him...listen to me.'

A second cut. Blood ran.

'Fuck you.'

'You ungrateful bitch. I got you what anyone else in the bloody world would die for and you throw it back in my face!'

'I had what I wanted.' She sawed the blade over her flesh in time to her words.

'You've got something better.'

'How do you know? How do you fucking know? Who are you anyway? I wish you'd just leave me alone'

'Skin, please, I love - '

Blood fountained.

Jesus, she had hit something vital.

Black-red juice squirted in pulsing gouts across the room. I grabbed her and rammed a handful of bed sheet over the wound.

The sheet was instantly transformed into a sodden, red mass. Skin's face whitened, she fell back. I shouted her name, sobbed her name.

Then just sobbed.

For her, for me, Christ knows.

YOU CAN JUMP

Mat Coward

So many people die. That's the main thing I've learned from life; so many people seem to die. And when they're not busy dying, they generally pass the time being unhappy, or else making other people unhappy, or else getting drunk and dancing and throwing up.

Which puts getting drunk and dancing and throwing up in a whole new light, when you think about it.

*

I was never much of a dancer, to be honest, except for very briefly, when I was seventeen. I lacked the ability to just let go and let it happen. But my mate Andy danced. I'm not saying he was a *good* dancer, necessarily; not saying he had any particular talent for it. That wasn't the point: he enjoyed dancing, so he did it. Andy had a true punk rock soul, by which I mean that he didn't give a toss what other people thought of him. As long as what he was doing was right by his lights, then that was all he needed to know. And if you didn't like it, then that was your problem, not his.

For a while, in the late summer or early autumn of 1977, there was a sign in the window of one of the West End venues - the Vortex, possibly - which showed a picture of a punk rocker in all his glory (bondage trousers, ripped leather jacket, safety pins, spiky hair) and written underneath was the message: 'If You Don't Look Like This, Fuck Off.' The police made the club take it down eventually. I think there might even have been a threat of prosecution. I thought it was brilliant, hilarious. It was tribal, and aggressive, and punky and it said *Go to hell* to the entire Establishment - to anyone who wasn't us. Andy thought it was stupid.

'If they want to wear a uniform,' he said, 'why don't they join the army?' Next time we went to a punk gig, Andy wore a sports jacket and tie.

The dance that everyone associates with punk wasn't really a dance at all. Pogoing didn't involve learning any steps; it didn't require an ability to keep time, or to coordinate with a partner. That was the point of it, really. If you could jump up and down, you could pogo. If you could jump up and down even though your trouser legs were linked at the ankles by a short length of khaki fabric, or black mock leather, then you could *really* pogo. Not that it would have mattered; those were not competitive days, punk was not a competitive scene. To be better at pogoing than someone else - or rather, to have tried to be better - would have been to miss the idea entirely. Can you jump up and down? So; you can pogo. I even remember seeing two kids in wheelchairs, at one gig, bumping their wheels up against the side of the stage, pogoing away with the rest of us. Even if you *can't* jump up and down, you can pogo.

Slamming and choking are not as well remembered today, but were just as important at the time, and both were a little more involved than pogoing, a little more demanding. Slamming required timing. As you hurled your body at your mate - or he hurled his at you - at distances ranging from a few feet to a few inches, depending on whether the floor was illegally overcrowded or catastrophically overcrowded, if you didn't time it right you could end up with all sorts of trouble. Not that anyone ever did get injured, as far as I know. Those were wild times, and in wild times the wild children are protected. Today, people live more safely, and children are killed everywhere.

The choke (I'm not sure if we actually called it that, or even if we called it anything - 1977 was more a time of doing than of branding) - was a frenzied dance, even more so than the pogo or the slam. There was a strange sense of thrill to choking a total stranger; how would he react?

To an uninitiated onlooker, seeing two teenagers gripping each other about the throat and shaking each other back and forth, while simultaneously leaping into the air, bouncing on the rubber soles of their French kickers, it must have looked like a fight to the death. It is this one image of the punk era - of my friend Andy strangling Jamie Holmes, holding on and tightening his wrists even after Jamie's hands had dropped to his sides - that stayed in my mind over the years more than any other.

*

I hired a room for the reunion above a suitably dingy pub near Waterloo. That wasn't as easy as it sounds; dingy pubs were not so plentiful in 1997 as they had been twenty years earlier.

I got there first, to set up. I had a few homemade tapes of the classics: Elvis Costello, The Clash, The Pistols, Wreckless Eric, Eddie and the Hot Rods. There was a small bar in the functions room, staffed by a friendly teenage girl. She asked me what it was, a stag night? A works do? I told her. She was delighted.

'Oh, wow! I love all that old punk stuff, it's so naff isn't it? So camp? Like, you know, so *Seventies*.'

I wondered when irony had become the only acceptable response to anything; when, precisely, people had decided that it just wasn't safe to actually feel anything any more.

The girl passed me the clingfilmed plates of sandwiches I'd ordered, and I distributed them around the room. I stuck a few treasured old posters to the walls: creased fold-outs of the Pistols in their pomp; red-and-white handbills advertising gigs at the Marquee or The Other Cinema.

I drank a quick half, and smoked half a cigarette. I was nervous. The fact was, I hadn't kept in close touch with any of the old crowd. I'd seen Andy maybe once or twice a year for a quick drink in town; most of the others I'd seen even less than that. The last time we were all together in the same room was ... well, shit, *forever* ago.

'Can you keep an eye on things for a moment? I just need to change.'

'Sure,' said the barmaid. 'No problem.'

I took my holdall into the Gents, locked myself in a cubicle, and took off my jeans and jacket and shirt. I put on my Army surplus straights held together with an old bike padlock and chain, and a black t-shirt, faded to grey. I took off my slip-ons and replaced them with French kickers. I hadn't needed to visit a barber - my hair, these days, being short enough by nature - but I did spike up what remained of it with a comb and a blob of gel; I'd have used Brylcreem, or perhaps sugar water, back then.

'Oh, wow!' said the barmaid when I emerged. 'Where did you get all that fantastic stuff?'

'I don't know. Just stuff I never threw away.'

'Wow, you mean it's *authentic*! Hey, you know, that stuff might be worth something.'

'I don't know. I wouldn't think so.'

She looked at me more closely. 'But shouldn't the t-shirt be, like, ripped?'

I just shook my head, smiled; I couldn't be bothered to explain. A ripped t-shirt was one that *got* ripped; a t-shirt ripped on purpose was for posers.

Well, I was dressed. The posters were up. The tapes were standing by. The sandwiches were sweating. Everything was ready. I'd invited seven blokes, those I still had fairly recent addresses for, and asked them to invite anyone else they thought of. How many would turn up? Just me? Or, just me and Andy ... I didn't fancy that. That would be even worse.

The first bloke to arrive wasn't a bloke. It was Anne. I must have looked as astonished as I felt (perhaps even - though I hoped not - as *horrified* as I felt), because she laughed and said 'Hi, Steve. Hope you don't mind? I know I wasn't really invited, but ... '

She obviously had been invited, I thought, because otherwise how would she have known about it? But who had invited her, I couldn't imagine.

'Of course not, Anne, I'm delighted to see you. It's - you look wonderful.' She did. She was dressed up like Gaye Advert, black leather jacket and tight PVC trousers. Long black hair, and black eye make up. She looked stunning.

We kissed awkwardly. You didn't kiss when you met people in the old days; that's something of the modern age, of who we've become.

To my relief - and Anne's, no doubt - the door banged again, and three men walked in. I recognised one of them (Chaz, he'd been in the Hammersmith squat with me and Andy), but I didn't know his companions. All three had dyed hair: green, with yellow highlights. It looked as if someone had been sick on their heads - someone with a streaming cold, at that - which I suppose was the idea.

Chaz introduced his nephews. Now I came to look at them, they were a good bit younger than him - nearer the barmaid's age. I was annoyed: this wasn't supposed to be a fancy dress party, for heaven's sake. But I tried not to show my annoyance, not even to myself. After all, it was only a reunion, not a sacred rite.

More people drifted in over the next half-hour or so. Old friends, old acquaintances, wives and girlfriends, friends of friends. Almost everyone had made some effort with their clothes, though the results were astonishingly varied. It seemed to me (though I don't pretend my memory's any better than anyone else's), that most of them were dressed according to 1990s ideas of what 1977 looked like.

I reckoned I was the only one wearing his own original clothes from back then - and I wasn't sure what that said about me. The worst word a modern kid can use about anyone is 'sad,' which seems to mean something like 'enthusiastic.' But the barmaid had said I looked fantastic, hadn't she? Well, no ... she'd said my *clothes* were fantastic.

In the end, there were more people present than I'd feared might be the case: must have been getting on for twenty-five, which was about right for the occasion. A few I didn't know. A few, to be honest, I didn't remember, or barely. Rob was there; I was glad to see him, we'd been good mates. He hadn't lived in the squat, but he had got me a job in a pub near Whitehall, which had become our HQ. He was wearing straight black jeans and a long, thin tie and he was completely bald, smooth as a shaved egg. I'd pretty much lost contact with Rob some time in the late 80s, but when you've been close to someone when you were seventeen, the years don't matter that much.

'How you doing?' I asked him, and he just shrugged and said *Oh, you know, mustn't grumble,* and then we talked about old times instead. Which - fair enough - was the reason we were there. I noticed he could hardly take his eyes off Anne. I wasn't sure if that was because he shared my shock at her presence, or just because she looked so sexy.

I was pretty busy acting like a host, so I didn't notice Andy had arrived until he tapped me on the back while I was turning over a cassette and said: 'Wotcher, Stevey-boy. Good turnout.'

His hair was slightly longer than was fashionable; he was wearing blue jeans, a sports jacket, and a smart denim shirt. We went up to the bar to get him a drink. While I ordered, Andy looked around him, smiling. 'I see Anne made it,' he said.

For the second time that night Anne caused my jaw to drop. 'You knew she was coming?' I handed him his pint.

'Cheers. Yeah, I invited her.'

'*You* invited her?'

'Sure. Who wants to spend the evening at a stag do?'

'No, right. No, I'm glad she's here. I just - I didn't even know you were still in touch.'

'Why wouldn't we be, Stevey? We were married, you know, albeit briefly.'

A hand fell on his shoulder from behind, and Chaz said: 'Andy, mate - is that you? Oh man, great to see you. Great!'

'Chaz.' Andy put down his beer, and they shook hands. I got the impression Chaz was trying to do some black-kid thing with fingers and thumbs, but if he was it crumbled inside Andy's firm, conventional grip.

Chaz fingered one of Andy's lapels. 'But mate, shame on you - you're not dressed up.'

'Never mind, Chaz. You're punk enough for both of us. Nice hair.'

Chaz ran his fingers through his Day-Glo spikes. 'Oh, yeah. Well, no harm in a little nostalgia, right?'

Andy shrugged. 'Sure.'

'You don't agree?' Chaz smiled in the fixed way people do when they're not going to have a fight, but they're not going to let it go, either.

'I just think being nostalgic for punk is maybe a contradiction in terms.'

'Sort of un-punk?' I said. I felt I knew what he meant.

'If you like. Besides, life is better now than it was then. We had a revolution and it worked - so why look back?'

'Surprised you turned up, then,' said Chaz. 'Still - great to see you.' He moved further down the bar, and began waving a tenner to attract the barmaid's attention.

'Always was a bit of a poser,' I said.

'Bloke's entitled to his point of view. They're *his* memories. Tell you what, I should have come in my work gear.' Andy worked as a nurse in a busy casualty department. 'Head to toe in blood and vomit - he'd have liked that.'

'So. Why did you come, if you're not into All Our Yesterdays?'

He clinked his glass against mine. 'See some old mates. It's good to keep in touch. No, all I'm saying is, punk wasn't a fashion, something that can be reproduced by wearing the right clothes or dyeing your hair. It was about how you walked, stood, the expression on your face, your tone of voice. Your outlook.'

'Fair point,' I said. But I couldn't help wondering if there was another reason why Andy didn't feel nostalgic about 1977; because that was the year he killed a kid with his bare hands.

*

When I first arrived at the squat, all I knew about punks was what I'd seen on the news, or read in the *Daily Mirror*. They couldn't play their instruments, they looked like freaks, they had no respect for anything and they were violent. When Andy persuaded me to go to my first punk rock gig I was nervous, frankly. Excited but nervous.

I never knew Andy's full story; his accent was from somewhere up in the Midlands, maybe Wolverhampton, but it soon faded, and he ended up speaking the kind of universal sub-Cockney that was youth's Esperanto. He never admitted to a surname, not in those days, and he never offered much in the way of biography, except to say that he'd come down to London for the music, and because back home everything and everyone was 'dead.' I took this to mean that, like the rest of us, he wanted a few laughs before he got old and died. Obviously, there was something he wasn't talking about: a violent dad, maybe, or a juvenile criminal conviction. It wasn't a mystery that I found interesting enough to pursue. I was simply glad that he wanted to be mates with me, this quiet, rather serious-minded, grown-up man (he was nineteen, I was seventeen), who always knew where things were happening, and shared his knowledge without condescension. As a new boy in the big city, I felt safe in his company. In part this was because there was, behind his wry eyes and hidden in his understanding smile, an unmistakeable glint of danger. The first time I met him, I remember thinking: 'You wouldn't want to be his enemy.'

My own story was a simple one. Born in Kent, didn't much take to school, moved to London as soon as I could. I got on OK with my parents; even phoned them, every now and then. I wasn't a runaway - I was just a teenager who'd moved to London. Where else was there to be, if you were young in the summer of '77?

Andy, Jamie and Rob were already regular attendees at various of London's mushrooming punk venues. They'd seen all the bands I'd heard of, and many that I hadn't. Chaz used to tag along as well, although I don't think he really had any close friends at the squat. He was in some ways the opposite of Andy: he tried to be a mystery man, and failed. Jamie's summing-up of him was blunt, typically Glaswegian, and generally accepted: 'He's a middle-class tosser, thinks wearing anarchy symbols makes him cool, but he's harmless enough.'

If I'd been on my own at that first gig, I would never have got into the dancing. In fact, if I'd been on my own, I'd quite likely have turned tail the moment I passed through the weapons search in the corridor, and walked through the doors into a living definition of claustrophobia.

There were a few hundred kids there, mostly boys, and their collective *thrum* of newness and rebellion was something the press reports could never have prepared me for. It was alien and frightening and my stomach walls were squirting cold-hot liquid at each other ... and as my heartbeat and my breathing gradually attuned themselves to this new world, I began to think that maybe I'd come home.

Between us and the small stage there were rows of tip-back chairs, and there was hardly room to get into the place, let alone to move around. Drinking from the plastic beer glasses was difficult enough, hemmed in by elbows and hips; rolling a cigarette would have required a dexterity far beyond my skills.

The lights went down, and Jimmy Pursey yelled *One two three four!* and Sham 69 leapt into - I don't know, I don't remember exactly. It could have been 'What Have We Got,' though I seem to remember they used that as a closer, so maybe it was 'They Don't Understand.' Whatever it was, it was big and strong and hard and relentless, and I'd never in my life heard music so driving, so physical. The guitar chords raced each other up the hall and tore holes in my body.

'Come on,' Andy shouted in my ear. 'Let's go down the front.'

I'd have preferred to stay put, not too far from the illuminated exit sign. Apart from anything, getting to the front would involve fighting through an almost solid mass of leaping, screaming flesh. But the others set off towards the stage, and I had either to follow them or lose them.

You couldn't actually stand in the space immediately in front of the stage. It was too crowded for that; the only way that many people could all occupy such a small floor simultaneously, was by jumping up and down, taking turns to annex the vertical so that your neighbours could occupy the horizontal. In 1977, choreography wasn't an art or a science, it was a force of nature.

That's how the pogo was born, I would guess; from teenagers full of uncontrollable energy, responding to music that could never be listened to static, played in venues designed for audiences half the size. That - and the sheer speed of the beat. The conduits of information between brain and limbs weren't up to a job like this. By the time the message had travelled from head to knees, the beat had gone - and you were already too late to catch the next one. Just jump up and down: that's all there was time for.

I'd never done it before, or even seen it done, but it seemed as if my legs were veterans of the pogo while my brain was still back at the box office queuing for a ticket.

I jumped, jerking my body upwards from the hips, twisting and writhing at the point where my ascent peaked, forcing out an extra inch of flight, then using my landing to shoot me back up. It sounds effortful, but really I seemed to be hovering more than jumping. A teenager is a kind of furnace, who burns his childhood inside his belly for fuel.

My glasses flew off my nose. I caught them and shoved them in my pocket. Andy grabbed me round the throat and began to shake me.

Oh Christ, I thought. *Here's the violence.*

His eyes were pure danger now, all rage and no wry. I didn't want to do it, but I had no choice - to save myself, I put my own hands around his throat, trying to hold him at arm's length. It was only as his mouth split into a wild smile, and then as he goggled his eyes and lolled his tongue, making believe he was choking, that I realised: my neck didn't hurt. I could breathe normally. I relaxed my own fingers, suddenly embarrassed and afraid at the force with which they'd been digging into him.

Locked together, we took it in turns to jump and kick our legs out, leaving our weight momentarily on the other guy's shoulders. We caromed around the floor, bouncing off other people, knocking them sprawling, sweat flying from our hair, and at the song's peremptory end, we spun away from each other, ending up on our arses amid a million legs.

I wondered how that was possible: how did we have enough space to fall over? I looked at Andy's laughing face and saw the answer: we'd made our own space.

The singer was swearing at the people who were still standing at the bar, clutching pints. 'Tossers! Why ain't you dancing? This lot down here, they're the ones that count. They're the only ones we're playing for!'

And he pointed at me and my mates. We were the ones they were playing for. If you've ever been seventeen, you'll know how good that felt.

*

About half an hour after the last tape had finished, no-one at the reunion had bothered to turn it over - including me. It wasn't that sort of evening. There wasn't going to be any pogoing tonight, let alone throttling.

By ten o'clock there were only half a dozen of us left, sitting round a couple of the tables, chatting, drinking moderately. Andy and Anne seemed relaxed, courteous with each other, though they didn't have much to say to each other. Chaz had left early, with his cousins - to go on to a Seventies disco that one of them ran. Chaz at least had the decency to look a little embarrassed when his cousin let that slip. They offered us free tickets, but no-one took them up. I might have been arrested for assault if anybody had.

Nobody had mentioned Jamie all night. I hadn't expected anyone would. For all I knew, I was the only one who remembered him.

I looked around at my old punk rock comrades: a nurse, a computer guy, a plumber. Anne was a housewife, with two children at school. Having spent twenty years doing crap jobs, I was halfway through a non-graduate-entry teacher training course. I was proud of that; didn't like to say so, didn't seem very punk to say it, but I was a not very academic bloke who'd left school a few days before my sixteenth birthday. I wanted to be a teacher because almost all the teachers I ever had were sadists or morons or defeatists.

The conversation at first was of the catching-up type you'd expect, and then, as the alcohol did its gentle work, we moved on to soul-searching. Rob and Andy held the floor mostly, while the rest of us listened and nodded and contributed the occasional affectionate insult. I gathered from what they said that the two of them had seen quite a bit of each other over the years, though I'd never had them down as big pals, particularly, in the old days.

Rob was the punkiest of us, so it seemed, despite his bald dome and the fact that he was on orange juice. He'd never had a steady job, never been married, still went to gigs, still lived the punk life. 'Unlike you load of BOFs,' he said, and we all laughed at Anne, who had to have the phrase *Boring Old Fart* explained to her.

Andy was as I remembered him; calm and quiet, serious but always amused. Never a shouter, but never one to say something just to make people comfortable. 'For the record, Andy,' I told him, 'I reckon you're the only authentic-looking ex-punk here.'

He gave me a puzzled frown, though I'm sure he knew what I meant.

I gestured at his sports jacket and clean jeans. 'Well, that's what real ex-punks look like when they're knocking forty, isn't it?'

Amid the jeers, and cries of 'Never trust anyone over thirty,' Andy said: 'I'm not an ex-punk. I'm a punk. I always was punk, and I always will be.'

Someone said: 'In *those* shoes?'

'DIY,' said Andy, and we all fell quiet, ready to hear something worthwhile. 'Do-it-yourself, use the materials at hand to make the world a place you want to inhabit, that was punk. And you can do that all your life. I don't just mean music - any aspect of life. Give you an example. I'm a good cook, you know? Dab-hand with the old wok, maestro of the flung-together stir-fry. But I've never read a recipe in my life.'

*

Anne and Andy met in an all-night snack bar not far from Big Ben. She was working there, he was eating there. He asked her out and she said, 'Yeah, why not?' It was two a.m. Their first date, later that morning, consisted of having sex in an empty car park. For the second date, she took him to the pictures.

She was never into punk, which would have made her all but invisible to the rest of us except that she was too pretty to be invisible.

The announcement of their wedding came as a shock; getting married wasn't a very punk thing to do. As wedding announcements go, it wasn't very formal. One evening, Anne came into the pub where I was working and asked me if Andy had been in yet.

'Not yet. You supposed to be meeting him here?'

She shrugged. 'Yeah, you know. Talk about the wedding and that.'

'What, you're going to a wedding?' I gave my lips a little twist as I released the words, like a bowler putting on spin. We didn't go to weddings, our sort. Funerals, maybe, they might be quite cool. But not *weddings*!

'Yeah,' said Anne. 'So are you - you've got to be a witness.'

'What witness?'

'At the registry. Yeah? You and one of the others. Jamie, maybe. Me and Andy, we need two witnesses, when we get married. You've got to have two, it's the law. I don't know why. In case one of them's lying or something, I don't know.'

It was mostly Andy's friends at the registry office. A cousin of Anne's did attend, wearing a hat, but she cleared off as soon as she decently could, and that was it for family on either side.

After the ceremony, about half a dozen of us went off to somewhere in the country, on a train. A cottage in Kent, or somewhere, owned by some old hippies that Anne knew. They'd lent her the place for a sort of combination wedding party and honeymoon.

Speed was the true punk drug - a fast, urban buzz, harmonising with the fast, loud guitars of the music - but for that occasion it didn't seem appropriate, so we compromised our principles and stuck with dope and cider. My only big memory of our rural sojourn is of staying up all night - the weather was very hot, must have been high summer - and at one point, sitting outside the house on the front step of the cottage watching the sun come up. Feeling tired, but completely awake. Shivering slightly from the brief period of chill that comes at the dawn of even the hottest day. Pulling my jacket across my chest, and putting my hands deep in the pockets: we'd all worn hired suits to the wedding, as a laugh. (Oh,

God - is *punk* responsible for irony?)

Then, about six in the morning, going into the little house, seeing a pile of people snoring and farting on the living-room floor, going up to use the bog, looking out of the landing window and seeing Anne and Jamie, kissing in the back garden. She was wearing his jacket, and she had one hand behind his head, a cigarette between the fingers.

It was a very short marriage. I never said anything to Andy, so I can only assume that Anne did, or Jamie maybe, or perhaps Andy himself looked out of a window and saw what I saw. At any rate, by the time we headed back to London that evening, they were no longer a married couple in any but the legal sense.

*

These days, the 1970s is packaged as a fashionable, cherishable decade, the greatest flowering of a sweetly naive kind of cool. That's not how those of us who were there remember it. Before punk rock, with its snarling singers and its rude graphics, the mid-70s were cold and grey, unfriendly and above all *boring.*

Let me tell you about punk music, about what it meant to us. Or to me, at least. It wasn't about anarchy - we weren't anarchists, you have to study to be an anarchist. It was simpler than that: for the first time, or at least the first time for white kids since skiffle, pop music became something you could *do* instead of just something you consumed.

Just before punk detonated, you could buy a Yes concept album, and listen to it - and that was it, that was your part of the process finished. Punk was as different as it could have been. If you liked the noise, you just *became* punk. Thousands of kids formed bands, about ten minutes after hearing their first punk single. People used to say 'But they can't play their instruments,' not realising that was the whole point! Music isn't as hard as people make out - that's something all the young punks discovered, as bluesmen thirty or forty years earlier had discovered.

All you needed was two chords on the guitar, a bassist who could count up to four by tapping his feet, and someone who could shout loud enough to be heard over the drums - the technical, musicological term for this latter Herbert being 'lead vocalist.'

The lyrics; that was the easiest bit of all. You just said what was going on in your life, in your head: 'I'm bored. Working is crap. School is crap. I want excitement. I'm scared.' Same with the dancing. You can jump up and down, can't you? Fine, then you're dancing - so get down the front and dance.

You didn't even need to be in a band to be part of punk. If you wanted to be part of it, believed you were part of it, acted like you were part of it, you were part of it. If you felt punk, you were punk, whether you were the editor of a Roneo'd fanzine in the heart of punkland, or a school kid in rural Wales. There was no distance between the band and the crowd; they were just the same as us, except they'd managed to get hold of an amp from somewhere, and we hadn't, or hadn't yet, or didn't want to. In 1977, all the bands were garage bands.

If you wanted to be a punk, the only thing that could stop you was death.

*

The night Jamie died, about a fortnight after the wedding, we'd been to see an all-girl group in the cellar of a pub near Kings Cross. By then, just about every space in London was putting on gigs, live music was alive again for the first time in ages.

This particular place was even less suitable as a venue for a music club than most: the sound was dreadful, the heat was unbearable, and the beer was warmer than the fug. We were having a great time; me, Andy, Rob and Jamie. Anne had been there - not with anyone as far as I could tell, just hanging around, almost as if the wedding, and the break-up with Andy had never happened. But it wasn't really her sort of place, and she left well before the end, saying she'd meet us later at a pub down the road.

‘I’m going outside,’ Rob told me, though I understood him mainly by sign language. ‘Get some air.’

‘Right,’ I said, thinking I might follow him, but just then the band went into a number that was even faster than the stuff they’d been playing so far, and I decided to have one last jump around the floor.

Andy and Jamie were already on the floor, slamming into each other, ricocheting off strangers. One of Jamie’s slams pretty near knocked Andy off his feet, and I felt a flash of unease; neither of them was smiling. I pogoed over to them, with the vague idea of doing some kind of peace-keeping, but I was too late. They had their hands around each other’s throats, and even if no-one else in the place noticed it, I could tell they weren’t dancing.

I couldn’t get to them through the crowd, so I just had to watch as Jamie’s mouth worked - to take in air, or to expel curses, or both - and as his fingers lost their hold on Andy’s neck, and dropped to his sides. Andy was smiling. Jamie’s teeth danced and his bones rattled, and Andy smiled.

*

Two guys I didn’t know very well were at the bar getting a round in, and Rob was lost in conversation with Anne, when Andy put his arm along the back of my chair and leaned forward and spoke directly into my ear.

‘I didn’t kill Jamie, you know.’

I couldn’t quite manage to say *‘What?,’* so I just looked at him.

‘All these years it’s been bothering you, Stevey-boy, and you’ve never said anything, and I thought tonight might be the time to get it sorted.’

‘All right.’

‘Not now, obviously. Later - when everyone else has pissed off. I’ll stay behind, help you to pack up. All right?’

‘All right,’ I said, and was surprised I managed to say that much.

*

One long, distorting chord ended the set, and a bunch of punks rushed the stage. The girls in the band beat them off with kung fu kicks and spittle.

The lights came up, and Andy dropped Jamie - dropped him, I mean, like you'd drop a bag of rubbish into a swing-bin. I caught Andy's eye. He just shook his head, and marched off towards the exit.

'You all right, mate?' Jamie was slumped against a big speaker, holding his throat with one hand and rubbing at his ribs with the other. I reached out a hand to help him up.

'Just sod off, Steve,' he said. So I did. I deliberately didn't catch up with Andy.

The next morning, Jamie was found dead in an alley, in amongst the dustbins of a Chinese restaurant, a few yards from the club we'd been in. It said in the *Evening Standard* that he'd been throttled.

Most people remember pogoing as the punk dance, but to me, the choke has far greater symbolic resonance. It epitomises so much of that era: the desire to break with the past, the need to shock, the way everything was a laugh, even though everything was deadly serious; the pretend violence. Except, of course, that violence never is pretend.

*

Rob was the last to leave the reunion, apart from the two of us. He drained his final orange juice, smacked his lips as if it had been best ale, and got up to go. We'd already told the barmaid to get off home, not to worry about the clearing up.

'Well, lads,' he said. 'That was a quick twenty years. Not bad, but a bit quick.'

Twenty years, I thought. *Bloody hell.* 'Let's make the next twenty count more, yeah? I mean, I really wish we'd kept in touch better. You know? This time, let's do it, not just say it.' I held out my hand for a handshake. I really meant what I was saying. How had I virtually lost touch with someone who used to be such a mate?

Rob blinked, and his cheeks crinkled. He put his arms out and around me, and I could feel his bald scalp against my ear and his dry lips pressed for a short second against my neck.

I was amazed. I'd never have expected to see him act so emotional, especially when he hadn't been drinking. It took me a moment to recover, but when I did, I patted his back, squeezed his shoulder. 'Look after yourself, Rob. Keep the faith, eh?'

Andy didn't wait to be asked. He enfolded Rob in a solid embrace, and said 'I'll phone you.'

We sipped at our drinks when he'd gone, and smoked a couple of cigarettes, and then I said: 'So?'

Andy nodded. 'I want to thank you for organising tonight, Steve. It's been good for me.'

'Despite the nostalgia?'

'Reminded me what it's all about.'

'Which was?'

'Is,' he said. 'What it is all about. Breaking up the established order. Bringing music back to the kids.'

'Yeah, but did it work?' By 1978, people were saying punk was just another fashion. You'd see trendies wearing expensive bondage gear. Genuinely individual, rebel New Wave bands were being turned down by major labels for being 'not punk enough,' despite the fact that the real punk rockers had always admired, and worked with, musicians from all sorts of different styles. 'I mean, look at the kids nowadays - '

'Look at the kids nowadays,' said Andy, and we both laughed.

'Yeah, I know, it's what every generation says. But don't you reckon? We set out to murder boredom, but boredom's become a lifestyle option. It's all satellite TV and computer games and music that would have sounded tame half a century ago! Even the drugs are boring. You've got kids of nineteen talking about careers, for Christ's sake. They either put up with boredom, or they actively *treasure* it - because life's so dangerous and horrible that a bit of boredom is a relief.'

'Sure,' he said. 'But their children won't. I'll bet you. You can't keep the kids quiet forever. One tame generation, maybe, then it'll turn again. Seventy-year-old punks and their grandchildren'll be out to all hours smashing up clubs and getting arrested. Don't you worry, Stevey: boy bands and tribute bands contain within themselves the seeds of their own destruction.'

I hoped he was right, and listening to him tell it, I was far from sure he wasn't. I drained my glass, and said: 'If it wasn't you, who was it?'

*

For me - for all of us, I would guess - the punk summer disintegrated the day we heard about Jamie's death and everybody split up. The way we lived, the way we thought, it was only natural that we'd run rather than talk to cops, innocent or guilty.

The punk explosion was more or less dead by that autumn, in any case. Which was no bad thing. Previous youth movements had made the mistake of thinking they were going to go on forever; we believed the exact opposite right from the start. We didn't despise people for selling out, we despised them for pretending not to sell out.

I found another squat for a while, then a bedsit, and eventually I got a council flat near my parents. I took a job in a local factory, and helped my mum look after my dad while he was dying.

I never went to the police with what I knew, the half-strangling I'd seen in that club. I never mentioned it to anyone, and never confronted Andy with it, after we'd met up again by chance three or four years later.

At the time, my silence was instinctive, but as Rat Scabies once said 'You can't help growing up.' So, after twenty years of growing up, I held a punk reunion above a pub near Waterloo, and they all came.

*

'It was Rob,' said Andy, and I knew at once that it was true.

'Why?'

'Rob's never gone into details, and I've never demanded any, but my belief is that when Rob left the club, he went to meet Anne at that pub. He made a pass at her, she turned him down. He headed back towards the club, met Jamie coming out, and - well, you know old Jamie could have quite a sharp tongue on him.'

'You think they had a row?'

'More likely Jamie figured out where Rob had been, what he'd been up to, and taunted him about it. Rob went for him, and of course Jamie was in a weakened state, because of...' He spread his fingers, like a manual shrug.

'You and him, choking each other on the dance floor.'

'You thought I'd killed him because of him and Anne. Well, Stevey-boy, I almost did.'

'I know. I thought you had, for a moment.'

'But I didn't.' Andy stubbed out his cigarette, and his face looked as serious - and yet as happy - as I had ever seen it. 'It just came to me, from nowhere. Lack of oxygen to the brain, maybe, I don't know. But I had a sudden realisation - that I didn't have to be like that any more. I was a *punk*: I could be what I wanted. I was a self-made man, made of safety pins and glue.'

'Who else knows?'

'Not Anne,' he said. 'She probably still thinks it was me. Or maybe she doesn't. She's never talked about it. For her, it's something that happened in the past, and therefore something that doesn't exist.'

'How do you mean?'

'You never saw her wearing punk gear before tonight, did you? She was more into disco back then. As far as she's concerned, you're a kid, then you grow up, and whatever happened when you were a kid doesn't count when you're grown up. If she didn't think that, she'd never have agreed to come tonight.'

'Just you and Rob?'

Andy smiled. 'And Chaz.'

'You're joking!'

'Chaz knew. He was there when Rob told me. He knew, and he's never said a word.'

'Just like Anne.'

'Except that with him, what happened when we were young is nostalgia. Same result; the past isn't real.'

'And you?' I asked the inevitable question. 'Why didn't you ever say anything?'

'What good would have it done? Rob was just unlucky.'

'*Unlucky* to have killed a mate?'

'Sure. Millions of lads fight over birds and booze, all over the planet, every day of every year. A boy doesn't deserve to have his life destroyed for a bit of bad luck - not if he's fundamentally a good man.'

'And Rob is?'

'I've kept an eye on him, over the years. If he'd disappointed me, I might have acted differently.'

'But what's he done that's so great? What's he done with his life?'

'He's stuck to being who he thinks he ought to be. You can't ask more than that of a man.'

'So why tell me now?'

Andy paused, as if waiting for me to catch up, and then said: 'He asked me to.'

'Rob did? Why?' But even as I put the question, I saw the answer. 'Oh, God ... '

'Yeah. He won't be around for the next reunion, I'm afraid.'

'Oh my God.' Bald Rob with his orange juice and his dry kiss.

'He wanted you to know, because he wishes he'd told you years ago. Because he's never stopped thinking of you as a friend.'

The weight of twenty years wasted on occasional acquaintanceship, where there might have been constant friendship, almost crushed the air from my lungs. Rob, Andy - even Chaz and Anne, maybe, who could say? It wasn't going to happen again. 'Andy. You said that when you were strangling Jamie in the club, and you stopped, it was because you realised you didn't have to be like that any more.'

'Yeah. That's something else I came here to tell you. Before I moved to London, all those years ago, I killed a man.'

'Why? I mean - who?'

He shook his head. 'Doesn't matter. It was a - a *friend* of my mother's. Point is, I'm giving you my secret for the same reason Rob gave you his.' He leant forward, locked onto my eyes. 'You understand?'

'Sure. Yes, I do.'

'Good. I was thinking, maybe you could come round and meet my family some time?'

'Yes. I'd like to.'

'You've never met my wife. My little daughter.' He laughed. 'The flat that eats my wages up, paying off the mortgage. You've never met my life. And I'd like you to, because it's a good life.'

'Redemption through punk rock,' I said.

He shook his head, lit another cigarette. 'If you like. I don't know about redemption, but ... I don't know if I told you, I'm a union rep. I led a strike last Christmas. They wanted to reduce the number of emergency beds at our hospital, and we weren't having it.'

'What happened?'

'We won.' His face glowed. 'We were fierce and full of rage and acting unafraid, and they backed down and we won. You see what we were doing, Steve? You know what we were doing?'

I nodded. I did know. 'You were jumping up and down.'

'*Right*, Stevey-boy! We were pogoing in their faces and gobbing on their shiny shoes and shouting in their ears and shocking them with our war paint. The fact that half of us couldn't have *actually* pogoed if our lives depended on it, because our old knees are too knackered, and the other half were too young to have ever *heard* of pogoing, didn't matter. We were punk, and that's why we won.'

*

Let me tell you about punk rock. For an exhilarating few months, the kids controlled the music. The business, the media, they had no influence over what was happening. They recovered quickly, of course, and re-established the status quo, and they learned from it - they determined never to let things get out of hand again.

They learned from it; but so did we.

'No future' was the big slogan back then, and it's only taken me half a lifetime to figure out what it means. The future never arrives, and the past never departs, and what matters in between isn't *how* you dance - it's *why* you dance. And the day you realise that, is the day you go punk.

We're still out there, us old punk rockers. We don't bother with the safety pins any more, or the bondage trousers, or the gobbing. But you'll know us when you see us. We're the ones jumping up and down.

THE LAST MOHICAN

Andrew Hook

Each morning when Laura was alive she used to lay my clothes out on the bed whilst I had breakfast leaning against the front door jamb; looking down the row of terraced houses on our street: a cigarette.

Now I watch from a chair in the corner of the room as Tatyana – one of my regular carers – pushes her soft hands into my underwear drawer searching for a sock matching the one she has draped over the bedpost. She tuts under her breath: 'Can't you fold them into one?' despite being aware it's my granddaughter who does the laundry. The two of them have a good relationship though, and she doesn't like to argue.

Through the thin curtains sunlight glows as though viewed through a yellow toffee wrapper. It's the 4th June, 2069: a Tuesday. It would be a good day to be outdoors, drawing heat from a cigarette to kick-start my lungs, just as the day draws fire from the sun. But the blue morning light can't be sullied with smoke, the ban isn't simply national but personal.

When Tatyana handles my underwear I wish I could feel a pull of attraction, even lust. Instead memories fold into each other of Laura, head over heels as though falling down a stairwell. The little things: her half-smile tilting her head, the energetic way she danced, mouthing song lyrics in the mirror. I push out the thoughts of the later years. They only serve to make me feel lonelier than I already am.

Tatyana is talking: 'A big day, Mr Read, no?'

I nod. I want to talk but I know there's a cough brewing at the back of my throat, and I don't want the embarrassment of hawking up phlegm. Instead, I continue watching as Tatyana lays my clothes on the bed. Socks at the end, then black skinny jeans with my underpants laid where the crotch would be, a torn white t-shirt with *Punks Not Dead* scrawled over it with a permanent marker, and my favourite long black leather jacket hung on a stand. I dislike how she places the clothes as though I can't remember how to put them on. But I suppose it doesn't really matter considering it is Tatyana who will be dressing me anyway.

Finally, at the back of the underwear drawer she pulls out a metal box containing what I consider to be medals, my badges of pride. In the old days, when there was war, there were 11th November Armistice celebrations at the cenotaph. Those old boys standing proud with polished medals over their lapels. At the time I used to wonder how they could commemorate those battles that they fought, as Spitfires flew passed strafing the crowds with noise instead of gunfire. Now, today especially, there is some kind of understanding.

What didn't matter was what you had done or that you had survived it. What mattered most was that you were there.

Tatyana takes the badges out of the box and I try to ignore my irritation at the fingerprints she will leave on their smooth surfaces. I'll be polishing them again later, before the event. She places them down on the table beside me. I let her choose, and she chooses rightly: The Damned, The Buzzcocks, The Fall, The Stranglers, Joy Division, and – of course – the Sex Pistols.

Technically speaking, The Stranglers and The Damned shouldn't be included, of course. Them being Southerners and all. But apply that logic and the Sex Pistols wouldn't be there either. And that wouldn't cut it. Besides, being punk means that the only conventions are that there are no conventions. No doubt the major newspapers will run articles at great length on what it means to be me - the last survivor of the Manchester Lesser Free Trade Hall gig of the 4th June 1976 – but I won't read them. Once this year's parade is over I want to be *over*. There's no fun in being the last man standing. And anyway, Laura is waiting for me.

*

Later I'm downstairs. Tatyana is at my feet, but not in supplication, she's re-threading the laces on my black monkey boots after having applied a polish that sends memories up my nose faster than a sniff of cocaine. The yellow and red alternate spikes of her Mohawk haircut nudge against my knees. She finishes and looks up, smiles through black lipstick, her lip piercing gleaming in the low wattage energy saving lightbulb over the kitchen table.

'Done,' she says, with that accent of hers that reminds me how global punk became. Not that the Eastern Europeans really understood it, even if they had more to rebel against than we had.

1976: Britain was run down, rubbish piled high on the streets, electricity flickered intermittently due to strike action, unemployment reigned, and the education system taught you to keep your place. What did Rotten say? *Out of all that came pretentious* moi *and the Sex Pistols and then a whole bunch of copycat wankers after us.* Well, he would say that, and he had the right to say it. But whatever way you looked at it the Pistols were the catalyst for what had been brewing for a very long time. And – surprising us all – it worked. It bloody well worked.

The front door opens and my only surviving son, Steve, shoulders his way through. He's approaching eighty himself, but a six-pack of beer is held within the crux of his arm. Behind him come his two daughters, Magenta and Columbia, their husbands, Gary and Clive, and my two great-grandchildren, Scooby and Iggy. For a moment there's a cacophony of noise but Tatyana – bless her – quietens it without looking like she's imposing; although I do see her place a hand over her heart at the same time as she holds a finger to her lips.

Shortly afterwards, Chrissie, my daughter is also here. I try to look through the crowded kitchen to see if she's brought anyone with her but as usual it appears that she's alone. I remember buying her white X-Ray Spex t-shirt almost three decades ago, but it still looks good on her. Just like the music, these things were built to last.

'We're all here,' Steve says, cracking open the first of the beers although it's just after ten in the morning. 'So's the press. They're three deep outside.'

'It's an important day,' says Tatyana, speaking for me. I realise then there's as much pride in her voice as there is from my own children, perhaps more so. I guess for my kids I was a father, whereas for Tatyana I'm approaching an icon. Even if I was never an actual musician.

History splits us into two groups. The Southerners and the Northerners. The Southerners had the Saint Martins College gig and we had the Manchester Lesser Free Trade Hall. Ok, so the Southerners got the Pistols first, on the 6th November 1975, and out of that came Billy Idol with Generation X, the scream that was Siouxsie Sioux, and the rest of the Bromley Contingent, but the Pistols hadn't even played any of their own material before the plug was pulled. To all intents and purposes they might as well have been a covers band. Whereas we got a proper gig, and out of that we got the Buzzcocks, Joy Division, The Fall, and eventually The Smiths. Oh, and Paul Morley. Journalists were always wankers. You just had to look at the way they treated The Stranglers. But the point is the most important gig in the North had been played. There couldn't have been more than 40 in the audience, but it was the 40 that mattered. Although reading about it for years afterwards you would think there were thousands there. Add everyone together who claimed they were there and you'd have the half-million who were at Woodstock. Tell anyone though, size doesn't matter, it's what you do with it that counts.

*

Spiral back ninety-three years, scratch the surface of memory.

Laura is fourteen and I'm fifteen. We're standing opposite each other in the grey hallway at school, in two distinct groups of boys and girls. Matt, the long-haired Adonis that he is, nudges me and says: 'Hey Pete. You ain't had a girlfriend yet? What's with that.' I shrug. I hadn't really thought about it. I remember my eyes scanning the crowd of girls. They were alien to me. Then I was about to mumble something placatory when I caught Laura in profile, at the back, looking to the floor. Something tugged inside me, as though all my interior organs were laced together and they had just been pulled tight.

'Who's that?' I said; my voice sounding different, as though I were hearing it recorded.

'Who's what?'

'That. *Her.* At the back.'

Matt looked over. 'That's Laura,' he said. 'Fuck knows what she's done with her hair.'

What she had done was cut it short and dyed it black. It made her stand out like a Negro at a Klu Klux Klan convention.

'You like that do you?' Matt continued. Then before I could answer he'd crossed the divide between the boys and the girls and was whispering something in Laura's ear. That was the first time I saw the half-smile.

Four weeks later, after we'd been going steady for a while, I held two tickets for a gig at the Lesser Free Trade Hall. The Sex Pistols supported by Solstice, some heavy metal rock band from the Midlands who everyone then forgot about. But Laura couldn't go. Her parents forbade it. So it was me who caught the revolution and whilst she attended the second gig six weeks later there was always a wedge between us – just like the dividing line in the school corridor – that I could never actually cross. She didn't hold it against me – how could she? But it was there.

It remained that way through the following eighty years, four children, several grandchildren and the two great-grandchildren. Even now I get sad about it. She had the ticket. She should have gone. I don't even remember what happened to that spare. I just know that I didn't sell it and if I had it now then it would set my family up for life.

*

Through the window I can see the reporters, the white vans of the television crews, and the other equipment that I don't quite understand now that technology has past me by. I'm holding a warm can of beer in one hand, and my head in the other. A few sips of the beer have settled in my stomach like oil on water. I'll put it down somewhere discretely when I get the chance. Alcohol doesn't agree with me anymore, but I can't let my family know that.

I remember the first time I saw Laura naked. We had pulled aside a corrugated metal sheet that half covered the entrance to a deserted warehouse in Moss Side. I don't think either of us knew what our intentions were other than just to get away and be together. We were outsiders, we knew that: at home, at school, in the city. People looked at us askance. There was no edge to us; I won't pretend we knew violence. But the difference was there and we could feel it beyond the pull of puberty.

Laura wore a mohair jumper, black and red, like Dennis the Menace. When she pulled it up over her head I remember being shocked that she wore no bra. Her tiny breasts appeared as pale clay moulds against her skin, the nipples even paler. Cupped in my hands the centres of my palms connected with a jolt. She reached around behind her and undid her pleated skirt that fell to a floor covered in brick dust and odd pieces of rusted metal. I remember pulling down her white knickers until they were around her ankles and standing back and looking at her and not knowing what to do.

Another day she touched my penis until it hardened and I came with my head arched back looking at a bright blue sky through the jagged smashed glass of broken windows. I swear a bird flew across the view; but as a silhouette I couldn't tell if it were a dove or a raven.

Tatyana used to hold me as I went to the toilet, but she doesn't do that anymore. I now have to sit down regardless, but I don't miss her touch, which I know embarrassed us however matter-of-fact she made it.

My other carer, Daina, is as rough as they come. My skin bruises easily and I won't show my family but Tatyana tuts when she sees it although she says there's nothing she can do.

If my body has had a chequered history then so did the Lesser Free Trade Hall. Finished in 1856 – well over two hundred years ago – it's been a public hall, a concert hall, a bombed out World War II shell, another concert hall, a hotel, and now a museum. Certainly it doesn't have the extended kudos of a venue such as New York's CBGB's, but at least it remains standing.

I always thought it pertinent that it was built on the site of the Peterloo Massacre: that date in 1819 when cavalry charged into a crowd of 80,000 who had gathered to demand a reform of parliamentary representation, killing a handful but wounding more than 700. And that in 1905 the Women's Social and Political Union activists, including Chistabel Pankhurst, were ejected from the building during a meeting from which began the militant WSPU campaign for women to vote. Maybe there was something in the ground that echoed upwards and instilled the crowd during the Pistols gig. And if that sounds like a contrivance, then I'll answer it's just my memory assimilating how such a tiny event could have triggered both a musical and political revolution that has led us to where we are today: a free country independent from the constraints imposed by the capitalism and faux democracy lauded by America and the rest of Europe and the ever-emerging Third World Countries. We welcome all and repel none. We have true power held by the masses where individuality can make a difference. And a government unbound by convention or artifice: where each decision considers the rights of everyone. Unequivocal freedom of expression.

'You alright, dad?' Chrissie is on her knees, beside me, and I realise I've been rehearsing parts of my speech in my head in my own little world; the eye in a storm.

'I'm fine,' I say, my voice crackling like burnt leaves underfoot. 'Just reminiscing.'

'You're lucky you've still got your memories,' she says, and I know she's thinking of Morrissey, who, until last year and for the previous six years before it, was the only other survivor to join me for this march. I barely knew the man. We had exchanged but a handful of words over the years. But he had a right to attend, just as all of them did. In the final years, of course, he didn't even *know* he was there. What was it that they used to say about the Sixties, that if you can remember them then you probably weren't there? Much the same was true about any decade, because despite the drink and the drugs or the lack of them, memory will be your ultimate enemy. The loss of it an erosion of everything you know, of history.

Chrissie's right. I am lucky I have my memory. And this is it, now:

Despite what you might think from the myth and stories that sprung around afterwards, the only thing you could have been sure of at the gig was that you were about to witness something you'd never seen before. And whilst perhaps half of the audience went on to do something within the punk movement, that didn't alter the fact that for the rest of us, the schoolboys and schoolgirls, the people who worked for the Manchester Dock company, the plasterers from Denton, the *ordinary* people, it was no less than remarkable.

The front that was the Seventies: the propping up of tired systems, the patching up of old establishments, the inherent class system, the popular rock music that was a soporific opium to the masses, the traditional values of inherited decency which no longer belonged to our age, the outrage that anyone might question *anything* – all this was about to be torn down.

I'd be lying – and I will lie to the papers, the television, later today – if I said I could remember the gig note for note. So many gigs have been and gone in the intervening years. For a time I even tried to forget it. I wanted my first gig with Laura – the Pistols second, on 20th July 1976 – to be my moment of epiphany. But history is a brush with tar that will never wash off, and I remember enough of the gig to know I was there. And that's the important thing. I know I was there and I can prove I was there.

Everyone says they remember where they were when Thatcher's government came down. Of course, we were all post-punk then, but the ragged sentiments from the three-chord thrust were still running through our veins. And by that time we had the whole country behind us. Whoever said the revolution starts at closing time had been right. We had a black and white TV in those days, but I swear you could see the orange flames flickering at the Houses of Parliament.

The rest, as they say, is history.

*

I'm exhausted by the few questions I answer leaning over my garden gate, a veritable Medusa's head of microphones pushing towards my face. The parade itself will follow in an hour's time, but for the moment I bask both in the sunshine and in my moment of glory. A glory tinged by sadness, of course, not only for Laura who would have been proud of this moment, but for all the fallen soldiers I've left behind: Pete Shelley, Howard Devoto, Ian Curtis, Morrissey, Peter Hook, Mark E Smith and the regular gig goers. Not to mention those who were crucial to the revolution: Ian Dury, Poly Styrene, JJ Burnel, Joe Strummer, Dave Vanian, Captain Sensible and Steve Severin. And of course, John Lydon himself. The only one that ever really mattered, because he was smart and he knew it. No wonder the old government had tried to suppress him. He was a dangerous Molotov cocktail that threw himself back into the audience.

Later, with Tatyana taking my arm, I walk a few faltering steps at the start of the parade, my monkey boots reflecting the harsh light off streetlamps in monochromatic photography, my long black leather jacket moving in a soft wind around the tops of my knees, my t-shirt proclaiming what we always knew, my jeans hugging my legs like paint. Of course, after those initial steps I'm back in the wheelchair, deafened by the accompanying applause. It's fitting that the parade takes place at night, around the time that the gig would have occurred all those years ago, but also it conceals my frailty from the harsher light of day.

I look out into the faces of the crowd, almost half with hairstyles extending skywards like space rockets. Of course, back in the day, hardly anyone styled their hair like that. Few wore bondage trousers. Few had safety-pins pushed through their noses or earlobes. What we had was what we stood in. I remember one of the thousand documentaries about the punk revolution where an Irish record shop owner recalled his amazement at seeing the Undertones on Top Of The Pops *wearing their own clothes*. Yet every movement has a uniform and so long as it's funded by the independents and not the multi-national companies that seem to have sewn up the rest of the world then that's fine with me. In my day, we removed the logos from our clothes. I've heard in some countries the *population* is now physically branded.

By the time we've reached the Lesser Free Trade Hall I'm exhausted. I stand again, receive the applause. I think of those November Remembrance parades of yore, watching a dwindling number of ex-army men year after year after year. Now, I'm one of them, but representing a worthier cause. What will happen, though, after I'm gone?

For I was only there. After the gig I married Laura and we had our kids and I went out to work for the rest of my life like everyone else. And I built my world around myself. And – like the best of them – I remained me. But I held no greater role at the gig than a cook might have in a forgotten army. And after me, what comes next? Could tonight be another catalyst, or will another group come and usurp us. Steve told me a rumour that a collective known as the New Romantics are waiting in the wings. But after 93 years of successful revolution, and with myself in my one hundred and eighth year, I can't quite believe that.

They call me The Last Mohican but it's a misnomer; yet the media like a sound bite even if we're a long way off Bill Grundy.

*

Much later, back home, with only the crumbs of meat patties, sausage rolls, crisps and tiny orange flakes of cheese remaining on the paper plates; with the bin choked by flattened beer cans emptied by the adults and squashed Kwenchy Kups drunk by the great-grandchildren; with the echoes of my extended family's goodbyes resonating in my ears; and with Tatyana upstairs making my bed, I close my eyes. And when I open them I see Laura.

She's sitting across the table from me. Her elbows create circles in the tablecloth and her head is resting in her hands.

'How did it go?' she asks. As though her voice is coming from a long way away. From the other side, perhaps.

When I sigh I feel something unpick my heart, a stitch unstitched.

'It was ok,' I breathe. 'But I wish you were there.'

'You always wished I was there,' she says. 'My bloody parents.'

I force a smile across the table, across the years. How different would it have been if she had been there too? Regardless, I would have remained the last one standing. The last one standing even as I sat. Even as I watched the crowds pogo to God Save The Queen at the end of the parade: from the Lesser Free Trade Hall right around the country to the museum dedicated to the sins of the past which was once Buckingham Palace.

I reach out across the table, fingers outstretched.

Laura does the same.

When we connect, the music is there. A simple beat with a simple lyric. And it's just as valid as ever. Because punk – true punk – isn't just about nostalgia. It's about being us, now. And being us, always.

I won't hear Tatyana return downstairs.

CONTRIBUTORS

Joe Briggs is 27. He writes about punk at *Some Days the Thunder Gets You* and *Oi! Is This Punk Rock*, co-writes the comic *Nothing Nice to Say* and co-hosts the *Fullthrottlelazy* podcast. He knows that Hickey are the best band ever.

Gio Clairval is an Italian-born writer and translator who has lived most of her life in Paris and is now based in Edinburgh. Since she started writing short fiction four years ago, she has sold more than 20 stories to magazines such as *Weird Tales, Galaxy's Edge, Daily Science Fiction, Postscripts,* and several anthologies, including T*he Lambshead Cabinet of Curiosities* (HarperCollins) and *Caledonia Dreamin'* (Eibonvale Press) among others. You can find her at GioClairval.blogspot.com and on Twitter @gioclair.

Gary Couzens has had stories published in *F & SF, Interzone, Black Static, Crimewave, The Third Alternative* and Midnight Street amongst others. His collection *Second Contact and Other Stories* was published in 2003 by Elastic Press. He edited *Extended Play: The Elastic Book of Music* (2006) which won the British Fantasy Award for Best Anthology.

Mat Coward's short stories have been nominated for the Edgar, shortlisted for the Dagger, published on four continents, translated into several languages, and broadcast on BBC Radio. He's gardening correspondent of the Morning Star, and one of the "elves" behind BBC TV's "Ql." Ellery Queen's Mystery Magazine has called him "One of the funniest writers in the history of crime fiction.'

Sarah Crabtree is currently working on a crazy notion to transform an as yet unpublished novel into a screenplay. Also, she cannot quite believe it has been ten years since her first novel, *Terror From Beyond Middle England* (ENC Press) was published. Where does time go?

Adam Craig has had fiction published in a number of places, including anthologies from Dog Horn and Alchemy Press.

He is currently taking part in Cinnamon Press' mentoring programme, putting together a short story collection. One day he promises to get a website. Until then, you can contact him at adamcraigsmail@gmail.com.

Richard Dellar is author of *Splitting in Two: Mad Pride & Punk Rock Oblivion* (2014), co-editor of *Mad Pride: A Celebration of Mad Culture* (2000), co-author of *Seaton Point* (1998) and editor of *Gobbing, Pogoing and Bad Language: An Anthology of Punk Short Stories* (1996). Aside from books, beginning with punk fanzine *Breach of the Peace* he has produced underground magazines prolifically since 1980, most recently *Southwark Mental Health News*. He works in the mental health sector and lives in South London.

Prog rock and twenty-minute guitar solo enthusiast, **Terry Grimwood**, authored the novels *Axe, Bloody War*, novellas *The Places Between* and *Soul Masque*, co-wrote an electrical installation text book and is proud owner of theEXAGGERATEDpress. He also edits *Wordland* (on-line and free), teaches at an FE college and plays harmonica.

Andrew Hook is the author of over 100 published short stories, with several collections and novellas in print. His most recent publication, *The Immortalists,* a neo-noir crime novel, was published earlier this year by Telos, with *Church of Wire* to follow from them in 2015. He is also co-editor of the irrealist magazine, *Fur-Lined Ghettos*. He resides at andrew-hook.com

Alexei Kalinchuk is a practicing novelist and published cartoonist and short-story writer. He's been published in *The Bitter Oleander, Amoskeag Journal* and other outlets. He is bilingual and has Lone Star dreams even when he lives in other places in America.

Born East London but now residing amongst the hedge mumblers of rural Suffolk, Pushcart nominee **P.A.Levy** has been published in many magazines, from *A cappella Zoo* to *Zygote In My Coffee* and stations in-between. He is also a founding member of the Clueless Collective and can be found loitering on page corners and wearing hoodies at cluelesscollective.co.uk

Richard Mosses has told stories all his life, from early zombie films he scripted for friends, to stories and novels infused with magic, fantasy and horror. Richard has worked for a number of technology companies but now works for SUPA, encouraging companies to explore what Scottish physics has to offer and runs the Scottish Technology Network. He's a member of the GSFWC. His website is khaibit.com.

Douglas J. Ogurek is a dink. He hides Christian themes in the glop that he writes. Though it has been banned on Mars, his work appears in the *British Fantasy Society Journal, The Literary Review, Morpheus Tales, Gone Lawn,* and several anthologies. He lives on Earth with the woman whose husband he is. They are owned by five pets. More at douglasjogurek.weebly.com.

Stephen Palmer is the author of seven published SF novels, with his eighth, *Hairy London,* out now from Infinity Plus. He is best known for his green/environmental novels. His short stories have been published by NewCon Press, Eibonvale Press, Spectrum SF, Wildside Press, Solaris, Rocket Science and Unspoken Water.

Jude Orlando Enjolras is a half Polish, Italian/British fiction writer and performance poet. He has a BA in English & Philosophy and two MAs in Shakespeare Studies. 'The God Fearing Crack Dealers' Songbook' is a re-imagined excerpt from his novel in progress, *Angels & Anarchists.* Jude's collaborative poetry project, *Poems for the Queer Revolution,* is out now.

Mark Slade has appeared in *Diabolic Tales III, Flash Fiction Offensive, Tales of the Undead-Suffer Eternal 1-3.* Horrified Press released his first book, *A Six Gun and the Queen of Light.* He lives in Willamsburg, VA, with his wife and daughter.

L A Sykes is a writer from Atherton, Greater Manchester UK. He has appeared in *Nightmare Illustrated Magazine, Shotgun Honey, Blackout City* podcast, *Deaththroes, Lurid Lit, Blink Ink, Bones Anthology, The Big Adios, Linguistic Erosion* and others. Thunderune Publishing released his first book of short stories entitled, *Through A Shattered Lens, I Saw,* and Northern Noir novella, *The Hard Cold Shoulder,* with two more releases scheduled for late 2014.

Douglas Thompson's short stories have appeared in a wide range of magazines and anthologies, most recently *Albedo One, Ambit, Postscripts,* and *New Writing Scotland.* He won the Grolsch/Herald Question of Style Award in 1989 and second prize in the Neil Gunn Writing Competition in 2007. His first book, *Ultrameta*, was published by Eibonvale Press in August 2009, nominated for the Edge Hill Prize, and shortlisted for the BFS Best Newcomer Award, and since then he has published four subsequent novels, *Sylvow* (Eibonvale, 2010), *Apoidea* (The Exaggerated Press, 2011), *Mechagnosis* (Dog Horn, 2012), *Entanglement* (Elsewhen Press, 2012), *The Brahan Seer* (Acair Publishing, 2014), *Volwys* (Dog Horn Publishing, 2014), and *The Rhymer* (Elsewhen Press, 2014). He can be found at douglasthompson.wordpress.com.

Out Now: Women Writing the Weird I & II Edited by Deb Hoag

WEIRD
1. Eldritch: suggesting the operation of supernatural influences; "an eldritch screech"; "the three weird sisters"; "stumps . . . had uncanny shapes as of monstrous creatures" —John Galsworthy; "an unearthly light"; "he could hear the unearthly scream of some curlew piercing the din" —Henry Kingsley
2. Wyrd: fate personified; any one of the three Weird Sisters
3. Strikingly odd or unusual; "some trick of the moonlight; some weird effect of shadow" —Bram Stoker

WEIRD FICTION
1. Stories that delight, surprise, that hang about the dusky edges of 'mainstream' fiction with characters, settings, plots that abandon the normal and mundane and explore new ideas, themes and ways of being. —Deb Hoag

Women Writing the Weird I features
Nancy A. Collins, Eugie Foster, Janice Lee, Rachel Kendall, Candy Caradoc, Mysty Unger, Roberta Lawson, Sara Genge, Gina Ranalli, Deb Hoag, C. M. Vernon, Aliette de Bodard, Caroline M. Yoachim, Flavia Testa, Aimee C. Amodio, Ann Hagman Cardinal, Rachel Turner, Wendy Jane Muzlanova, Katie Coyle, Helen Burke, Janis Butler Holm, J.S. Breukelaar, Carol Novack, Tantra Bensko, Nancy DiMauro, and Moira McPartlin.

Women Writing the Weird II features
Merrie Haskell, J.S. Breukelaar, Nicole Cushing, Sandra McDonald, Janett L. Grady, Victoria Hooper, Tantra Bensko, Rachel Kendall, Roberta Chloe Verdant, Amelia Mangan, Alex Dally MacFarlane, Michele Lee, Deb Hoag, Janis Butler Holm, Nancy A. Collins, Sarah A.D. Shaw, Lorraine H McGuire, Nikki Guerlain, Peggy A. Wheeler, Aliya Whiteley and Charie D. La Marr.

Out Now:
Nitrospective
Andrew Hook

Japanese school children grow giant frogs, a superhero grapples with her secret identity, onions foretell global disasters and an undercover agent is ambivalent as to which side he works for and why. Relationships form and crumble with the slightest of nudges. World catastrophe is imminent; alien invasion blase. These twenty slipstream stories from acclaimed author Andrew Hook examine identity and our fragile existence, skid skewed realities and scratch the surface of our world, revealing another—not altogether dissimilar—layer beneath.

Nitrospective is Andrew Hook's fourth collection of short fiction.

RRP: £12.99 ($22.95).

Acclaim for the Author

"Andrew Hook is a wonderfully original writer" —Graham Joyce

"His stories range from the darkly apocalyptic to the hopefully visionary, some brilliant and none less than satisfactory"
—*The Harrow*

"Refreshingly original, uncompromisingly provocative, and daringly intelligent" —*The Future Fire*

ND - #0487 - 270225 - C0 - 229/152/18 - PB - 9781907133893 - Matt Lamination